PRAISE FOR *THE*

OF AVA A

T0013145

"Banash's sublime new stunner immerses us in an intoxicating female friendship between two young singers, each striving for pop stardom, until one of them suspiciously dies, later leading a *Rolling Stone* journalist to dig out the truth no one seems to want uncovered. A psychological why-done-it about the glittering allure and tragic cost of fame, and the heady bliss of bonding, all set against an unforgettable soundtrack of love and deception."

—Caroline Leavitt, *New York Times* bestselling author of *With or Without You* and *Pictures of You*

"Gritty, propulsive, and complex, Banash paints a vivid picture of two young women navigating their way through the dark side of the music industry and the journalist who uncovers their shocking truth years later. I found myself completely transported into Banash's world of glittering stages, bright city lights, and deeply nuanced, compelling characters. *The Rise and Fall of Ava Arcana* is an addictive read that will leave you wanting more."

—Julia Spiro, author of *Full* and *Someone Else's Secret*

"I devoured this suspenseful and perceptive read about the price of fame, the dangerously blurred boundary between envy and admiration, and the tantalizing pull of those who recognize your potential and your desires. Urgently narrated in dual timelines, *The Rise and Fall of Ava Arcana* introduces us to three unforgettable women: the passionate, dogged Kayla; the dreamy, yearning Ava; the irrepressible, brazen Lexi. I'll be thinking about them for a long time."

—Caitlin Barasch, author of *A Novel Obsession*

"*The Rise and Fall of Ava Arcana* is one of the sexiest novels I've ever read. While it is a thriller, a mystery, and an excavation into the backstabbing glamour of the music industry, Jennifer Banash is also first and foremost an absolute master of sensual details and whip-smart dialogue, making her female protagonists leap off the page in an electrical storm. This novel is one part propulsive beach read, one part feminist deep dive into the ways women ferociously love, impulsively betray, and ultimately redeem each other. And did I mention that it's hot?"

—Gina Frangello, author of *Blow Your House Down* and
A Life in Men

"I binged this twisty mystery thriller that probes the darker side of fame and female friendships. *The Rise and Fall of Ava Arcana* is as addictive as any Netflix series."

—Liska Jacobs, author of *The Pink Hotel*

"This dark, sexy novel combines the rocker-chick moxie of *Daisy Jones & the Six* with the psychological-thriller plot twists of *Social Creature*. Banash's clear, lush prose makes *The Rise and Fall of Ava Arcana* a gripping read."

—Kate Christensen, author of *The Last Cruise* and *The Great Man*

The RISE
and
FALL
of AVA
ARCANA

The RISE and FALL of AVA ARCANA

A Novel

JENNIFER BANASH

LAKE UNION
PUBLISHING

Text copyright © 2023 by Jennifer Banash

Published by Lake Union Publishing, Seattle

www.apub.com

Amazon, the Amazon logo, and Lake Union Publishing are trademarks of Amazon.com, Inc., or its affiliates.

ISBN-13: 9781662505416 (paperback)
ISBN-13: 9781662505423 (digital)

Cover design by Ploy Siripant

Cover image: © Oleksandr Nagaiets / Shutterstock; © KPPWC / Shutterstock; © Hayden Verry / ArcAngel

Printed in the United States of America

"We are all in the gutter,
but some of us are looking at the stars."
—*Oscar Wilde*

KAYLA

Jeff Logan's voice was scratchy and strained with smoke as he gave me that same wry grin I'd seen on album covers and in countless videos, the kind of smile that would have most women willingly peeling off their clothes in a matter of seconds. "When I'm in the moment, I'm really *feeling it*, you know? And I just want the audience to feel it too. Especially the ladies."

Or for me, the lady in his hotel room, a writer at *Rolling Stone*, inarguably the most respected magazine in the history of rock journalism—who he clearly expected to sleep with him mid-interview—to feel it. This was by no means the first bit of innuendo I'd heard on the job, but the whole situation was starting to feel a little over-the-top. We'd gotten off on the wrong foot the moment he'd answered the door of his suite at the Carlyle hotel, clad in only a pair of black leather pants that looked like they might've been slept in for days.

He scrunched down a bit in his chair, shaking his shaggy mop of blond hair from his face and reaching deep in one pocket of his pants to pull out a silver lighter. His bare chest was tanned the color of dark honey, a thin silver hoop gleaming in each nipple. He brought the cigarette to his lips and lit it, his narrow blue eyes squinting through a veil of smoke. I knew from my research that he was in only his late twenties, but he was starting to get that leathery look rock stars were prone to after a few years of nonstop hedonism.

He's the lead singer. He should quit, I thought in annoyance as I sat motionless in a rose-colored wingback chair. Even the way I reached forward slightly with my left hand, which held a digital recorder, felt way too close for comfort. I knew that most women would be thrilled to be in such close proximity to one of the hottest front men in rock and roll, but at the moment, all I wanted was for Jeff to shut up, which would probably defeat the entire purpose of the interview I was currently conducting.

I'd been at the magazine for three years, slowly making my way up the ladder. But sometimes when my boss, Keats, assigned me this kind of throwaway story, I couldn't help but wonder whether he really believed in me at all. Nitro, Jeff's band, was talented enough, but there was no real story here—just that they had a new album coming out in a few months. I'd listened to the rough cut his manager had sent over, and it was more of the same ego-driven posturing that had made Jeff famous in the first place. And worse yet, this piece was only slated to be around five hundred words or so, a long paragraph at most.

"Tell me a little about the concept for the third album. Did you settle on a title yet? Your manager told me when we spoke on the phone that you were still playing around with a few ideas."

I watched as, instead of answering immediately, he let his eyes trail across my face and then move slowly down the length of my body, the tailored white button-down I wore, an oversize leather jacket, and the black skinny jeans ending in a pair of Chelsea boots. There was a coffee stain on the collar of my shirt, a tan splotch, but that morning I'd just thrown the jacket over it, running my fingers through the dark bob that grazed my shoulders, a heavy line of bangs marching defiantly across my forehead. Lately, my pale skin appeared sallow, jaundiced, as if something inside me had gone rotten overnight. There'd been too many evenings spent hunched over my computer, too many cups of coffee in place of water and sleep, my brown eyes burning and gritty with exhaustion.

"The new album?" he said, leaning toward me, thick, bare forearms pressed against his leather-clad knees. He blew out a drag as he spoke: "Get this . . . *A N V I L*." He stopped for dramatic effect, and I had to force myself not to roll my eyes. "It's hard. It's metal. It *bangs*. I really think this could be it, the record we've been waiting for, the *Slippery When Wet* for a new generation," he said, a huge yawn swallowing the end of his sentence. "Did you know that Jon Bon Jovi's been married to the same chick for like, twenty-five *years*? Like, what a trip, man."

As I listened to Jeff blather on, I knew I already had what I needed to write the story I'd been assigned. I stayed put out of mere politeness, allowing his voice to fade into the background, my thoughts drifting back to the less-than-inspiring first date I'd had the night before. Eric, who I'd met on Bumble, had taken me to a sports bar in Midtown. When he wasn't droning on about his career in arbitrage, his eyes were glued to the blaring TV above my head. I'd sipped my glass of lukewarm draft beer, shifting uncomfortably in the hard wooden booth as the minutes crawled by in innings. Before that it had been Jared, an independent filmmaker who "dabbled" in erotic photography and asked me what my kink was before our drinks even arrived. I was glad in some small way for the interview with Jeff Logan, if only to distract myself from the pathetic state of my love life. I was starting to wonder if maybe I just wasn't cut out for romance, if it might be better to bury myself in work the way I always did.

Better to feel nothing at all.

After I'd gotten home from sports-bar hell, I'd stood at the kitchen window looking out into the dark sky, a sliver of moon hanging low over the row of brownstones directly across the street. "At least you got out for once, Mikayla," my mother said as I pressed the phone to my ear, as if I could somehow will her into my orbit. "Doesn't Keats usually act like you're covering the Pentagon Papers or something?"

"Hardly," I said dryly.

There was a sudden, familiar rustling of paper, and I knew she was probably flipping through the pages of a book, something dense and thick, with a word like "Origins" in the title. It wasn't unusual for my mother, a professor of anthropology at Michigan State, to multitask, especially while on the phone. The only thing capable of capturing her complete attention, it seemed, was work. After my dad walked out on my third birthday, she'd started spending every waking hour at her desk writing a new book or sequestered away in her office with students, shuddering at even the slightest suggestion of a romantic entanglement. She preferred the solidity of objects to people, had spent most of her life uncovering the layers of meaning in things, turning an Aztec pot over in her hands and holding it up to the light.

In my own way, I wasn't so different. I did the same thing with my subjects, delving into their personal lives and ferreting out tiny details and long-gone history—the origins of a song, the genesis of a world tour. I'd hidden behind words for decades, distracted myself with them. It was why I'd become a journalist in the first place. There was comfort in words, in the solidity of them. Once something was written down and published, it felt irrefutable, as if I'd somehow managed to inject some semblance of truth into the world—even if it was only a few hundred words on Madonna's next tour. Writing allowed me to lose myself, gave me a place to leave my own narrative behind and focus on someone else's instead. When I was immersed in a story, I barely ate or slept. I forgot the outside world even existed.

It didn't exactly make me an ideal romantic partner by any stretch of the imagination.

"Men are little boys," my mother would often say, peering out from behind a pile of student papers ringed with coffee stains. "First you marry them, then you raise them. Who has the time?"

Maybe she was right. At least work was a place where I knew my strengths—and where most of the time they actually worked for me. I was twenty-nine years old, on the cusp of thirty. I didn't have time for the distractions, including yet another depressing reverie about my failed attempts at online dating. I'd perfected the art of running away before I could disappoint anyone, and the older I got, the more I was convinced that I was ultimately someone who looked better in the metallic sheen of a rearview mirror, receding into the distance. Better to keep to myself and not let things go too far.

Better to not find out.

When I looked up again, Jeff was asleep, his head thrown back, his mouth slightly open. For the first time I noticed the empty decanter on the floor next to his chair, the cut glass shimmering in the light from the chandelier overhead. How had I missed that? *You're off your game,* I admonished myself as I shoved my recorder back into my tote and stood up, walking quietly across the sea of thick beige carpet until I reached the door.

After a forty-minute subway ride sandwiched between two teen girls yelling into their cell phones between stops, I finally made it back to Brooklyn. When I stepped into my apartment—the ferns tucked into corners of the living room, the midcentury furniture that I'd refinished piece by piece, the large, earth-toned wool rug strewn across the floor—a sense of relief washed over me. I'd found the apartment, the top floor of a brownstone on a tree-lined street in Bushwick, nine months ago and been immediately smitten with the honey-colored, wide-planked wood floors and the tin ceilings that winked silver in the light that poured through the huge windows. Light was a luxury in New York City, and I felt lucky to have so much of it. Most of the time I felt lucky to live here at all, in this city of dreams where the cliché was real, where everyone was trying to make it in one way or another—myself included.

I shrugged off my jacket, throwing it on the worn, moss-green velvet sofa I'd picked up at the neighborhood Goodwill, and sat down at the desk I'd placed strategically under one of the windows, pulling my laptop from my bag and opening it. No time like the present to transcribe my interview with Jeff, despite my feelings of loathing toward him. Just then my cell phone rang, the sound shrill and intrusive, snapping me out of my thoughts.

"How did it go with Jeff? You still alive?"

Keats never bothered with anything as pedestrian as a hello, just got right to the point. Not that I blamed him. He was editor in chief at *Rolling Stone* and the busiest human I'd ever come in contact with. But even with the latest issue about to close, he always made time to talk over a story until we'd exhausted every angle or possibility, something that made him a rarity in a business largely run by men who were at best unavailable and at worst predatory and abusive. A business that was becoming as obsolete as dinosaurs with every passing moment. *Print is dead.* I heard the phrase nearly every day, and it always made my blood run cold. If it was true . . . then what did that make me—and thousands of other journalists just like me?

Sitting ducks.

"That could have been a phone call, Keats," I said. "You really want to run the risk of one of your writers having to #MeToo another rock dude for a front-of-book blurb about *Nitro*? I'm going to have to make a new rule: I'll only hang out with assholes for a feature."

I could hear him stifle a laugh. Of course, I shouldn't have been saying things like this to Keats—hell, he shouldn't have been checking up on me after reporting such a nothing story. Keats knew that I could take care of myself, and he also knew that I filed clean *and* on time, which was more than could be said for some of the more marquee names at the magazine. But for whatever reason, Keats seemed to actually care about my career, even if he hadn't always given me the best opportunities to shine. Maybe that was because I was always telling him exactly how the magazine should be run.

Not that he ever listened.

"OK, Kayla," he said, and I could hear the telltale creaking sound his desk chair always made when he leaned forward, as he often did when he was excited about something. At that moment my heart began to pick up speed, beating faster. "Though I'd love to while away the afternoon discussing the cultural irrelevance of Jeff Logan and Nitro, I'm calling because I've got another asshole for you to follow for a feature—your first cover story: Lexi Mayhem."

I sat there for a moment in silence, his words spinning through my brain, wondering if I'd somehow misheard him. My first cover. I'd dreamed of this moment for years, and now that it had arrived, it didn't seem quite real. I'd wanted this opportunity for as long as I could remember. Wished and worked for it so hard that sometimes late at night, bent over my desk in our Midtown office, engrossed in a story, it was all I could think of.

And now it was here.

"Kayla? You still there?"

"Of course," I replied, aware that my pulse was now thudding in my ears. I switched Keats to speaker and put the phone down, willing my heart to beat normally.

"I thought you'd be a bit more excited," he replied, and I could hear a hint of disappointment creeping into his voice.

"I am," I said quickly before he could pivot and pass the assignment on to someone else. "Keats, I *definitely* am."

"I thought you'd be perfect for this. Wasn't Lexi Mayhem your first concert?"

"How do you even remember these things?" I mumbled, shaking my head as though he could see me. "I think I mentioned that like, two *years* ago on the company retreat."

"Professional hazard." He chuckled, and all at once the memories came flooding back, the feeling so strong that I had to remember to breathe. Mayhem's howl filling the stadium like a war cry, the hair on the back of my neck standing on end. The reassuring weight of Astrid's hand in mine and the musky haze of the patchouli incense she burned in her room, snow piled on the sidewalks like powdered sugar . . .

"For a cover, it's a cakewalk," Keats said, the low timbre of his voice breaking into my thoughts.

"What's the angle?" I asked as I stood up and walked the few feet to the kitchen, grabbing a can of sparkling water from the fridge before making my way back to my desk, banishing the past the way I always did whenever it arose, forcing its way into the present.

"She's got a new album out in a few months and a tour scheduled. But that's not really the story. She's starting her own record label—one exclusively devoted to female artists. It's unprecedented, really. We know Lexi Mayhem the pop star, but I want you to get at Lexi Mayhem the mogul. She's more powerful now than any suit in this business. What's she going to do, who is she going to take a risk on . . . who has she already pissed off?"

"Interesting," I said, flicking open the can with my thumb and forefinger and taking a long swallow. "Is she here in town?"

"Nope. She's in LA right now. Your point of contact regarding all things Mayhem is her manager, Ben Reynolds. I've emailed you all the details."

"Got it," I said, nodding as though he could somehow see me. "When am I leaving?" I raised the can to my lips and took another sip.

"This got pushed up at the last minute, so you fly out of JFK tonight. Mayhem wants to meet with you tomorrow at, get this, her bungalow at the Chateau Marmont."

I stopped dead, spitting out the water and wiping my mouth with one hand. "Tonight?"

"Get packing," Keats said, and then before I could say another word, the line went dead.

AVA

It was early September when I first met Lexi Gennaro, the air hot and stagnant, stinking of the garbage that littered the sidewalks, that rotting-sweet scent almost compelling in its intensity. The sun beat down on my head as I walked the streets of the Lower East Side, a sudden breeze tangling my hair. The cutoff denim shorts and black crop top I wore were no match for the heat that pressed in on me insistently, like an unwanted tap on the shoulder.

You'd think I would've been used to it. I'd lived in New York since I was five years old, when my mother and I left Kyiv. But that Slavic coldness seemed to have settled deep in the marrow of my bones. Ever since, my body rejected any temperature that threatened to climb above seventy-five degrees. *I've never seen anyone sweat so much,* my mother, Irina, would proclaim disdainfully, running one hand across my slick, bare shoulders and shaking her head, as if my perspiration itself had disappointed her.

I remembered so little about Ukraine. The snow that fell endlessly outside the windows of our tiny flat. How the shelves of the grocery stores were sometimes inexplicably bare. The way that, as we boarded the plane to America, a flight attendant bent down and pinned a set of silver wings to the collar of the starched cotton blouse I wore. Even now I could almost still feel the weight of those wings, see the endless expanse of blue sky outside the window, feel the wave of excitement that rushed through me as the wheels of the plane touched down on American soil.

But the afternoon I met Lexi, I wasn't thinking about any of that. I was worried that I'd end up arriving at the café soaked in sweat. I needed this job. I'd finally moved out of Irina's Staten Island apartment a month ago, and the meager savings I'd managed to accumulate from summers babysitting for neighborhood kids dwindled with every passing day. Manhattan was impossibly tall buildings, the scent of roasting nuts, sirens, hot asphalt, and unlimited possibility, a kind of danger simmering below the concrete surface of the city. But Staten Island was different. Safer. More suburban.

I couldn't wait to get away.

But now that I lived in the city, I couldn't seem to leave my tiny studio apartment on Ludlow Street without buying something. A Snapple Peach Tea. Sunglasses from a street vendor in Chinatown. A slice at Ray's Pizza. It all added up, and every time I logged in to my bank account, I felt like I was drowning. Even on the way to the café, a table of bracelets outside the subway station caught my eye. One in particular, a wide, woven, vaguely tribal design in black and white captivated my attention, and before I even knew what I was doing, I'd handed over my last ten dollars, the cuff laced firmly onto my wrist, its dangling strings like an exhalation of breath tickling my skin.

I needed a job, and fast. I'd applied at a few coffee shops in SoHo, but I was intimidated by the customers with their hip, expensive clothes, the fancy espresso machines behind the counter, gleaming silver. The clouds of steam escaping the top reminded me of a woman screaming. So even though I'd never waited tables in my life and the thought of having to talk to strangers made me want to die inside, when I saw the job posting on Craigslist, I was desperate enough to call the number right away. A gruff male voice told me to come down for a "pre-interview." That was New York for you. Even to get a shitty waitressing gig, you had to make it past a random series of gatekeepers. Whatever arbiter of cool I ended up meeting would probably take one look at the battered Converse sneakers on my feet and immediately show me the door.

I wasn't cool. I was secondhand clothes. I was watchful eyes. I was silence. I sang only when no one was home, and I generally preferred my own thoughts to other people. *You don't live in the real world,* Irina sniffed whenever she caught me daydreaming out a window or burying my nose in a book. *This is America!* she'd say, throwing up her hands in exasperation. *You will get nowhere without ambition!* But so far, drifting along had suited me just fine. Until that sweltering summer afternoon. As I approached the red awning of the Cornelia Street Café, I was twenty-two years old, unsure of every step I took. And whether I knew it or not, my life was about to change.

When I walked in, the place was empty, the tables scattered around the small room all set for a dinner rush that, on that night, felt like it might not ever come. Onstage at the front of the room stood a girl in a tight, cropped black T-shirt and a pair of low-waisted, faded jeans. Her dark hair cascaded to her shoulders, and black liner ringed her wide-set eyes. Her mouth was a generous slash of red, and the bones in her narrow, angular face could break your heart. Both wrists were loaded with silver bracelets that jangled when she moved, and she had the kind of frenetic energy that reminded me of a champagne bottle that had been recklessly, flagrantly shaken before the cork was finally released.

In the middle of the stage, which was really more like a low platform, was a microphone stand that the girl intermittently flung herself onto, her bangled arms rattling, and she hung both hands off it and stared out over the empty tables. Each time she repeated the move, she added a new little gesture, a flip of her raven hair, a curled lip. She didn't seem to notice me, so I just watched as she pounced on the microphone again—her eyes sweeping the empty room, a low growl emitting from her throat—and it slowly dawned on me that she was practicing.

And that she was good.

I took a deep breath and walked on toward the bar, my eyes still adjusting to the dimness. The back of my shirt was wet with sweat, and I had never been so glad to be dressed in black in all my life. The girl held one last long, high, plaintive note before it faded away. I watched, my arms dimpled with gooseflesh, as she stepped down from the platform and toward the bar. When she saw me, her eyes narrowed, and she walked over, her steps purposeful, militant, as if I were a problem to be solved.

"What can I get you?" Her voice was husky and low, a spoonful of honey and ground glass, but her tone was guarded, as if she were waiting for me to disappoint her.

"No," I said, aware that I was flushing red and thankful for the muted light that concealed it. "I'm sorry. I mean, I'm here for an interview? A pre-interview, actually? I'm Ava?"

I was always apologizing back then, as if just by existing I'd done something unforgivable.

She stood there, still sizing me up while I squirmed uncomfortably, looked down at the wooden surface of the bar, then back up, afraid to meet her eyes. Even in the shadowy dimness of the room, I could see how green they were, like lichen clinging to stones.

"Come with me," she said, walking from behind the bar and over to one of the small tables shoved into a corner, out of sight.

After we sat down, she leaned back in her chair, appraising me coolly. "So," she said, and I wondered if I was imagining it, but her voice maybe seemed a bit friendlier. I took the moment and leaned into it. "Who are you, anyway?"

She crossed her arms over her chest and stared at me, daring me to respond.

"I'm Ava."

"You said that already." And then she smiled, her eyes softening at the corners. "Ava what?"

"Petrova."

"Russian?"

"Ukrainian."

"Do you have any experience working in a restaurant, Ava Petrova?"

"Not much. Not really. Well, not at all. But I'm a fast learner," I added in a rush, afraid she might immediately show me the door.

"Are you now."

"I like to think so. But I'm probably exaggerating."

She cocked her head to the side, staring at me thoughtfully. "What do you *really* want to do? No one comes to the Big Apple to be a server."

"Well, actually I grew up on Staten Island. But I sing a little," I mumbled, looking down at the table, hoping that would be the end of it. "But not like you or anything. Not professionally."

She pushed her thick mane of hair back with one hand, exposing the sharpness of her jaw, the twin slashes of cheekbones. A dark mole lay at the base of her throat, pulsing with every beat of her heart. She looked at me and smiled again, but this time it was tight, her lips flattened into a thin line. "I've been doing this since I was seventeen, dragging my ass to Tisch every day—you know, the music school at NYU? Anyway, seems like a lifetime ago now." There was a flash of vulnerability as she looked at me that disappeared as quickly as it had arrived.

I nodded as if I understood, as if guys walked up to me every day wanting to make me a star, when in actuality, no one in my life knew about the songs that I scribbled on sheets of lined paper late at night when I couldn't sleep, the streetlamps outside my window flooding the room with soft yellow light. I'd never had any real vocal training, never performed in front of anyone but my cat, Mr. Pickles, who only blinked his yellow eyes at me lazily as if to say, *So what?*

"Nice bracelet," she said, gesturing at the cuff on my wrist. "Can I see?"

I held my arm out, and she took my wrist in her hands deftly, gently. Before I knew it, the cuff was firmly laced onto her own wrist, looking as if it had always been there. She held her arm out, admiring herself, tilting her head thoughtfully to one side in consideration. "It suits me," she said, matter-of-factly.

"It does," I replied. Mostly because it was true.

"Can I borrow it?" She turned to me, her expression still as a mid-day pond, and I knew it was a test, this moment.

I shrugged nonchalantly. "Sure. I mean, you can have it—if you want."

I regretted the words the minute they slipped from my mouth, but it was too late.

She nodded, as if things like this happened to her every day. And they probably did.

"Thanks," she said coolly. "When can you start?"

I hesitated for a moment, unsure of what had just been offered. "So . . . I have the job?"

"We'll try you out," she said, standing up and abruptly pushing her chair back, and I knew I'd been dismissed. "It's not a guarantee, though. So don't get your hopes up, OK?" She eyed me warily. "Does tomorrow night work? Five o'clock?"

I nodded. "But . . . can I ask you something?" The words were out of my mouth before I'd even had time to stop myself.

She raised that eyebrow again, almost imperious. *She thinks her shit don't stink,* Irina would've said. I didn't know it at the time, but she wouldn't have been wrong.

"Why me? I mean, I'm sure you could throw a rock and find a hundred people who have way more experience than I do. Why take a chance on me?"

"Why not?" she said with a shrug. "What do I have to lose, right?"

But that was the thing. We had so much to lose. The both of us. We just didn't know it yet.

"By the way," she said as she walked me toward the door, "I'm Lexi. Lexi Mayhem."

Now it was my turn to raise an eyebrow, though I was nowhere near as practiced as her. It probably looked like I was having a stroke.

"My stage name," she explained. "Tough, right?"

I just nodded as she opened the door and I stepped out into the night air. The air had cooled, and the street outside the café was teeming with life. Everything seemed amplified, the blare of car horns, the NYU girls giggling as they passed by, weaving drunkenly through the crowd, the smell of smoke and salt in the summer air mixed with car exhaust. For one brief moment, the city felt like home, full of possibility, the night opening up before me like a gift, my heart inexplicably light.

"See you tomorrow, little Ava," she said as I turned to face her. She was leaning in the doorway, propping the door open with the length of her body. She looked like she'd always been there, like the doorway had been constructed around her in her honor.

"I'll be here."

A lock of hair obscured my face in the summer breeze, a strand settling in the corner of my mouth. Without missing a beat, she reached up and pulled it away, her touch gentle as a puff of milkweed, fleeting and delicate.

"Don't I know it," she said quietly, a sudden edge in her voice, and then before I knew it, the door swung shut and I was alone in the street, the stars above my head blotted out by the lights of the city.

From: Ben Reynolds <b.reynolds@avantentertainment.com>
Sent: Sunday, April 14, 2019 6:35 PM
To: McCray, Kayla <kayla.mccray@rollingstone.com>

Subject: Avant Entertainment, Inc. - Interview Memo

Kayla,

On behalf of myself and Team Mayhem, welcome to LA! I hope the flight wasn't too tiring. In preparation for your meeting with Ms. Mayhem tomorrow afternoon at her private bungalow at the Chateau Marmont, I've prepared a list of questions/topics that, if possible, should be approached delicately:

—Ms. Mayhem's recent divorce from Anders Andersson. While yes, his settlement did grant him the Wyoming estate, they remain cordial.

—The delicate nature of her relationship with Katy Perry. (Please note that we prefer "frenemies" over "feud.")

—The cupcake-licking incident.

Ms. Mayhem will be awaiting you in her bungalow at the Chateau at approximately noon tomorrow and is greatly looking forward to it!

Best,

Ben

From: McCray, Kayla <kayla.mccray@rollingstone.com>
Sent: Sunday, April 14, 2019 9:57 PM
To: Ben Reynolds <b.reynolds@avantentertainment.com>

Subject: Re: Avant Entertainment, Inc. - Interview Memo

Hi Ben,

Thanks so much for your email. I'm still in transit but wanted to send a short note addressing your concerns. You can trust that as a representative of *Rolling Stone* magazine, I will approach the story with the utmost care and consideration. However, to produce the caliber of journalism our publication is known for, I will need to ask Ms. Mayhem a few probing questions. Rest assured, the feature will of course be thoroughly fact-checked and details doubly and triply confirmed.

Looking forward!

Best,

Kayla

[CAUTION] This email originated outside Avant Entertainment.

KAYLA

2019

Maybe it was something about being out of New York, away from those rainy, wet days of early spring, that slight chill still hanging in the air like a ghost. But the minute the plane touched down at LAX and I walked out into the blinding sun, I felt instantly lighter. As I waited for my Uber, I turned my face up toward the sky, rays of sunlight warming my cheeks. I imagined it moving through layers of skin and muscle, all the way down to my bones, purifying them in radiant light. When the car arrived, we lurched along for almost forty-five minutes in traffic, winding down Santa Monica Boulevard before turning onto Sunset, where the Chateau Marmont rose like a castle in the mist, its white towers and lush gardens hanging over the smog-filled city.

The Chateau was known for the privacy it offered its high-profile clientele, and even the tropical foliage surrounding the pool seemed to whisper secrets—and encourage the keeping of them. Everything—from the faded furnishings in the lobby, to the obsidian piano where musicians settled in long past midnight for an impromptu set, to the rosy pink lighting in the lounge, to the gilt-edged mirrors adorning the walls—made you want to move closer and stay awhile. It was no wonder that some stars practically lived there. It was as much a respite from the real world as it was a microcosm of it.

My room was in one of the slightly newer wings, and by the looks of the chipped yellow tile in the bathroom and the slightly pilled bedspread, it was clearly one of the cheapest the hotel offered. Once inside, I showered, standing under the hot spray until a wave of sleepiness washed over me, drug-like, and I forced myself to turn off the comforting heat and get out. Ignoring the siren song of the bed, I changed into what I hoped was my smartest-looking ensemble: a pair of high-waisted black pants and a boat-necked black top, the cut minimalist—bordering on severe. I rubbed my eyes, dry and gritty from the stale plane air and a lack of real sleep, then leaned into the mirror to apply a few coats of mascara and some blush to my cheeks, so I didn't look as dead as I felt inside.

I opened my tote, pulling out the notes I'd managed to jot down in a leather notebook on the flight, the detailed list of questions I planned on asking during the interview. I'd taken advantage of the in-flight Wi-Fi and googled everything I could find on Lexi Mayhem, and her presence was now burned into my brain, the platinum hair, her voice the screech of an impending car crash. Lexi Mayhem had growled her way onto the Billboard charts well over a decade ago with songs that combined the grime of Lower East Side clubs with the glittery sheen of mass-produced pop. Her 2007 hit, "Stiletto," was a dance-club banger about a murder-suicide. In the video, she played both roles in the narrative, that of the killer and of the victim, and in the chilling final scene, she donned a pleather catsuit, raising a gun to one temple, closing her eyes before the screen went black.

But as the years passed, and with each new record she released, the music became more mainstream, the art-punk edge that made her seem so fresh eclipsed by higher budgets and brand-name producers who made her sound indistinguishable from everyone else's. But by that point it almost didn't matter. Lexi Mayhem had become such a massive star that she created her own weather systems, spinning off rumors, scandals, and singles that kept her squarely in the center of the zeitgeist, no matter what. The tabloids were obsessed with examining every facet of her dating life, and while her marriage to Anders had been a surprise, the subsequent divorce certainly was not.

No one, it seemed, was able to stay too close to Lexi for too long.

———

"Kayla. So nice to meet you. How was the flight?"

A tiny, glamorous creature stood in the doorway of the bungalow, holding out one hand for me to grasp. As I took it, her fingers, long and cold as icicles, curled around my own with surprising strength. She was shorter than I'd imagined, almost frail-looking in a loose pair of black drawstring pants and a soft black shirt knotted at the waist, highlighting a sliver of taut navel. A gold medallion gleamed at her throat, and her platinum hair grazed her shoulders, catching the light.

"It was fine," I managed to say, conscious of the fact that her hand was still in mine, soft as water but hard as steel. Up close, Lexi Mayhem's skin was flawless, dewy and without a single line, though I knew she'd recently turned thirty-eight. There'd been a masquerade party at an infamous LA hot spot with a celebrity guest list that had rivaled that of the Met Ball. She wore no makeup that I could discern, and her cheekbones were sharp and high, forehead smooth, her green eyes bright and youthful. But there were dark circles beneath them, lavender half-moons that suggested she was no stranger to sleepless nights.

"Come in already," she said with a low, throaty laugh, swinging the door open wide so I could follow. Moroccan glass lamps in deep jewel colors of cobalt and rose hung from the ceiling, and a large crimson kilim rug was strewn across the hardwood floors. Large french doors flanked by sheer white curtains led out to a courtyard of palms, and the couch was covered in indigo velvet that looked soft enough to sleep on. When she turned to face me, I realized for the first time she was barefoot, her slim white feet marred only by a slightly chipped black pedicure. Her fingernails, I'd noticed when she shook my hand, were black as well, but filed sharp, long and pointed as talons.

I stood awkwardly in the middle of the room as she walked over to an elaborately stocked bar and stood behind it, filling a gold cocktail shaker with ice. She picked up a bottle of whiskey, measuring it out into the shaker, her movements sure and precise. "I thought you might like a drink," she said as she added sweet vermouth, held the cocktail shaker aloft, and began to move it with a series of sharp, staccato motions of her wrist. The clattering of ice on metal drowned out any words of protest I might've had, and I watched as she strained the amber liquid into a pair of short crystal glasses.

"I don't normally drink during interviews," I said carefully, not wanting to get off on the wrong foot.

"What's normal, anyway," she replied, as she sliced a lemon rind into a curly strip, perching it on the rim. "Normal," she said with another dazzling smile, walking over to me and holding the drink out in one hand, "is boring."

I took a deep breath, my fingers grazing her own as I took the glass. *Just one sip to be polite,* I told myself. *You can't afford to be drunk for your first cover story.* Even at a publication like *Rolling Stone*, there were strict codes of professionalism. The days of the renegade gonzo journalism Hunter Thompson had made the magazine famous for were long over.

I brought the glass to my lips, her eyes on me, waiting for my reaction. The drink was perfectly balanced, sweet without being overtly so, with a tart freshness that lingered on the palate.

"What is this?" I asked curiously. *And why am I the only one drinking?*

"Oh, just a little something left over from my days as a working stiff," she said with a wave of her hand. I knew she was referring to her tenure as a bartender at the Cornelia Street Café; I'd seen it mentioned in a few articles about her early career, though little was said beyond the fact that she'd worked there for a few years as she got her footing in NYC. I wondered briefly what it was like for her back then, grinding away at her music, struggling to make rent, just like every other aspiring artist in the city. Did she know back then that she was headed for greatness? Did she ever slump dejectedly on the subway late at night, staring blankly into space, wondering if she'd mix drinks for handsy drunks forever as the stations outside the windows flashed by in the fluorescent glare?

She walked over to the couch, pulling her legs up under her as she sat. She stared at me, a half smile gracing her lips. I could hear faint music coming from the pool area, the wind rustling through the palm trees outside the front door.

"How was your trip?" she asked, as if she really wanted to know.

"It was great," I said quickly. "I've never flown first class before."

"All the warm nuts you can eat, right?"

"The free champagne doesn't hurt either," I said. "Not that I had any."

"I never liked champagne," she said, wrinkling her nose distastefully. "Too many bubbles. It gives you the *worst* hangovers." She laughed, leaning forward slightly, pushing her hair back with one hand.

I reached into my bag and retrieved my notebook. "That it does," I said, placing it in my lap and opening it. "So, Ms. Mayhem, I'd like to ask a few preliminary questions, just to get some background. Does that sound OK?"

"Call me Lexi," she said warmly.

"OK," I said slowly, smiling despite myself. "Lexi it is."

"Ask me anything," she said, leaning back and crossing one leg over the other.

"Anything? Ben mentioned several—"

"Oh, fuck Ben," she said with a wave of her hand. "I pay the mortgage on his ridiculous house in Bel Air. So I think that means I'm in charge, right?"

Her words were harsh, but there was fondness there too. It reminded me of the way I teased Keats about his ridiculous elbow-patched blazers.

"Have you worked with Ben for a long time?"

"Too long." She rolled her eyes. "Let's see . . . about thirteen years now? Give or take. Before that I was basically my own manager. I used to call venues and pretend to be my own booking agent." She drew herself up, her spine straight as a broomstick, holding one hand up to her ear as if it were a phone. "I represent Lexi Mayhem," she said in a clipped British accent. "She's incredibly hot right now, and we'd love the ten p.m. slot for her if it's available?"

"Was this back in New York?" I asked as I reached into my bag, pulled out the small voice recorder I used for interviews, and turned it on, setting it between us on the coffee table.

"I was banging on doors and getting nowhere," she said, twirling one ankle in a slow circle so that I caught a glimpse of the bottom of one foot, shadowed with dirt, as if she'd been walking around barefoot for days. "Having a manager—even a fake one—got me more gigs. And then I finally gained some momentum."

"You got signed."

"Eventually. After a showcase with some record execs, a lot of sweat and shows in dive bars and leaving a pint of my own blood onstage every night."

She wasn't bitter, just pragmatic about it all, that this had led to *this* and *this* and *this*. A long chain in her history, one door opening onto the next, all of them unlocked.

"Was that the genesis for the new label?"

"Underworld? Definitely. If I can save another talented female performer some grief, then I'm going to do it. I mean, now that I *can*, you know?"

"Can you talk about the impetus for the name?" I asked. "Why Underworld Records? What's the significance there?"

Lexi got up suddenly, grabbing her phone from where it sat beside her, shoving the voice recorder aside and sitting down on the coffee table so that we were inches apart. I watched as she tapped the screen with one pointed nail, her face set in concentration before holding out the phone for me to view.

A drawing of a pomegranate filled the screen, the scarlet flesh split open, seeds in a darker red spilling out in a messy profusion, the words "Underworld Records" circling the perimeter of the logo in a baroque black script. "The goddess Persephone was the queen of the underworld," Lexi explained, her voice hushed, almost reverent. "Back then, the pomegranate was considered the fruit of the dead, and anyone who ate it—like Persephone—was condemned to stay in the realm of darkness forever. When Hades fell in love with her, he forced her to remain there against her will."

She plucked the phone from my hands and scrolled through it once again, stopping on another logo mock-up, this one depicting a woman in a flowing vermilion robe, her back turned to the viewer, the perimeter swallowed by blackness, a faint light glimmering off in the distance. "Her mother, Demeter, was so grief-stricken that she turned all the lands barren, causing the upper realm to live in eternal winter. But eventually, Hades agreed to allow Persephone to return to the land of the living once a year . . ." Her voice trailed off, and she looked up with a faraway smile, as if lost in her own thoughts.

"Bringing spring with her," I finished. "And restoring balance to the world."

"Exactly," she said, as if she were relieved to be understood. I could smell the heady jasmine and musk of her perfume, and though I hadn't ingested more than a drop of alcohol, I felt momentarily dizzy, intoxicated by the nearness of her.

"Going back to the origins of the label—there's clearly a feminist agenda afoot with the backstory of women bringing balance to an unjust world. I take it that it's important to you? Supporting other women?"

"Well, *yeah*. Isn't it to you?" She stood up, walking back over to the couch and sitting down again, her phone resting in her lap.

"Journalism—and publishing—is a business largely dominated by men," I said, aware that the explanation sounded thin, even to my own ears. As I pondered her question, I couldn't help but wonder why I hadn't made any real, supportive friendships with women over the years. Sure, I'd managed to develop a mentoring relationship with Keats, and with almost every male boss I'd ever had. But not with the women I'd worked alongside for years. There was Simone, with whom I shared the tiniest cubicle on earth, who blinked at me in terror if I dared to ask about her weekend, sputtering a two-word reply before turning back to her computer. We weren't exactly what you'd call close.

"If you haven't noticed, so is the music business." Her smile was tight now, a thin line. "Which is why I wanted to start my own label— to give women artists a fair shot, so they might be judged on the quality of their talent. Not on how big their tits are."

"I would imagine that you experienced that kind of sexism and scrutiny in the early days of your career," I said, thrilled to have an opportunity to turn the conversation back to Lexi and away from myself. "Can we talk about that a bit?"

She nodded, pulling her legs up and crossing them beneath her, resting her elbows on her knees. She was still for a moment, silent, and I was reminded of a sphinx, her eyes lowered as she contemplated the floor in front of her. "When I was starting out," she began slowly, "I had a lot to prove. Women in this business always do. I was expected to be sexy. That was a given. I mean, every suit that wanted to sign me ended up hitting on me—they didn't even try to hide it. They'd buy me fancy dinners, clothes. But there was always a price. I played the game for a while, until I got where I wanted to go. But for me it was always about the music, pushing boundaries with it. Making people . . . uncomfortable."

"Uncomfortable? In what way?"

She looked up, and I marveled at the extraordinary bottle-green hue of her eyes, the murkiness shot through with flecks of gold.

"Well, I don't just use my body to seduce. Not exactly. Sure, it's part of drawing the audience in, but I try and push beyond it, take them somewhere they never thought they'd go. It's a trick. A kind of bait and switch—and a form of provocation. All the best art is."

"Like the year you appeared at the VMAs wearing that long black dress, walking"—I searched my brain for the reference—"a skunk on a leash?"

"A *diamond*-studded leash," she said, leaning forward in her seat. "You should've seen the looks on everyone's faces when that skunk sprayed on the red carpet under those bright lights—they all thought it was a mishap. But it was part of the performance too." She leaned back, laughing softly. "I really thought Ben was going to quit that night. My whole team was ready to have my head, but I didn't care. That's the thing—you can't worry about what anyone else thinks. You have to trust your gut and do what feels right. Because at the end of the day, it's *your* career. And you need to protect it. It's the only way to survive."

I nodded slowly. "That makes sense. So I guess my question is . . ." I paused for a moment, trying to find the right words. "Is that the lesson you're imparting to the up-and-coming artists you'll sign? That they need to be completely self-reliant?"

"I think it's a good lesson for everyone." She shrugged. "When you start depending on other people . . ." Her words trailed off, and she looked away, her profile sharp, as if it had been etched on glass. "You become weak," she finished, her voice low, almost a whisper. "You lose your independence. You lose *yourself*." She turned to face me again. "You know what I mean?"

I nodded, swallowing hard, and looking down at the coffee table. I knew what she meant all too well. Ever since my friendship with Astrid had fallen apart so spectacularly, I'd kept my distance from people, building a fortress out of words, sheets of paper that cut the hands of those who reached for me too closely.

We'd met in third grade, Astrid and I, but in a way, she'd always been there, just a few blocks from the little white bungalow where I lived with my mother, the shingles on the roof curling in perpetual disrepair, the proliferation of rosebushes climbing the weathered fence in the front yard in the hot gasp of summer. I'd never had a best friend, someone who was so willing to be mine. I was confident and outwardly cool, but inside I overthought every syllable that left my lips. Astrid had always been shy, the girl in the corner of the library, a tower of books beside her, who would smile if you caught her eye, then look away sharply, her cheeks lit by roses.

We completed each other's sentences. Thought each other's thoughts with a kind of telepathy that scared and elated us. Slept in twin beds at night, the phone pressed to one ear until it grew hot and pink, falling asleep to the sound of one another's breath, rhythmic as the ocean. The years passed, her hand clenched firmly in my own. Boys couldn't penetrate the scaffolding we'd created out of sticks of sugarless gum and song lyrics, the private jokes we doodled in each other's notebooks.

And then, as things often do, one summer, everything changed.

There was a high-pitched protest of springs as Lexi shifted her weight on the sofa, and I blinked rapidly, hoping she hadn't noticed the momentary lapse. "I'd love to hear more about your plans for the label," I said as I reached over and grabbed the voice recorder from the table, checking the battery life. "And maybe cover some of your life back in New York—before fame and fortune came calling."

Lexi stood up and strolled back to the bar, plucking two bottles of Evian from the minifridge, before making her way back over to the couch and handing me one. "There's plenty of time for all that," she said declaratively. "I'm flying to New York next week for a press conference, so I'll be happy to meet with you then and fill in the blanks of anything we don't cover today. But in the meantime, why don't you tell me a little about you."

She sat back down on the couch, looking at me expectantly.

"M-me?" I stammered, the plastic frigid in my hands. "What exactly would you like to know? I've written about—"

"I'm not interested in your writing," she said, cutting me off. "I want to hear about *you*."

"But we're not here to talk about me," I pointed out. "We're here to talk about *you*. As a journalist, I live my life behind the scenes. Not on the front page."

"How boring."

"It's not boring," I said gently. "It's part of my job. And I take it seriously."

She rolled her eyes, and I couldn't help but smile. She was wearing me down and she knew it. Just sitting in the same room with her made everything seem as if it had been brushed with gold. Even the air inside her bungalow felt different on my skin, voluptuous and seductive.

"OK, OK," I said with a short laugh. "What do you want to know?"

"Well . . . ," she began, drawing out the word like caramel on her tongue, "why were you interested in this story, anyway? Just because it's the cover?" She raised an eyebrow. "Did you even have a choice, or was it assigned to you?"

I uncapped the water bottle, taking a swig before answering, my lips dry from the recycled air of the long flight. "It's my first cover story for the magazine, but I think you already know that, right?" She nodded, a quick dip of the chin, and I went on before she could interject. "I've been working toward this kind of feature for my entire career. But I also knew the assignment wouldn't be boring, and . . . well, someone I knew a long time ago was a big fan of your music."

Astrid's face flashed through my mind again, but quickly, so quickly, and then it was gone. I took a deep breath, banishing her presence from the room.

"Does that answer your question?" I asked, clearing my throat.

"I suppose," Lexi said grudgingly, a slow smile stealing over her lips. "For now."

Was she mocking me? Daring me? It was hard to tell. And it was then that I saw the faintest glimmer of satisfaction pass over her face, like a light winking on in the darkness.

AVA

2005

"Picking up!"

There was a voice at my back, sharp and gruff, and I moved to the left quickly, just in time to see Lexi push past me, plates she'd just grabbed from the kitchen now balanced over her head, her movements as graceful and sure. I concentrated on rubbing a damp cloth—bar mops, Lexi called them—in circles on the scarred wooden surface as the sounds of the café closing for the night swirled around me. I'd made it through my first shift, if only by the skin of my teeth.

My feet ached inside my battered pair of black Converse sneakers, and my hands were red and roughened already from the harsh disinfectant we used. A small burn stood out on the top of one hand where I'd bumped into the espresso machine while grabbing a latte, and I rubbed my fingers over the raised red welt, wincing. I was tired. So tired that it was almost a challenge to stay vertical. *Will it always be this hard?* I wondered, feeling daunted already. But that's how I was back then. Sidelined by the smallest challenge. I liked to think of myself as brave and determined, but I wasn't. It was in my nature to fold like paper at the smallest setback.

Earlier that evening, I'd been completely frazzled, the bar packed three rows deep with customers, all angry, all impatiently waiting for me to take their order. I'd turned to Lexi, my heart beating wildly, trying to stifle the anxiety that was probably written all over my face and asked, "Stoli and cranberry. How do I make it?"

She just stared at me uncomprehendingly while I babbled my inane request yet again, the pitch rising in my voice. *Stoli and cranberry,* I kept repeating, as though if I said it enough times it would somehow magically make sense. *Stoli and cranberry.* The words sounded jumbled in my mouth, like I was speaking a foreign language. I felt my heart fluttering ominously in my chest, and I knew if I didn't find a way to relax, I'd spiral into hysteria right there in front of Lexi, in front of the entire bar.

"Ava," she finally said, reaching over and grabbing a bottle of clear liquid with a red-and-gold label emblazoned on the front. "It's just a vodka cranberry. Stoli is a type of *vodka.*" She pushed the bottle into my hands. "Just add cranberry juice, OK?"

I nodded, the shame leaving high circles of color in my cheeks, and I turned away, filling the glass with ice, pouring two jiggers of vodka over it, then adding the juice, which turned the drink almost fuchsia in the dim light.

"Jesus," Lexi grumbled at my back, laughing softly under her breath, "a Russian chick who doesn't know what Stoli is?"

"Ukrainian," I mumbled, pushing past her and grabbing an orange slice for the rim. I had no idea if that was standard, but it made the drink look a little more professional, and at that point, I'd take what I could get.

She just shook her head disdainfully, moving over to the register and depositing a wad of bills inside.

"About time," the surly, middle-aged guy who'd ordered it said as I placed the drink on the bar in front of him. I watched as he took a swallow, grimacing, and I fought back the urge to pull off the towel I'd thrown over one shoulder, walk out of the café, and never come back.

I grabbed my purse from behind the bar and stepped out the back door into the alley. The night air settled on my skin, cooling it, and there was the scent of smoke in the air, faint but present, the first sign of fall. I lit a cigarette, leaning my head back against the brick wall and closing my eyes, the tension of the night slowly ebbing away. For a moment I couldn't feel my throbbing feet or the pain in my hand. When I opened my eyes, there were only the stars overhead, I knew, their light hidden by the neon city.

My cell buzzed, the sound unrelenting, and I rummaged endlessly through my bag before I finally found it, buried at the bottom. As I looked at numbers on the screen, my stomach tightened. I'd deleted the contact so many times now that his name no longer showed at all. I hit "Play" on the voice mail he'd left, and when I heard his voice in my ear, I wondered if I'd ever have the strength to break free entirely.

Hey . . . it's me. Maybe you think you're all that in the big city now. Maybe you don't miss me anymore, huh? There was a pause and a rush of wind, and I could picture him standing outside his mother's house on Staten Island, the red front door with its peeling paint, his silver Mustang in the driveway, glowing under the streetlights. *We belong together,* he said, his voice low and slightly menacing, the way it got each time I'd tried to leave him. *Remember what happens when you fight me—*

The call ended abruptly, and I dropped the phone back into my purse, slinging it over my shoulder and taking another drag off my cigarette as if it were oxygen. *You're done with him for good this time,* I told myself sternly, exhaling a thick cloud of smoke. *And you're never going back.* A siren wailed in the distance before fading away, and the alley was suddenly quiet again.

The sound of the door creaking open made me jump, and then Lexi was there, looking at me expectantly. I tried to smile, bringing the cigarette to my lips for another drag, willing my hands to stop shaking. Her dark hair was pulled back in a high ponytail, making her cheekbones appear higher and more sculpted than usual. She leaned against the wall next to me, looking down at the cigarette in my hand. "Got one for me?" she asked, arching one eyebrow. Her lips were crimson, rouged expertly, even after a long night of lugging plates and slinging drinks.

I nodded, reaching into my bag once again and shaking another from the half-empty pack. Every day I told myself I'd quit, and every day I found myself walking to the bodega and buying another pack. It was a vicious cycle, but one I couldn't seem to break. There was something about the heaviness of the smoke in my lungs that made me feel calmer, more centered.

Lexi popped the cigarette in her mouth, then leaned closer to me until she was an inch away, touching the tip of her cigarette to mine, her eyes closed. She was so close that I could smell the medicinal reek of the patchouli oil on her skin. She breathed in, and the tip bloomed cherry red. She opened her eyes, so close to mine, and I could see flecks of gold inside, a sprinkling of glitter.

She pulled back, inhaling, then breathing a cloud of smoke into the air, leaning her head back against the brick wall. "Thanks," she said. "This shift was fucking interminable." I was quiet, and after a few seconds, she turned her head to look at me. "You OK?" But before I could answer, she went on. "The first night is always the hardest, but don't worry, you'll get the hang of it."

"It's not that," I said, still shaken by the way Ian always seemed to pop up every time my life was even remotely on the right track. She took another drag, then crushed the cigarette out under a bootheel.

"Trouble in paradise?" she asked quietly, staring out into the alley, at the dumpster directly across from us. I tried not to think about how many rats might be inside, scavenging for food. I'd read somewhere that there were more rats in New York City than people, and the thought made me shiver.

"It's over between us, but he . . ." My voice trailed off helplessly, and I wondered if the words were even true, if some tiny piece of me still wanted him, even after all that had happened between us.

"Won't take the hint?" Lexi asked, nodding slowly. "All you can do is move on. Eventually he'll get the message."

But Lexi didn't know how dogged and persistent Ian got when there was something he couldn't have. She didn't know that he was always right, always telling me he knew better. How he'd fight like hell, just so he didn't lose.

That he'd rather destroy something completely than be denied it.

"You still love him?" she asked, and I exhaled another cloud of smoke, unsure of how to untangle the question. It was worse than love—it was two people bonded by the hurt they'd done to one another, caught in a never-ending dance, one I didn't know if I'd ever have the strength to break free of entirely.

"You can love someone . . . and still know they're wrong for you," I said, the pain in my voice like a tightly knotted rope. "He turns me on and off like a switch."

She looked over at me sharply, and I knew from her expression that she was busy filing away what I'd said for later. And then, as was her way, she changed the subject, switching gears. "I'm taking you out tonight," she proclaimed. "You need a distraction—and I need a drink."

She looked at me expectantly, waiting for an answer, and suddenly my exhaustion faded away in a rush, and I was ready for whatever the night might hold. I would've followed her anywhere without question, just because she asked me to. And she knew it.

As sure as she knew she'd be a star.

"OK," I said, my face breaking into a smile. "Take me."

———

The room spun. Low red light, pounding bass, the glass of Jack Daniel's in front of me melting into ice. Lexi chased the light, bathed in it, entertaining everyone who approached her while I shrank from the eyes that sought me out. But on the dance floor, the music pulsing through us, our bodies moved in sync. She grabbed my hands, our fingers interlocking, and held them above our heads as our hips twisted below. She threw her head back, and I mirrored her, my body responding automatically. When we finally left the dance floor, I was spent, and slick with sweat.

I pushed the damp hair from my forehead, while at the bar, Lexi ordered us each another shot. I liked the way she drank, throwing her liquor back easily, as if even the sting of alcohol couldn't touch her. She leaned her head on my shoulder periodically, and I could feel the insistent pounding of her heart through her skin.

"Let's get out of here," she yelled in my ear around two a.m., and I nodded, following her as she pushed through the crowd and out into the maze of the city. There was a slight chill in the air, a hint of fall beneath the last gasp of summer heat. We walked down Tenth Street and then continued farther downtown, making our way home, passing the Hells Angels' headquarters; Ray's Candy Store, where I sometimes stopped in the heat of the summer afternoons for a soft-serve cone or an egg cream; and then heading into Chinatown, the storefronts all shuttered except for the twenty-four-hour dumpling shops and restaurants.

But I wasn't hungry; I was whiskey drunk and spinning, my blood racing with excitement. The energy of the city made me manic, unable to sit still, the wail of sirens in the night air, all of New York at my feet. Some nights I'd prowl the alleyways like a stray cat, peering into lit windows of apartments, inventing stories about the people who lived inside, envying their seemingly happy lives. But tonight, I didn't envy anything or anyone. Tonight, I didn't want to be anywhere but exactly where I was—arm in arm with Lexi.

"Sing me a song," she commanded as she pulled me along the street, the heels of her boots clicking sharply against the pavement. Suddenly she stopped for a moment and looked at me, her gaze fierce and commanding. "Sing," she ordered, lifting her chin slightly, daring me.

The idea was preposterous. Sing here? *Now?*

"No way." I laughed nervously, breaking free of her grip and continuing to walk, hoping she'd just let it go but knowing that she wouldn't. That in her own way she was like Ian. Once Lexi latched on to an idea, she wouldn't give up until she got her way.

"C'mon, Ava," she pleaded, her steps quick and light behind me until she caught up. "I want to hear one of your songs. Sing for me."

I shook my head violently from side to side. I didn't sing for anyone. I'd never shown anyone my songs, not even Ian. I didn't even much like singing for Mr. Pickles. I only did because he seemed so totally indifferent, barely awake as he lounged in the sunlight.

"Ava, *stop*," she said, reaching out and grabbing my arm again, roughly pulling me to a halt. We stood on Canal Street, downtown mostly deserted at this hour but for the occasional crowds of drunken revelers walking by. "Just do it," she said fiercely, her green eyes boring into mine. "All of New York is a stage, you know. If you can't perform here, right now, then how will you ever do it for an audience?"

"Who says I even want to?" I muttered, looking down at my feet.

"I do," she said firmly. "And I'm hardly ever wrong." When I looked up, she smiled seductively, and I felt my resistance beginning to crumble. Something about being with Lexi made me feel almost brave, as if her very presence gave me the will to break out of the prison of fear I'd built for myself. Or maybe, like everyone else she encountered, I was incapable of saying no to her.

Neither would've surprised me.

I leaned against a streetlight, the metal on my skin cold and reassuring; closed my eyes; and began to sing, the words coming slowly, then faster as the melody took flight. *She flips off her teachers, makes out on the bleachers. Her boyfriend's a loser, he lives to abuse her . . .*

I could feel Lexi hovering near me, the weight of her presence, agitated, like the spreading of wings. But I was lost in the moment, in the notes that spilled from my throat, the words that moved through me thick as blood. *Heartsick, hot chick, left of the middle, suburban damage . . .*

If crowds pushed past, I was oblivious, transported somewhere else entirely, the city disappearing into the melody I wove around me like a cloak. When I finished, I stood there for a moment, eyes still closed before I opened them slowly, cautiously, and the night snapped into sharp focus. There was Lexi's face, her reddened mouth agape, eyes wide, and a smattering of applause from a coterie of drunk college kids who walked by. Lexi and I stared at one another, my cheeks flushing hotly until I had to look away.

"You *wrote* that?" she said, walking toward me. There was disbelief in her eyes, to be sure, but also something that glittered dangerously below the surface, turning her hard and impenetrable. As soon as I saw it, I pulled back into myself, wanting to hide inside the soft meat of my body.

"It's nothing," I said quickly. "It's just a little—"

"Nothing?" she breathed, her expression incredulous. "That was not *nothing*, Ava. That was *everything*. Do you know how good you are?"

There was something aggressive in her demeanor, and I could see her entire body tense, taut as a wire. I didn't understand it, but I shrugged, feeling my eyes moisten, the tears coming from a place so buried in the furthest corners of my being that it almost hurt to access it at all. A place that thought I wasn't good enough, battered and blackened as a bruise. But I somehow managed to smile through it, hoping my expression said what my words couldn't.

That I was happy.

"You need a better stage name, though, if I'm going to introduce you to my manager. Ava Petrova? That'll *never* work." Lexi laughed, linking her arm in mine as we began to walk again. She stopped momentarily, lighting a cigarette, and I noticed her hands were shaking, fluttering around her face, briefly illuminated by the flick of her lighter. She inhaled sharply, as if the nicotine were medicine, and for the first time since she'd demanded I use the sidewalk as my own personal stage, I saw her face relax slightly, a small softening. "I like Ava. Ava's good," she said declaratively.

"It means 'bird,'" I offered. "In Latin."

"What's your middle name?" she asked, exhaling a plume of smoke.

"My middle name? Why?" I asked, immediately ill at ease for reasons I couldn't quite discern.

"Just *tell* me." She laughed, rolling her eyes in annoyance.

I took a deep breath. "It's . . . Arcana." She stopped in her tracks and looked at me, but before she could speak, I went on. "I hate it," I said quickly. "It means 'secrets.' Or 'mysteries' maybe? I looked it up once. I can't remember now," I finished with a nervous laugh. "Before I was born, my mother was a bit of a hippie, into tarot cards and crystals." I remembered the photographs I'd seen of Irina in her twenties, a knit poncho draped over her thin frame, a colorful scarf wrapped around her head, hiding the mane of black hair that fell to her waist, clear quartz and obsidian punctuating her wrists and throat.

"That's the coolest name I've ever heard," Lexi said, an envious glint in her green eyes. "It's perfect: Ava Arcana," she proclaimed as we kept walking. "But Ava Arcana Petrova? Good god." She cackled.

"Wait," I said, hoping to change the subject. "You have a *manager*?"

"I do!" Lexi said, turning to grab my arm, giving it a small squeeze. "I'll introduce you."

"You think I'm good enough for that?" I said hesitantly, afraid to speak the words aloud.

"Yes!" Lexi exclaimed, looking at me as if I'd momentarily lost it, her voice ringing with annoyance. "What have I been *telling* you? I mean, you were off-key in a few places—you really need to work on your technique," she said chidingly, Miss Know-It-All, "but if you weren't good enough, trust me, I wouldn't even suggest it. This guy likes having his time wasted even less than I do." She stepped nimbly over a pile of trash on the street. "He's gotten a few local acts signed and thinks

I'm next. I've been doing this for *so* long, Ava." Her voice had turned bitter now, her eyes hardening. "But I think this is my big break."

I could see the desire rising from her skin like perfume, hovering in the air around her, charging the very molecules and rearranging them. I could almost smell it, the sulfur that lingers just before an electrical storm. And maybe, just maybe, some of that magic would rub off on me too.

Maybe, for once in my life, I was right where I belonged.

KAYLA

2019

On the way back to New York, I was sure I'd pass out from sheer exhaustion the second I sat down on the plane. But ever since the interview, I'd been too wound up to sleep. Something about Lexi Mayhem made me feel shockingly alive, but also slightly unsettled, and I'd spent the entire six hours of the flight staring out the window into impenetrable blackness, my eyes growing leaden as the hours passed and sleep continued to elude me.

Once I made it back to Brooklyn, I dropped my duffel bag on the living room floor and headed to the deli on the corner. I ordered a bacon, egg, and cheese and a black coffee, grease running down my wrist as I walked to the subway, ducking into the station as a light rain pelted my head and shoulders. I could hear the train approaching from below and I ran for it, my shoes clattering on the long flight of stairs as I hurled my body inside just as the doors were closing.

The *Rolling Stone* office was housed in a giant steel building that gave me anxiety every time I walked through its doors. The lobby was always a sea of humanity, the elevators just as packed. I exited on the twenty-fifth floor, making my way toward the bullpen, where my desk was located. I waved hello to Miles, the junior reporter who sat behind me, and slid into my chair, wrestling the AirPods from my ears.

Simone was already in our veal-fattening pen, as Keats had affectionately dubbed it, bent over her laptop, the intricate rows of braids that hung halfway down her back swaying as she typed. She was one of the last vestiges of *Rolling Stone* as a magazine that covered anything other than pop dreck, writing features about plotting generals and cybersecurity—all the journalism-with-a-capital-*J* kind of stuff.

As usual, she was dressed head to toe in black, and her dark, slightly hooded eyes were magnified by the lenses of the thick black glasses she wore, a pearl chain dangling from each earpiece. With her smooth brown skin, she could've been anywhere between twenty-five and forty. And after my meeting with Lexi, I couldn't seem to shake the why of it all. After Astrid, I'd shut other women out. I hadn't even wanted to try. Simone hadn't exactly laid out a red carpet in welcome, but it wasn't like I'd made any kind of effort myself either.

Although we'd never exchanged more than a few pleasantries, I was pretty sure she'd bought me a cupcake on my last birthday. The plastic container had been waiting on my desk when I'd returned from lunch that day, the swirls of pink icing almost completely obscured by a prolific shower of rainbow sprinkles. I'd looked around for a note, finding nothing on my desk but the usual mess of papers and empty coffee cups, then craned my neck to search the perimeter, but no one so much as nodded in my direction. "Is this . . . from you?" I asked tentatively, wincing as the words left my throat, as though waiting for a blow. Simone didn't even look up from her screen. Her long nails, polished key-lime green, tapped the keys authoritatively.

"Don't know what you're talking about," she said when she finally answered. "Baked goods materialize all the time. The world's a mysterious place."

I stifled a laugh, biting the inside of my cheek to keep a straight face, even though she had her back turned. Ever since then, even though most of the time Simone acted as though she were merely tolerating my presence, the tiniest shred of warmth hung there, suspended between us. One I had done nothing to stoke the embers of.

Until now.

I took a deep breath, and before I could change my mind, I swiveled around to face her, waiting for a break in her typing. As if she could feel the impending words before they'd even left my mouth, her hands stilled on the keys, and without turning around, she spoke.

"Well?"

My mouth dropped. Simone and I were having a conversation! Or at least half of a conversation. "Well . . ." I trailed off. It was amazing how I could make a living talking with sources, and yet, whenever I was put on the spot with a regular person, it suddenly all felt so impossible. "I did my Mayhem interview—you know, for the cover." I hesitated, wondering if Simone would know anything at all about what I was saying. Why would she even care about my assignments when she was probably writing about Muammar al-Qaddafi's lost gold?

"How'd she look? She's gotten so *safe* over the years," she said, chortling to herself. "Nothing like the days when she'd show up on the red carpet looking like she hadn't even bothered to brush her hair."

"She was in the plainest clothes imaginable." I shrugged. "But somehow it worked. It still looked like it had all cost thousands of dollars."

"No doubt," Simone said with a snort. "Sounds like you were pretty charmed by her."

My cheeks flushed in protest, but just as quickly, I realized she was right. After so many years of interviews, I should've been immune to Lexi's charms. My brain flashed back to the bare feet, the expertly mixed drink, the fierce look in her eyes when she spoke of upending the music industry like one of the amps she used to tip off the edge of the stage nightly in the early days of her career. Most celebrities were disappointing in the flesh. But Lexi Mayhem in person had been every bit as compelling as I'd hoped.

"You have to watch it with people like her," Simone said as she swung her chair back around and started clacking away at the keyboard again as if I'd suddenly vanished. "Your problem, McCray, is that you don't get out enough. Grab a drink with a friend. Go out for brunch. Hell, go to a movie once in a while. That way you'll be able to see this for what it is—just another performance. Lexi Mayhem is not your buddy. None of them are. And a celebrity interview is no different from a sit-down with a high-ranking politician. It's an act, designed to lull you into subserviency. Don't let any of it fool you, and don't forget you're there for the truth. Not some PR spread."

"Wait a minute," I said, with as much indignation as I could muster. "How would you know anything about my social life? Or lack thereof?"

"I've got eyes, don't I?" Simone retorted, her fingers still tapping without a break. Although I couldn't see her face, I suspected that her lips were curved in the faintest hint of a smile. "You'd probably move a damn bed in here if you thought you could get away with it."

"Like you wouldn't?"

Simone let out a sound that fell somewhere in between a grunt and a sigh, which I took as my cue to get back to work. I swiveled my chair around, pulling out my voice recorder and popping back in my headphones. As I replayed the interview, Lexi's gravelly voice streaming through my ears, I opened my laptop and began the tedious work of transcription. I could've used a service and often did, but for more important pieces, I preferred to do the work myself. Fewer errors crept in that way, and plus, it allowed me to relive the entire interview in my mind. I could see the bare spots clearly, the places I'd need to go back and ask follow-up questions to add more detail or where I needed to ask a source for more clarification. But as I listened, a pattern began to emerge, and with it a strange feeling overtook me, a needling I couldn't ignore.

Anytime I'd brought up Lexi's past, she'd deflected, changed the subject, or given me a surface-level answer. If her early experiences with sexism in the industry were part of the impetus to start her own label, then why wouldn't she want younger female artists just starting out in the business to benefit from reading about her struggles in print? It didn't make a ton of sense once I stopped to think about it.

I opened a new browser and began googling. *Lexi Mayhem. Early career. Lexi Mayhem. New York.* I clicked on link after link, all with only the bare bones of a past history. Scaffolding, really. There were the same lines I'd seen before about her working at the Cornelia Street Café, occasionally performing onstage there, but not much else. I was searching for footage of Lexi's first performances, interviews from the early days of her career. Anything to show how she'd gotten from there to here, which at the end of the day, I suspected, was the real story. But in one interview after another, Lexi repeated the same talking points, almost as if they had been rehearsed and memorized. The struggle to get noticed in the industry. The climb to the top. All recounted in the vaguest and most general terms possible. Whenever a journalist came too close, Lexi deftly skirted the issue, changing the subject.

Just as she had with me.

As I sat there mulling this over, I looked up to see Keats exiting his office and beginning to make his way across the room toward me. He was dressed in his usual professorial drag, his black hair cut short and silvery gray at the temples, and he wore the kind of rectangular black eyeglasses that had been popular around 1995. He'd told me once that his vision was perfect—he just liked the affectation. That was Keats all over. He was cool, but he wasn't *hip*, and there was a very big difference between the two—especially in the music industry. He was exceedingly well versed on every up-and-coming or indie band you could think of and a walking encyclopedia of pop music, but he wasn't the guy who'd take you to a warehouse in Brooklyn at two a.m. to see some obscure act. He resembled one of those ubiquitous dads on practically every corner of Fort Greene or Park Slope, skateboarding around with little Wolf or Hunter. But as far as I knew, the only kids Keats had were us writers.

"So, how'd it go?" he asked, coming to a halt in front of my desk. "You get some good tape out there?" He took a sip of the cup of coffee he held in one hand.

I pulled the AirPods out of my ears, even though the recording was paused. "It was a good start. We talked about pop as performance art and her new label. Being a woman in a male-dominated industry."

I paused, thinking back over the conversation, imagining what Keats would take away from it if he'd been there. He was always so good at seeing things from a thousand feet up. "Did you know she used to pretend to be her own manager? She didn't say much about the early days of her career—it's weird actually, I haven't been able to find a ton about that time period in print—but she did mention that."

Keats was quiet for a moment. I hated when Keats got quiet. It usually meant there was a problem. I sat back, wincing slightly. I was sore from the flight, and my horrible desk chair, which was more of a torture device than anything resembling actual furniture, wasn't helping matters.

"I'll save the fact-checkers some work on that one," Keats said, placing his cup on my desk. "Jamie Preston was her manager back then."

"What do you mean?"

"I'm sure Lexi probably handled some things herself in the very beginning, but Jamie entered the picture pretty early on."

"Jamie Preston? CEO of Rukus Records?"

"The very same."

I'd followed the label a little over the years. Rukus had a knack for signing unknown bands and artists, performers who would eventually go on to superstardom—usually with the clout of a major label behind them.

"But I've read every profile of her, and he's never mentioned. Not in any of her interviews."

"I've been in this business a long time, Kayla," Keats reminded me gently. It was true: legend had it that Keats had started covering shows back in high school, sneaking out of his parents' classic six on the Upper East Side, fake ID in hand, to the dive bars of the Lower East Side in pursuit of the next big thing. "Trust me. Jamie Preston was Lexi Mayhem's first manager. Not everything is online."

"But why would she lie?"

"You tell me," he said evenly, leaning against my cubicle as if he had all day, though I knew he was probably multitasking a hundred different things in his head all at once. "Maybe because it's a good story? The self-made Lexi Mayhem? It's mythmaking."

"Maybe," I muttered distractedly, reaching over and typing Jamie's name into the open search engine. Keats picked up his cup and took a swig, grimacing immediately, probably because it was lukewarm by now. Keats was always ordering coffee that he forgot to drink. Which meant his assistant, Vanessa, spent most of her young life waiting in line at Starbucks.

There was a pause while I turned the interview over in my mind, the pieces refusing to interlock cleanly. Even this early on in the process, I should've been able to draft the first few lines of copy, the ones that clearly showed the direction the story was headed. That I couldn't felt troubling.

"I'm just not sure where to start," I admitted, more to myself than Keats. As willing as she'd been to talk, I was beginning to realize that I hadn't walked out of that bungalow knowing anything Lexi Mayhem didn't want me to know.

"Never forget the first rule of journalism, Kayla," Keats said with a smile. "Begin at the beginning."

After Keats wandered back to his office, I grabbed a kale salad from the cafeteria on the fifteenth floor and wolfed it down at my desk, barely tasting it. I finished the transcription and placed it in a file I named MAYHEM. Then I did what all writers do when we get blocked—I stared into space for a while, thinking about what Keats had said. *Begin at the beginning.* But where was that? Lexi's childhood? Her teenage years? When she first realized she could sing? Maybe those early days in New York that she didn't want to talk about . . . with a man she'd all but erased from her history.

I turned back to my computer again and pulled up the website for Rukus Records. I clicked through a series of pages, not finding anything of real interest. The website was bare bones as far as design went. Just a home page with the word "Rukus" in electric violet, a contact email, and a phone number.

And an address.

I scribbled it down on a Post-it and crammed the paper into my pocket, grabbed my jacket, and headed for the elevator.

AVA

"Think fast."

I whipped around and ducked as a yellow object whizzed by my head, landing at my feet. Lexi grinned, grabbing a cocktail shaker from behind the bar where she stood, and gestured at the lemon still rolling on the ground beside me. "Gimme that," she growled, and I bent and picked up the fruit, the skin textured and pitted under my hands. I knew if I raised it to my nose, it would smell of summer, that unmistakable citrus tang that clung to the pads of your fingers.

Without missing a beat, I lobbed it back at her, but unlike me, she reached up with one hand and caught it neatly, placing it back down on the cutting board resting on the wooden surface of the bar. With a sharp little carving knife, she began fashioning the peel into concentric spirals. I'd been working at the café for less than a month, and already it felt as if I'd always been there. Not to say I was good at my job. I wasn't. "Every mistake brings you closer to perfection," Lexi repeated constantly, as if it were a mantra I'd need to adopt in her presence. But every mistake I made felt like abject failure, not a step closer to triumph.

I watched as she filled a silver shaker with ice, arranging the peel artfully on the rim of a cocktail glass, her hands practiced and sure. Her dark hair looped to her shoulders in snarls that seemed deliberate, and I saw flashes of the black tattoo on her forearm as she moved, a tiny, delicate symbol that I was too timid still to ask about.

Ever since I'd been hired officially, we'd spent nearly every day together, working at the café, in bars and clubs after hours, traveling down to Chinatown after our shifts for hand-pulled noodles and ice-cold beer. She taught me how to eat soup dumplings, to tear a tiny hole with my teeth in the tender dough, sucking out the broth that threatened to scald my tongue. My hours with her were jasmine tea, brunch at two p.m. in SoHo, her elegant bones hidden beneath a black hat, wide as a saucer. The nights grew colder. We wore hats, wound scarves around our throats, rough wool against the silk of skin. There were afternoons spent in the cramped living room of her studio on Broome Street, her hands in my hair, plaiting it, arranging the braids around my head so that when I glanced in the mirror, I was unrecognizable to myself.

You two look like sisters, everyone said. We were both dark haired, long limbed, and skinny, subsisting on the popcorn we served to customers at the bar and the one family meal of fried chicken and greens, tortillas and beans, a meal we were entitled to but usually showed up too late for anyway. Not siblings, not by blood, but an inexplicable energy connected us, our bodies moving in sync as we worked side by side behind the bar, a golden cord stretched between us, winking like a string of fireflies in the dark.

Kindred spirits, she'd whisper, reaching down and grabbing my hand as we walked the Lower East Side like the streets belonged to us. It was strange territory. I'd never had a best friend before, never opened myself up to anyone except Ian, and then only at first. I was afraid if I started to rely on her presence, she would evaporate into thin air. She could be tender, then suddenly cutting, shutting me out with a sharp glance that made my bones ache with coldness, like being plunged into a snowdrift, and I never knew which version awaited me. It kept me off-balance, never knowing when the ground might crumble unexpectedly.

Wherever we went, the drinks appeared as if we had conjured them, the sting of mezcal in my mouth or the flush of vodka. St. Jerome's. The Bitter End. Motor City. We could spend a whole night ducking in and out of doorways until dawn tinged the sky rose gold. On the way home, we'd sometimes buy a bagel and cream cheese from a bodega, our own low-rent *Breakfast at Tiffany's*. I'd watch Lexi kneel to pet the store's sly gray cat before it arched its back and hissed, running away from her. The cat knew what others did not: she was a time bomb, ready to detonate.

But even on my nights off, even when I tried to stay away, I'd somehow wind up back at the café. The pull was magnetic, my feet leading me toward that red awning, that smoky room like an irresist-ible, terrible lover. *You're here,* Lexi would say with a grin, sliding a shot of Grey Goose toward me across the bar, watching as it slipped easily down my throat. *I'm lonely, Ava,* she'd murmur, no matter how many people surrounded her.

Little bird. Stay with me.

Every night we wiped down tables, shrugged off the hands of drunks, stopping only long enough to stare at the stage tucked up at the front, hoping it might be one of us up there someday. But I was content to wait for things to unfold like a flower in the dark, while Lexi simply couldn't. Her impatience hovered in the air around her, rearranging the molecules and charging them with electricity.

She'd been especially restless tonight, agitated, fighting against the bar like it was a prison she needed to escape from. Her frustration was palpable, a living thing in the room, so around ten p.m., when she looked up and her face broke into a wide grin at the sight of a man walking through the doors, I exhaled in relief. That smile. It made you want to give her anything, just so it might stay.

She turned to face me, her face flushed with excitement. "Jamie's here," she breathed, and I watched as he strode across the room, pushing through the crowd in a dark pair of jeans and a black T-shirt under a leather jacket, the hide so dark and glossy it appeared oiled. His sandy hair was combed back from his face, and a smattering of stubble lined his sharp jaw. As he came closer, I noticed his eyes most of all, a hypnotic blue, almost feral. His skin was golden, as if slightly tanned, and I was surprised at how young he seemed. I'd always thought of managers as older, experienced, and worldly. But the man approaching us looked no more than twenty-five.

He walked up to the bar and leaned on it, grinning. Like Lexi, he seemed to have an effortless ease in his body, none of my own crippling awkwardness. With a smile, Lexi poured a shot of tequila and placed it in front of him. He drained it in one swallow, pushing the glass back at her across the bar.

"What do I owe you?"

"Oh, I'll take it out in trade," Lexi said, and they both laughed. There was a practiced banter between them, a familiarity that made me buzz with nervous energy, so I busied myself restocking the bar, refilling the trays of cut limes and lemons, tidying the jars of crimson cocktail straws.

When I looked over again, his eyes locked on my face, holding me there. I turned away in embarrassment and began polishing glasses. Anything to look busy. Anything to seem like I didn't care. For weeks it had just been our own little world of two. I'd fooled myself into thinking it was enough. But by the way she looked at him, I knew our little bubble, so protective and warm, had suddenly burst.

"Ava." Lexi's voice cut through the ambient noise of the café, the jazz playing through the speakers overhead. "I want you to meet someone."

When I looked up, she was beckoning me over, and I took a deep breath, placing the glass in my hand back down behind the bar, and walked toward her.

"This is my manager, Jamie," she said, a hint of pride in her voice. "Jamie, this is Ava, the one I've been telling you about."

He reached out a hand, and I stretched my own across the bar reflexively. "Nice to meet you, Ava," he said as his fingers closed around mine. "I feel like I already know you." His skin was warm and dry, and he held my hand just a beat too long. There was a sudden heat, and I pulled away as if I'd been branded.

Years with Ian had taught me that men lied and cheated as easily as they breathed. They told you what you wanted to hear. But that wasn't the worst of it. It was that sense of animal attraction, a hunger and lust so deep they felt almost primal. The most dangerous kind of man was one who could bring that out in you, unchecked. And I could see by the look of bewilderment on Jamie's face that he'd felt it too.

I stepped back, trying to hide my discomfort by pulling my hair into a ponytail and fastening it with the elastic I wore around one wrist, anything to avoid looking at him again. But I knew my luck would run out eventually.

"Lexi tells me you have some great songs," Jamie went on, and I glanced over at Lexi, who was busy making a screwdriver for some bridge-and-tunnel cretin in a polo shirt.

"Make it *strong* this time, girlie," he muttered, his round cheeks as pink as his hideous shirt, throwing a fifty on the bar as an incentive. "If I wanted orange juice, I'd go to a methadone clinic." Lexi rolled her eyes at me before I remembered that Jamie was waiting for an answer.

"I don't know," I muttered, my voice fading beneath the cacophony of saxophones. "She's just being a good friend." I glanced toward the stage at the front of the room, knowing that soon the music would be snapped off, only to be replaced by a live set. Tonight, it was Saxon Albright, a downtown folk singer with a mop of auburn curls who I'd admired for months. I'd played her EP so incessantly over the past few weeks that Lexi had threatened on more than one occasion to snap the CD in two. Before Jamie showed up, I'd been looking forward to getting off work and sticking around to watch the set, a beer bottle sweating in my hand. Now my shift seemed interminable, and I couldn't wait to escape out the front door of the café, where the throngs would swallow me up in a vortex of bodily heat and stomping shoes.

"Good friend or not," Jamie continued, "she knows talent when she hears it. I'd love to meet up sometime next week and hear your stuff. If you're game, that is."

Lexi finished with her customer and sidled up beside me. I could smell the heavy scent of her perfume, patchouli and musk, and something that smelled of the wet stone walls of churches. "What are you guys *talking* about?" she asked with a laugh, as if we amused her.

"I was just telling Ava that I should take a listen to some of her stuff," Jamie said nonchalantly. "Like you suggested."

"Right," Lexi said coolly, looking over at me.

"Lexi . . . ," I began weakly, feeling like I was on a subway car that had careened out of control, shuttling down the tracks and into the mouths of darkened tunnels. "This really isn't necessary."

"Of *course* it is," she said, a gentle chiding in her voice. "Jesus, Jamie, she's so modest it makes me ill. You'll see for yourself."

She seemed so sure of herself. Who could argue with her? Who could win?

"When's good for you?" He turned to me expectantly, those blue orbs taking me in.

"Well, Thursday's my day off. But I really don't think—"

The music cut out and the lights dimmed. At the front of the room, Saxon took the stage, striding over to a stool and sitting down, slinging her guitar across her small waist. I was thankful for the darkness, for the opportunity to evaporate.

"Let's shoot for Thursday," Jamie said, giving Lexi a wink, then looking over at me. "I'm in the studio this week. I'll get your number from Lex."

I nodded, suddenly tongue-tied. *This is business,* I told myself, *and he's probably just doing Lexi a favor anyway.* But then why did it feel like so much more? I swallowed hard, willing the lump in my throat to disappear.

"You're not staying for the show?" Lexi asked, her tone petulant, her hands placed defiantly on her hips.

"Not tonight, babe," Jamie said quickly, reaching across the bar to kiss her on the cheek. She closed her eyes, as if drinking in even that small moment of contact between them. Jamie looked over at me, and I felt my lips part, the blood rushing through my limbs as the music began, the strumming of the guitar mimicking the savage beating of my heart.

When Lexi pulled back and opened her eyes, Jamie and I were still staring at one another, and I forced myself to look away, grabbing a rag and looking around for something, anything, to clean. I rubbed the surface of the already pristine bar in frantic circles, as if I were trying to wear down the wood itself. When I dared look up, I noticed Lexi's eyes narrowing as she looked first at Jamie and then back at me. I turned away again so she couldn't see my cheeks, reddened and shamed. In that moment, I knew that if I wasn't careful, I would ruin everything that had been built so quickly. Trust was a thin line one walked each day. A tightrope.

One false step and it might smash to bits on the pavement.

KAYLA

I stood in front of an old brick warehouse in Williamsburg, right across the street from the hull of the old Domino Sugar factory, the rain pouring down in an unrelenting deluge. I buzzed the fifth floor, then pushed open the glass door and stepped inside. Everywhere I looked, there were echoes of the building's industrial past, from the steel girders crossing the ceiling to the cement floors underfoot. I took the elevator up and then walked down a long hallway until I reached a pair of frosted glass doors, the graffiti-like "R" logo emblazoned on the front.

I could hear a phone ringing continuously as I entered, the sound unrelenting. I looked around the waiting room, the walls lined with framed album covers and gold and platinum records. There was a long metallic silver couch along one wall, issues of *Rolling Stone* and *Spin* magazines littering the end tables. A young woman sat behind the desk, a phone pressed to one ear. Her hair was shaved to her scalp on one side of her head, while the rest hung to her other shoulder in a dark, silky curtain. A ring glimmered in one nostril, her brown eyes deeply lined with kohl, the word "Rukus" glowing in purple neon on the wall above her head.

As I approached, without even making eye contact, she held up the palm of one hand. "Yeah, I'll have him call you back," she said into the receiver and then with a sigh returned the handset roughly to its cradle. "Can I help you?" she asked, looking at me with suspicion, if not outright hostility.

"Hi," I said with a smile, hoping to get off on the right foot despite the chilly welcome. "I'm Kayla McCray, a writer with *Rolling Stone*. I'm working on a cover story on Lexi Mayhem, and I'd love to speak to Jamie Preston if he's available."

"He's not," she said curtly. "His schedule is full."

"I completely understand," I began, knowing that I had to keep my cool to get anywhere with her at all. "And I probably should've called before coming down here, but—"

"Yes, you should've," she said, cutting me off.

"But now that I'm here," I continued, "I'd really appreciate just five minutes." I dug into my bag, pulling out my wallet. I grabbed one of my business cards and extended it across the desk, but she waved me away impatiently, almost knocking the card from my hand with her sudden movements.

"That won't be necessary." She stared at me unwaveringly.

There was a long pause, and then I tried again. "Listen," I said slowly. "I get that you're just trying to do your job, and I'm not looking to make any trouble." She raised an eyebrow as if to say, *Oh really?*

Just then a door opened, and a man walked out, tall and lanky, wearing a faded gray T-shirt beneath a battered black leather jacket, distressed jeans, and a pair of black boots on his feet. He looked to be in his early forties, his angular jaw shaded by at least two days of stubble, his sandy hair unruly. When he moved closer, I saw that his eyes were ringed by darkness.

"Is there a problem, Dani?" he asked as he came toward us, frowning slightly.

"No, no problem," the receptionist said quickly. "She wanted to talk to you about Lexi Mayhem, and I explained that you're completely booked for the day."

"That's true," he said, looking over at me. His eyes stared holes right through me—the short trench coat I wore over my favorite pair of faded skinny jeans. The rose-colored lipstick I'd blotted, then blotted again, pressing my mouth to a tissue repeatedly until only the stain remained. My bangs were plastered to my forehead, and I had the sinking feeling that the liner I'd applied to my top lids that morning on the train was now pooling beneath my lower lashes.

"I'm so sorry," I said, holding out a hand to him. "I haven't had a chance to properly introduce myself. I'm Kayla McCray. I am a writer at—"

His expression was slightly amused as he reached over to take my hand in his own, but as soon as our fingers made contact, there was a sudden shock, a shower of blue sparks in the air. We both drew back immediately, and I placed my hand in the pocket of my coat.

"Wow," he said with a short laugh. "Quite the spark."

"More like boots and friction," I retorted. "You're Jamie Preston?"

"In the flesh," he said lightly.

"You managed Lexi Mayhem?"

He paused, looking more than a bit surprised. Probably no one had asked him that question in a long time. But if he was pleased by the recognition, he didn't show it. "I did," he said, looking down and digging his hands deep into the pockets of his jeans. "A long time ago."

"So how does it feel to be erased by the biggest pop star in the world?" I cocked my head to the side, smiling playfully.

"It comes with the territory." He chuckled, looking up and meeting my eyes again.

"I'm working on a cover story on Lexi for *Rolling Stone*. I was hoping you might have a few minutes to talk?"

"Come with me," he said, turning and walking back into the office, and I followed before he had time to reconsider. Once inside, I took in the large windows that stretched from floor to ceiling, flooding the room with a hazy gray light. His desk was a behemoth of a thing, fashioned from live oak, hopelessly strewn with stacks of papers and old bodega coffee cups. A row of metal file cabinets waited silently across the room, and the concrete floors underfoot echoed the silvery expanse of sky.

"I guess you're your own boss," I said, looking around. "Must be nice."

"It took a few years of sweat and shoestring budgets, and there were a lot of months where I didn't think we were going to make it," he said, picking up a pen from his desk and twirling it in his fingers like a drumstick. "Believe it or not"—he grinned, as if his own story amused him—"I used to do it all." He pointed back toward the room where Dani waited, presumably sharpening her knives. "Answering the phone, signing the talent, and booking the shows."

"After managing Lexi?" I walked over to the wall of windows and peered outside. The rain had stopped, but the sky was still darkened and full of thunderheads.

"Yep." He dropped the pen back on the desk, walking around behind it and sitting down, leaning back in his chair.

"What was that like?"

"Working with Lexi? It was . . . ," he began, his voice trailing off almost as soon as he had begun. I watched the emotions move across his face, darkening his expression until finally he spoke again. "A full-time job," he said with a dry laugh.

But there was something in the way he wasn't looking me in the eye that let me know he didn't want to discuss it further. I'd seen it before in subjects, how something deep inside them would switch off abruptly when I uncovered something they didn't want to confront.

"I bet," I answered. "What was she like back then?"

"Is this on the record?"

"If you want it to be. I'm just trying to get a better sense of who she was at the start of it all."

"I've got nothing to hide. But as Dani said, I am a little pressed for time." There was a long pause, and then he spoke again. "You've met her, right?"

"Lexi? Just once. So far."

"Then you know," he said, looking away. "Lexi is . . . unstoppable. She goes after what she wants. And she doesn't quit until she gets it. That's what it takes to make it in this business."

He stood up, walking around the desk before sitting on top of it, facing me. He had an ease in his body that only men who were comfortable in their own skin seemed to possess, a kind of feline grace.

"Would you be willing to talk about it sometime?" I asked, knowing that I was probably pushing my luck. "On the record, I mean?"

"It was such a long time ago." He glanced over at me, the dark shadows beneath his eyes almost purple in the light, even on such an overcast day. "But yeah. I suppose so. If you think it might help. She was doing some interesting stuff when she started out. Groundbreaking, I always thought."

"Do you have any of those early shows on tape? I'd love to take a peek," I said as I walked over to the desk, placing one hand on it to steady myself. The sound of my heart banging away in my chest seemed terribly loud.

"I probably do. I'd have to look for them."

"Could you?"

"Why are you wasting a cover on Lexi anyway?" He swung his feet to the floor and stood back up in one fluid motion. "She's gotten so pedestrian over the years."

"Well . . . for one thing, she's starting her own label."

"Is she now."

"From what she's told me, yes."

61

He walked back over and sat behind the desk, peering at the screen of his laptop, his fingers tapping against the keys as if I weren't even there.

"I digitized a bunch of old video a while ago," he said without looking up. "I can send you some files later today."

I looked at him in surprise. "Really?"

"Yeah, sure. I just ask they be kept confidential."

I reached into my bag, pulled out my wallet, and flipped through it till I found my stash of business cards, walking over and holding one out. "So you know how to reach me."

He took the card from my hand, his fingers grazing mine, and there it was again: that shock of recognition. "Well," I said, unable to keep the tremor from my voice, "I guess that's it, then."

"For now," he said, looking down at the card still in his hand. "I'll be in touch."

I walked to the door and opened it, the sound of a ringing phone infiltrating the room.

"Looking forward to it," I said, closing the door firmly behind me.

———

Later that afternoon, back at my apartment, I paced the creaky wooden floors, checking my phone every ten minutes. Finally, at 5:11 p.m., there it was: an email from Jamie. There was no message in the body of the email, just a link to a Google Drive. He'd uploaded three files, and I clicked on the first one.

The footage was dark and grainy, pixelated as hell, and I moved closer to the screen to see more clearly. There she was, Lexi Mayhem, howling through the speaker, her voice wavering on the high notes before descending to a throaty rasp. Her hair was long and black, hanging almost to her waist, her arms covered in silver bracelets. She leaned into the microphone, swaying there with her eyes closed until the music stopped and the audience erupted in a wave of applause. It was only then that she opened her eyes and smiled that dazzling smile before moving offstage. But just before she exited, I watched as she halted in the wings, throwing her arms around a young woman waiting there. The camera zoomed in shakily, and for a moment all I could see were two heads of dark hair pressed together, two sets of pale arms entwined around one another. But when she pulled back, my eyes widened.

The woman was a dead ringer for Lexi. They could've been sisters, the resemblance was that uncanny but for the hardness and determination in Mayhem's gaze, her chin slightly lifted. The mystery woman had the same long dark mane, the same lithe build and wide eyes. They were even clad in similar outfits—ripped jeans, leather wristbands, bare navels. But more than the resemblance, what struck me was the quality of their embrace, the intensity of it, as if it weren't clear where one ended and the other began. The slow smile they exchanged as Lexi pulled back. I rewound the footage, playing it back again, watching them in their world of two. But who was this mystery woman? And why had no one ever mentioned her before?

Without taking my eyes from the screen, I reached for my phone, dialing the number for Rukus Records, noticing with no small degree of satisfaction that Dani demurely put me right through.

"Miss me already?"

"I'm watching the videos you just sent over," I said, ignoring his flirtation, "and I noticed—"

"You're welcome." He laughed, interrupting me.

"Thank you," I said, stopping for a moment and taking a breath. "This is so helpful. But . . . there's this girl in one of the videos who's a dead ringer for Lexi. Dark hair, same style of clothing. Do you have any idea who I'm talking about?"

There was a pause, then that flat, tinny sound I knew so well, the sound of typing.

"Oh," he said slowly, "that's Ava."

"Ava?" I looked back at the screen. "Who's Ava?"

Another silence. One that felt heavy as concrete.

"They came up together in the scene a long time ago. They were pretty tight."

I grabbed the pad I always kept on my desk and a pen out of the drawer. "Ava, you said? She have a last name?"

"Petrova. But she performed under the name Ava Arcana."

"OK, thanks," I muttered, writing both names down and underlining them. "I appreciate it."

"Call me if you need anything else—and maybe even if you don't."

There was a click as he hung up, and I put the phone down, opening another window on my laptop. I pulled up Google, typing one name into the search function: Ava Petrova—and then her stage name, Ava Arcana. At that moment, I was so overtired that the room was buzzing with the strong sense of auditory hallucination that often accompanies days without sleep.

I stared at the screen in disbelief as I scrolled through the links. There was hardly any mention of Ava Petrova *or* Arcana on the internet. It was as if it had been scrubbed clean. But the journalist in me also knew that some people were skilled at covering their tracks and keeping their personal information offline. In this age where every last detail was routinely posted online, there were still those outliers who didn't want to be found.

I typed Ava's names into various search engines, garnering the same results every time. The first few links I found were old, bringing me to a series of dead ends, a missing page, or an error message. By the time I'd scrolled through three or four pages, my initial sense of excitement was beginning to deflate. *Maybe there's really nothing here,* I told myself as I yawned while clicking on yet another dead link. But then, at the bottom of page five, something caught my eye, an article in the *Staten Island Advance,* and I sat forward in my chair, my spine stiffening.

142 Broome Street, Apt. 4 . . . The body of a 22-year-old female . . .
possible suicide . . . roof access . . .

Why did that address seem so familiar? I grabbed the leather notebook from my bag, began flipping pages rapidly, suddenly wide awake.
I'd jotted down some notes during the flight, as I always did when
conducting research, and something was nagging at me, tugging at me.
And there it was: 142 Broome. Lexi Mayhem's former address, where
she'd lived during her years as an up-and-coming singer in New York.
Not only was Ava Petrova dead as a doornail, but she'd allegedly jumped
to her death . . . from the roof of Lexi's *apartment building?*

I went back to the Google search, clicking on the only clear photo
of Ava I'd been able to find. Long dark hair, silver rings on every finger,
a hoop shining in one nostril, and an almost pained expression in her
eyes. I looked closer, then clicked back to an image of Lexi Mayhem at
the beginning of her career, the tangle of black hair, faded jeans sliding
down, exposing her narrow waist, a diamond stud glittering in one
nostril.

Come at me, she seemed to sneer. *I dare you.*

I clicked back on Ava's pale, angular face, willing her to tell me what
she knew. Of course, there was no answer, only her plaintive expression,
imploring me to stay.

There was a story here. I felt it in my bones.

And I was going to uncover it.

AVA

2005

The day after Jamie's visit, Lexi barely spoke to me. As I mopped the bar and restocked the condiment trays in a trance, I desperately wanted to take it back, the look that had passed between Jamie and me, the thrill that had run through my body, illicit and strange and somehow so very familiar. But at the end of my shift, Lexi walked up beside me as if nothing had happened, linking her arm through mine, all seemingly forgotten.

Now there was a blue-black sky overhead, neon-red glow in the window along St. Marks Place. Stumbling drunk, we wandered along the sidewalk, broken glass at our feet shining like fragments of fallen stars. The street was alive, the crowd surging, punks mostly, their faces pierced with spikes, buckles on their leather jackets clanking metallically as they moved. It was nearing Halloween and the air smelled of burning leaves, the smoke of bonfires. Some kind of sacrifice.

We'd worked a double shift, and by four p.m. I was spent, my hair limp around my face, head drooping like a daisy on a broken stem. After I'd cleared what seemed like the millionth table, bringing the receipt up to the register, Lexi sidled up beside me near the bar, grabbing my arm and yanking me into the bathroom before I could so much as protest. She was gentle with me most of the time, petting my arms in long, smooth strokes that confused me with their overt seductiveness. But at other moments she could be rough, almost careless, shoving me around as if I were her own personal doll.

I always let her.

Inside the darkened space, lit by one low, minimalist light fixture over the sink, a row of lavender candles burned on a wooden ledge hanging over the toilet, the scent heavy as church incense, clouds of frankincense and myrrh. I watched as she nonchalantly tipped white powder from a folded triangle of paper she'd fished out of the pocket of her tight, ripped jeans, tapping it onto the back of one hand. She leaned down and inhaled quickly, standing up and rubbing her nose delicately before tapping the paper against the back of her hand again, then holding it out to me.

"It won't kill you," she said, a smile twitching at the corners of her lips.

"Cocaine?" I asked, my voice reverberating off the tile. I looked around at the black-painted walls and didn't know if I was nervous, afraid, or excited. What I was feeling was impossible to discern or even understand. But I knew that I wanted to do it, if only to feel what Lexi was feeling, the drug coursing through her bloodstream, her eyes glittering in the dark.

"What else?" Lexi laughed. If it were possible to look imperious while holding out a handful of drugs, she was pulling it off. "C'mon, Ava. It'll get us through this hell day. Don't make me be high alone."

I leaned down and pinched one nostril shut as I'd seen her do, then sniffed hard. The taste was sharp, medicinal, bitter as baby aspirin sliding down the back of my throat. I stood up and made a face, sticking out my tongue to show my displeasure. The rush was immediate, the tiredness evaporating completely, my limbs tingling. I was alive again.

"That's the drip." Lexi folded the paper back up carefully, then fluffed out her hair in the mirror. "It's the best part."

Now, after numerous trips to the bathroom during the last half of our shift, I felt euphoric, even after a twelve-hour day. I couldn't even feel my feet anymore; they were numb inside my boots. I liked that feeling, wanted more of it. I followed Lexi down the street, not caring where the night might take us. We owned the city, its concrete arms wrapped around us in a benevolent embrace.

"Are you meeting with Jamie tomorrow?" Lexi asked once we stopped singing, staring straight ahead. "I gave him your number."

"He called me," I admitted with a shrug. "I'm meeting him next week."

It had been a short call, no more than five minutes, but I didn't tell her about the electricity that crackled between us, even over the stale, dead air of the phone, that after I hung up, I sat down on the couch to slow the erratic beating of my heart.

Suddenly, Lexi stopped in front of a storefront: Psychic Readings. The neon blazed in the window, making her skin glow pinkly in the light, and she had never looked more alive, her eyes on fire, her forehead sheened with sweat. Lexi wasn't classically beautiful—her features were too narrow and sharp for that—but she had that *thing*. That ineffable quality that made you look . . . and then look again. It made you want to know her. To follow her every move, just to see what she might do next.

"We *said* we'd do this," she said excitedly. The temperature had dropped, and her breath hung in the air, a dense cloud. I shivered inside my leather jacket. Every time we walked by the fortune-teller's garish window Lexi would threaten to pull me inside, mostly to confirm what she already knew. For her, the future was as certain as if it had been written in the stars long before she was born. But I wasn't so sure I wanted to know what lay in wait. Now, as I stood there, the idea filled me with a sense of foreboding, as if the future were hanging just out of reach of my tentative grasp, my fingers coming up empty.

"*You* said," I pointed out. "Not me."

"C'mon! Don't you want to know?" she went on, hands on her narrow hips. But before I could even answer, she'd pulled me inside. The Nag Champa incense I recognized from the street vendors that lined the block swirling in dense, sweet clouds among the red lights and tangle of plastic plants, an altar in the corner covered in deities, a bowl of fruit placed in front of one statue, bananas and apples, a statue of a many-armed woman, limbs protruding from her body like snakes. I almost expected Irina to emerge from the shadows, crystals wound around her throat, her young, unlined hands carrying a tarot deck wrapped in a swath of purple velvet, bell-bottoms swishing around her slim ankles.

But it was an older woman who parted the beaded curtain, the sound rustling in my ears. Gray hair twisted back in a knot, brown skin, a loose white gown covering her slim figure and brightly colored scarves swirling around her as she moved. "You want a reading, yes?" Her amber eyes were kind, her voice gentle, and she beckoned for us to come closer, to sit down across from her at a small table. I shifted uncomfortably on my chair as she peered closer at the both of us. "Who will be first?"

"Can you read us together?" Lexi's voice sounded small in that room as she volunteered, but as she spoke, she raised her chin defiantly. I could tell that even through her drunkenness she was nervous, her hands twisting in her lap. I reached over and took them in mine to quiet them. I could feel her pulse thudding fast through her skin, relentless. Even back then, she was so much more driven than I was. I knew she'd do anything to make it. Sold-out stadium tours were in her blood. Nothing else was even an option. It was everything or nothing. And Lexi didn't like to lose.

"Yes . . . it is a bit more difficult, but . . ." The fortune-teller shrugged in assent. "Do you have a particular question you'd like to ask?" She shuffled the cards in her deft hands.

"Will I be a huge star?" Lexi said impulsively as we broke into a fit of giggles. Maybe it was the childlike way she said it, so full of hope and impatience, but once we started, we couldn't stop. I held my side, a pain deep in my abdomen as my whole body shook with laughter.

"You will need to quiet down," the fortune-teller admonished us, and we tried to straighten up. I bit the inside of my cheek, hoping the pain might sober me up, and little by little the room became still again.

The fortune-teller began turning over the cards, exposing pictures in soft, muted colors. The cards themselves looked well worn, as if they'd been shuffled for a lifetime. There was a chariot, a boy holding a cup, a pair of lovers intertwined, a pile of swords. But the card that drew my attention depicted a high stone tower, lightning zigzagging through the top, figures plummeting to the ground. I felt myself holding my breath as I stared at it, unable to look away. I could hear, as if through a wall of water, the fortune-teller saying the words "destruction, chaos, upheaval." But I concentrated on the feel of Lexi's hand in mine, how it began to shake as the fortune-teller's voice grew stronger.

"You both are talented, that is clear. I see much passion, much fire. You each have something to say, and you *must say it*, no matter the cost." The room, the cards, and Lexi's face swirled before my eyes. I looked back at the slightly gnarled hands of the fortune-teller, her voice coming from somewhere far away now.

"You will achieve your heart's desire," she said gravely, leaning forward as she spoke directly to Lexi. "But there will be a price."

Lexi nodded wordlessly, her hand sweating onto mine, our palms slippery and damp. And in that moment, she let go, pulling away, the shock of the absence of her flesh against mine sobering me up instantly.

"There are obstacles in each of your paths," the fortune-teller went on, her face darkening. I felt a shiver run through me.

"What kind of obstacles?" I blurted out, regretting the words the minute I spoke. I wasn't sure I wanted to know. I wasn't sure I wanted to know at all.

"Demons . . . ," the fortune-teller began, looking down at the cards, her eyes moving over the spread of them.

"Like . . . *literal* demons?" Lexi broke into a fit of giggles once again, putting her head down on the table as her shoulders shook.

I reached over and pulled her back up. *Stop,* I mouthed, our faces close, but she didn't, couldn't, her laughter infectious as always, and I found myself being drawn in once again.

"Enough!" the fortune-teller said sharply, and instantly we quieted, the air in the room suddenly charged with expectation as she leaned closer so that I could see the dark, wiry hairs protruding from her chin, the hardness in her gaze. "Only one of you will succeed," she said, her voice certain.

"What do you mean?" Lexi asked, her eyes narrowing.

"It is just as I said—there is only room for one," the fortune-teller repeated. "It is written in the cards. In your destinies, which are inter-twined—but separate."

"But that's silly," Lexi began with a laugh. "Ava and I—"

But before she could finish, the fortune-teller cut her off, her words slicing through Lexi's protestations with the precision of a newly sharp-ened knife. "Give me your hand," she ordered, turning to me, holding out her own expectantly.

I opened my mouth to protest, but before I could speak, I heard Lexi's voice in my ear, urging me on. *Give it to her.* I stretched out my hand, and the fortune-teller took it softly in her own, turning it over so that the meat of my palm was exposed.

She peered down at the lines crisscrossing my skin, and I saw her face grow pale. She looked up at me, her eyes dark as the watery surface of a lake at night. Without a word, she folded my fingers carefully into a fist and released me. I pulled back sharply, as if I'd been burned.

"I am sorry," she said, unable to meet my eyes. "I am a little tired now." She looked deflated, spent, as if her power had been stripped away without warning.

Lexi pushed two crumpled twenties across the table, and we rose to our feet like sleepwalkers and headed toward the door. But just as we were about to step back out into the street, the fortune-teller put a hand on my shoulder.

"Remember what I said." She looked intently at both of us, her eyes moving from Lexi's astonished face to my own.

And then we were out on the street, and Lexi was there beside me, her cheeks flushed with excitement. "What a bunch of crap." She laughed. Seeing my face, she stopped, grabbing my hands in hers, squeezing tightly. "You didn't actually *believe* her, did you?" I felt my expression turn apologetic. But I couldn't help what I felt.

And I couldn't ignore it either.

"She probably tells everyone who comes in there the same story. And it's not like she said anything we don't already know." The red light from the bodega we passed made a crimson ring around her head, like a slightly demonic halo.

"What do you mean?"

Lexi tilted her head to the side and regarded me almost pityingly. "Of course I'm going to be a star," she said simply. "Everyone knows that."

But if it were true, if I did know it, as she said, then why did I suddenly feel so cold, so unmoored, standing there?

"Let's get one more drink before bed." She grabbed my arm, hooking it through her own. I tried to release the dark cloud hovering over me now, following me as I moved. Instead, I tried to focus my attention on the meaty scent of the hot dog vendors on the corners, the clouds of steam rising from manhole covers in the street. I put my faith in Manhattan, prayed to it like a god. If the cacophony of the city couldn't drown it all out, nothing would.

Still. That fortune-teller's face haunted me, even as we walked into the darkness of the Bitter End and up to the bar. The glass of whiskey I downed in two swallows didn't stop the uncertain feeling in my gut or the words that replayed themselves in my mind, looping endlessly.

There is only room for one.

KAYLA

I clutched the steering wheel like I was afraid it would implode if I loosened my grip so much as an inch. I leaned forward, my sweater damp beneath my arms, towers of glass and steel looming over me as I navigated my way out of the Rent-A-Wreck parking lot in Downtown Brooklyn. It had been years since I'd driven regularly, and when I'd slid into the car, which smelled of vinyl seats and cinnamon air freshener, I'd hoped it would all come back to me as easily as everyone claimed.

It didn't.

As I white-knuckled it onto the freeway, I couldn't shake the feeling that I was chasing a ghost—one I wasn't supposed to be trying to find at all. But as I'd scoured the internet, attempting to patch Ava together from the few scraps that remained in the digital realm, it had felt almost as if she were leading the way, showing me where to go next. And in this case, it was the home of Irina Petrova, Ava's mother.

In all the years I'd lived in New York, I'd never once stepped foot on Staten Island or even taken the ferry across the water from Manhattan. What I knew about the place could be distilled to the image of Melanie Griffith in that eponymous scene from *Working Girl*, as she stood on the deck of the ferry, staring at the Statue of Liberty in the distance. Like many people who lived in New York, anything outside the general vicinity of Manhattan or Brooklyn seemed to fall off the map entirely.

Which was why I was surprised that, after thirty mind-numbing minutes sitting in traffic, I exited the freeway to a place that looked so, well, *suburban*, but that in actual mileage was alarmingly close to Manhattan. Staten Island felt like another world entirely with its cul-de-sacs and tree-lined streets, the neat rows of pastel-colored tract houses. As I drove, I looked around, trying to picture Ava's childhood in such a place and failing entirely. The few facts I'd managed to uncover about Ava hadn't amounted to much—that she'd been a fixture in the Lower East Side music scene and had shared the stage with Lexi Mayhem on more than one occasion. I'd read on one Reddit thread that had taken me hours to uncover that she had worked at the Cornelia Street Café alongside Lexi, and in my mind's eye, I could almost picture Ava wiping tables in dreamy circles, moving slowly and languidly as a sylph. But her music had somehow vanished without a trace.

Irina, on the other hand, had been easy enough to find. A few clicks on the internet and her address and phone number appeared in black and white. It always amazed me how much info there was to be found online about nearly anyone, if only one chose to go looking for it. But then again, Irina wasn't exactly hiding. Most people weren't, for that matter; they lived their lives in plain sight, not caring who came out of the woodwork to find them or why.

When I'd dialed Irina's number that morning, the phone had rung and rung, and I'd fully expected to get voice mail. Instead, on the sixth ring, a deep, mellifluous voice answered just as I was about to hang up.

"Yes?" She didn't sound unfriendly exactly, just a little gruff, her voice tinged with the hint of a Slavic accent.

"Is this Irina Petrova?" I'd asked, feeling my heart begin to beat a little faster. I'd always hated cold-calling, but unfortunately it came with the job. I didn't take it personally anymore, no matter what reaction I got.

"Who is this?" I could sense the suspicion, the mistrust beginning to take hold, and I spoke quickly before she decided to hang up.

"My name is Kayla McCray. I'm a writer from *Rolling Stone* magazine, and I'm working on a story about the pop singer Lexi Mayhem."

Silence. I could hear her breathing, low and even.

"In a video of a performance in the early days of Mayhem's career, I happened to catch a glimpse of your daughter, Ava."

There was a sharp intake of breath and then more silence. The seconds stretched on interminably as I waited for her to answer.

"What do you want?" she asked after a moment, not unkindly, but I could tell that she was on the verge of ending the conversation if I didn't reassure her—and fast.

"Just to ask you a few questions," I said.

"About Ava?"

"Yes. And her friendship with Lexi Mayhem," I added.

There was another long pause, and I could almost hear her weighing the possibilities in her mind. Should she tell me to take a hike? Or just hang up? But I'd probably call back, wouldn't I . . .

"You come see me, yes?" she said slowly. "You have a pen?"

I opened the notes app on my phone, even though, unbeknownst to her, I already had her address. I could've shown up at any time unannounced. But I'd learned over the years, through trial and error, that calling first tended to result in fewer doors being slammed in my face.

As I followed GPS, the streets widened, and I drove closer to the water's edge. I rolled down the window, letting in the damp wind and the briny salt air. I turned in to a gated community and gave my name to the guard, who glanced down at a clipboard and nodded before letting me pass. The road curved around, littered with mini mansions, the same generic, new-construction homes in an array of neutral colors and slightly different styles. *You have reached your destination,* the GPS informed me as I stopped in front of a large and imposing two-story home, the driveway smooth, jet black, and almost oily looking, as if it had been recently paved.

Given what I knew about Ava's background, which admittedly didn't add up to much after hours spent searching online, the grandeur of the house, as well as the gated community it sat in, surprised me, contrasting sharply with what I'd read of the Petrovas' humble beginnings in a one-bedroom apartment in a decidedly unglamorous part of town. How did Irina afford this place? I wondered, stepping out of the car and walking up to the front door. I rang the bell, setting off a loud series of chimes that immediately made me want to flee. Why were doorbells always so unnecessarily intense? Even my own buzzer back in Brooklyn made me jump out of my chair each time the UPS driver arrived with a package.

There was a series of footsteps, quick and light, the sound of heels tapping on tile, and then the door swung open, and Irina Petrova stood before me, smaller than I had imagined. A thin, dark-haired woman in her midsixties, hair scraped back in a severe bun. She wore a cream linen pantsuit, her neck wrapped in a series of heavy gold chains, and a ring with a large jet stone graced the finger of one hand. Her lips were vermilion, her skin white as new snow, the heavy face powder she wore accentuating the wrinkles around her eyes and mouth, the roughened texture of her skin.

"I'm Kayla," I said, holding out a hand, which she ignored, opening the door wider so I could enter. The foyer was dark marble underfoot and gilt-edged paintings of severe-looking women and brooding children. Just looking at them made me uneasy, and I wondered how she managed to live with those glowering presences staring down at her every day. I followed her into the living room, which was all red velvet and heavy wooden furniture, the kinds of antiques that looked like they might come alive at night and murder you.

"Sit," she ordered, pointing to the crimson love seat, and I obeyed, too intimidated to do much else. I wondered what it must've been like for Ava, living with a mother like this, who, at least so far, wasn't exactly warm or maternal by any stretch of the imagination. My own mother hadn't exactly been Carol Brady, but she'd always tried her best to make me feel loved.

I took out my phone and switched on the voice-recording app. "I'd like to ask you some questions about Ava," I began.

"So you said." She placed her hands in her lap, folding them into one another. "What would you like to know?"

"I was curious about her friendship with Lexi Mayhem," I said, placing my phone on the marble-topped coffee table between us. "Did Ava talk about her at all?"

At that moment, the gold clock over the mantelpiece, festooned with cherubs, began chiming incessantly, breaking the stillness in the room. Irina just stared at me, her lips twin slashes of blood on her pale face. I could see the echoes of Ava there just below the surface, the same angular bones and large green eyes. But where there had been an innate openness, a kindness, in Ava's delicate features, in Irina's visage there was none.

"From what I know," she began slowly, "the two were very close. Ava looked up to her, you see. But that was always Ava's problem." She stopped for a moment, smiling tightly. "Ava never believed in herself. Always looking outside of herself for what she thought she lacked." She shrugged her bony shoulders, which twitched beneath the thin fabric. "She never embraced the American way of being. I think it was something in her nature. Even as a little girl, she would spend hours creating imaginary worlds, kingdoms—but only to observe, never ruling over them. It was not her way."

"Was her musical talent evident from a young age?"

"I had no idea of Ava's talent until after she was gone. No idea at all."

"She never sang in front of you? Not once?"

The idea was unthinkable, and yet, I had certainly heard stranger things over the years.

"Ava was shy. Did no one tell you that?" Irina let out a short laugh. "Easy to push around by others. Her teacher told me once that she always ate lunch alone in the schoolyard. Sometimes the other children would gang up on her and steal her lunch money and Ava would come home hungry. But she never told on them. I could not understand it. *Ava,* I would say, *do not let them take advantage! You must get that money back! It is your pride that is at stake!* But she would just ignore me, my daughter. Stare into space until I stopped speaking and left her alone. It was in moments like these that I realized I did not understand my own child."

"Did you ever meet Lexi Mayhem?"

"No," Irina said, pursing her lips, as if the very words were distasteful. "Not then. Only after. After Ava was . . . gone. That Mayhem woman, she sent flowers to the wake. Lilies. Ava *hated* lilies. Too sweet, she always said. Like a moldering corpse. Like death itself." Irina sniffed once, delicately, disdainfully, as if the offending blossoms were still somewhere in the room.

"I'm sorry," I said quietly. Irina nodded, as if I'd passed some sort of test. And as I sat there, I thought of Ava, white silk beneath her in that wooden box, hands folded over her heart, the petals of a red rose clutched between her fingers, and the room ringing with silence. It was enough to break your heart.

"Ava never lived here," Irina said, her eyes sweeping the perimeter of the room, "so she did not have a bedroom of her own. At the apartment we shared long ago, yes. Here, no. But I have kept all her things. Would you like to see?" She stood up, waiting expectantly.

"Sure," I said, grabbing the phone off the coffee table and following her out of the room, then up the stairs that led to the second floor of the house.

With its thick ivory carpet and etched-glass sconces on the walls, the room looked nothing like that of an aspiring pop star, even a secretive one. Instead of the wall-size collage of band ephemera and magazine clippings that surely had been in Ava's childhood room just as it had in mine, there were two neatly framed flyers hanging on the wall just inside the door. She had played a 5:30 p.m. set at a 2005 show—the opener for the opener for some DJ named Spinning Bottles who'd headlined the party at a performance space in Williamsburg. A space that was probably some investment banker's condo now.

"More are here," her mother said, gesturing to the neat stack of cardboard boxes piled in the corner of the room. I slipped off the lid of the box at the top and began to flip through the manila folders nestled inside, each neatly labeled—PHOTOS, WINTER '05, FLYERS—and realized that here before me was everything I hadn't found online. In these boxes, preserved almost in amber by a mother who couldn't even begin to comprehend her daughter's life, never mind her death, was the story of Ava Petrova's short, meteoric rise.

The story that I realized I would now be able to tell.

"It's all yours." Irina's voice startled me back into the moment. "Take what you want," she said as she turned to walk away.

"Irina?"

She stopped without turning around.

"Are you sure about this?"

She sighed once, her chest moving with the exhalation, and then she turned and looked back at me. There was a weariness in her expression, the exhaustion of so many sleepless nights. "Ava," she began, "was very talented. You see?"

I nodded. There was a heaviness in the room, the same dark cloud that permeated the entire house, and I wondered if Ava were somehow here, watching us from above.

"There is truth and there are lies," she went on, the gold chains at her throat flashing in the light. "And we often bury the truth like the dead. You have everything you need now to reveal it. Stay as long as you like," she said, dismissing me with a wave of her red fingernails.

And with that she was gone, the bedroom door closing behind her with an almost imperceptible click. I was left alone with Ava's entire life, her possessions, her photographs, even her notebooks. I knelt in front of the nearest box and began sorting through it, pulling out brightly colored scarves that still smelled of musky perfume, concert ticket stubs, Polaroid pictures, their colors slightly muted with time. A marbled composition book lay at the bottom of the box, and I opened the cover and started flipping through pages of poems, song lyrics, daydreams, Ava's looping script covering the paper with funny little drawings in the margins: ladybugs, cats, monsters with rows of jagged teeth. She was funny, sharp, intuitive—someone I might have been friends with.

As I perused the notebook, turning the soft, worn pages, a photograph dropped to the floor, and I picked it up, cradling it in my hands. Lexi and Ava, standing outside the café, mugging for the camera. At first, I wasn't even sure it *was* Ava, as the girl beside Lexi was a platinum blonde, her hair just hitting her shoulders. All the photos I'd seen of Ava to date featured a mane of unruly dark hair. But here, it was almost white, floating around her face like a jagged cloud. Lexi was sticking her tongue out, making devil horns with her hands; Ava was down on one knee, looking up at her, holding on to one of Lexi's legs, encased in smooth black leather.

I brought the photograph closer to my face, studying it carefully, the studded belt slung around Ava's thin hips, the metal buckle spelling out the words "Rock Star." Why did that seem so . . . familiar? I wondered, racking my brain for the answer until it came to me in a flash. Lexi Mayhem had worn the same belt on the cover of *Spin* in the early days of her career. I could still picture her, that belt wrapped around the waist of the black leather pants that hugged her narrow hips. She stared straight into the lens, daring the reader to protest, her hands covering her bare breasts.

I looked again at Ava, the hair so light it was almost colorless, her eyebrows slashes of darkness framing the sadness in her eyes, even as she smiled obediently for the camera. Lexi Mayhem had dyed her hair platinum blonde early on in her career, never returning to the dark locks she'd sported in her New York days. My eyes darted from Lexi's face to Ava's, marveling at the resemblance. There was a sinking feeling in the pit of my stomach, but one tempered by the thrill that shot through me, the thrill of uncovering a story in the making. Of course, the two had influenced one another along the way, and who knew what bits of Lexi might've been found in Ava today if she were still alive? At least that was the logical explanation, the kind a seasoned journalist would favor. But my gut told me there was more. That I hadn't even begun to scratch the surface of what had really happened to Ava Petrova.

There was a rustling sound, and I looked up to see Irina standing in the doorway again. "You have heard how she died? My daughter?" she asked gently, as if she hadn't wanted to startle me.

"I read that she . . . fell," I said, choosing my words carefully. I knew from experience that parents could become quickly unhinged when discussing the death of a child, especially if it was a suicide, sometimes ending a meeting on the spot. There was also the fact that I didn't want to cause Irina undue pain if I could avoid it.

Irina just stared at me, the corners of her lips twitching as if she were trying to stifle a bout of laughter or maybe even a flood of tears.

"Is that right?" I added, waiting for her to confirm it.

"That is what they want people to think." Irina lifted her chin, her gaze haughty. "My Ava did not *fall*."

There was a long pause. She held my gaze unblinkingly, and I felt my blood run cold.

"My daughter was murdered."

AVA

The café before opening was another world. Without the bustle of the crowd, the gamy scent of broiling meat, the pressurized pop of a cork releasing from the neck of a bottle, it felt like a different planet. Eerily quiet. I closed the door behind me, shutting out the late-afternoon light, the smell of impending snow in the air, and flipped on the overhead lights that glowed a soft red. They buzzed warmly, the sound quieting my nerves. For days I'd thought of nothing but him. No matter how I tried to distract myself with work, balancing plates on my forearms and frothing milk with one hand or focusing on the melodies churning incessantly in the twisting labyrinth of my brain, he was always there. Waiting.

The days leading up to this moment had inched along like slow-moving insects, and each time I remembered his pale-blue eyes, my stomach dropped sharply, sweat breaking out on my skin. But there was always Lexi's face superimposed over the memory, coloring it with warning, and whether Jamie signed me or not, there was a sense of foreboding that I just couldn't shake. There was so much at stake, I knew.

Too much.

I flipped on the stage lights and pulled a stool dead center. If I had to sing, I knew I'd need to be still, to close my eyes and shut the world out. Otherwise, I'd never be able to go through with it at all. And with that realization, a wave of nervous energy shot through me. I threw my hair over one shoulder, and I thought suddenly of cutting it, lightening it to the color of the sun. I walked back toward the bar, stopping at a gilt-edged mirror on the far wall and pulling the strands up so that my neck was exposed, clean and long. I leaned closer to the glass, dropping the weight of my hair back down so that it fell over my shoulders. "Don't blow this," I whispered to the girl in the mirror, her eyes so murkily green, they looked almost black.

At that moment, I heard the front door creak open, the cold November air sneaking in, and then slam shut with a loud bang. I whirled around, startled by the sudden clamor, and there he was, a sheepish grin on his face. He shook the rain from his hair, then ran a hand through it and stepped toward me. He was wearing ripped jeans and a black leather jacket, a canvas messenger bag slung over one shoulder.

"Hey," he said as he arrived in front of me, nodding once, a quick dip of the chin, his jaw covered in at least three days of stubble.

"We only have about an hour before the staff gets here," I blurted out, trying to smile to cover my embarrassment.

"Then we better get started," he said with a slow grin, his eyes holding my own for a beat too long, and there it was again, that sudden drop in the pit of my stomach, that electricity mixed with a dizzying vertigo. He walked over to one of the empty tables in front of the stage, slinging his bag onto an empty chair. "You ready?" he asked, sitting down and looking at me expectantly.

"Why are we doing this here?" I fidgeted where I stood, aware that I was stalling. I didn't want to be exposed under the glare of stage lights, especially in front of him. *But what does it matter?* a little voice inside me pointed out. *He sees right through you anyway.*

"At the café?"

"Yeah. I mean, don't you have an office or something?"

"I do. But I don't spend a lot of time there."

"Why is that?"

"I find that kind of corporate atmosphere creatively stifling. It's not really my vibe."

"So . . ." I shifted my weight from one foot to the other. "What is, then?"

"This. The here and now. I stay close to the street because that's where the action is. I follow my instincts. And they led me straight to you."

"They led you to Lexi. Not me."

"Same difference," he said with a smile. "I trust my intuition, Ava. You should too."

"Trust you, you mean?" I said, trying to make light of it.

"Trust *yourself*."

"But you've never even heard me sing."

"Not yet. But I don't really have to," he answered, leaning back in his chair and crossing his arms over his chest. "I knew the minute I saw you."

"Knew what?"

"That you've got it."

My mouth dropped open in surprise, and I closed it again sharply. *Don't let your mouth hang open in one of your silly daydreams,* my mother had always moaned when she found me looking out the window, lost in thought, or at my desk staring into space, a pencil curled in one hand. But Jamie's words weren't a dream—they were real. For whatever reason, he believed in me.

"You can't know that just by looking at me," I said reluctantly, aware that I was doing what I always did, questioning everything until it all came apart like a ball of wet paper in my hands.

"Well, get up there and let's end the suspense," he said, pointing toward the stage.

The walk was only a few feet but felt endless, and when I sat on the stool I'd placed there, the lights overhead beat down on my shoulders and a sweat broke out under my arms. I didn't have a guitar. The only other instrument I could play was the piano, and not well at that. I was going to have to pull this off solo. I wasn't Lexi. I didn't have her bravado. I could only be myself. I could only hope it would be enough.

I shut my eyes, trying to tune out the room, Jamie, the lights, all of it, wiping it clean. I'd tossed and turned for hours last night trying to choose a song, but in the heat of the moment, sitting there on that stool, I just opened my mouth and let the music flow out of me.

It was a song I'd written when I first moved to Manhattan, the feel of Ian's fingers clamped around my wrist, how he would squeeze until it felt like my bones would snap. The way I'd sometimes catch him looking at me, his eyes alight with admiration and pride and then narrowing cruelly, the love turning to disgust. How when we first met, some nights we'd drive to the park that overlooked the harbor, the lights of the city far off in the distance, how they made anything seem possible.

I sang and sang, the notes flowing effortlessly, my voice breaking in only one or two places. As the last note died away, I opened my eyes, afraid of what I might see. But there was only Jamie, looking at me with astonishment.

"Was that OK?" I said hesitantly. "I know I'm not as good as Lexi . . ." My voice trailed off, and I felt the blood rush to my face. I looked down, biting my bottom lip.

I heard him stand up, a scraping sound as he pushed his chair back and then his footsteps as he walked over until he was right in front of me. "You and Lexi are different," he said, and I could feel the warmth of his body through the clothes he wore, filling the space between us. "She's not better. Just different. You're a songwriter. Lexi is a performer."

"I'm not a performer?" Despair washed over me, and I looked off to the side. Somehow forty minutes had passed on the clock over the bar, and I knew that soon the café would be bustling with servers and cooks dishing up the family meal, the sound of bottles clinking as the bar was restocked.

"Not in the same way, no. She lives for the spotlight. You're softer. A bit more reserved. But even so," he said quietly, "I couldn't take my eyes off you."

With those words, I stopped breathing. And when I looked over at him, I could see it in his eyes, the desire mirrored in my own. It was a living thing, a separate being pulsating with life. I could almost reach out and touch it.

"So . . . you want to work with me?" I asked when I could speak again. A few months ago, I was sitting in my room on Staten Island waiting for my life to change. And now here it was, opening up before me, bright as a box filled with tinsel. The whole glittering city reflected in his eyes.

"Hell yeah, I want to work with you." Jamie laughed, the sound melodious, deep barrels of honey shot through with amber. "I mean, this is exactly why I want to start my own label someday."

"What's wrong with being a manager?"

"Nothing," he said quickly. "But I want to make a home for artists that maybe don't quite fit in anywhere else—talent that might get lost in the crowd. Like yours. You deserve to be heard, Ava."

My cheeks flushed once again, and then there was a jangling, metal clinking on metal, the unmistakable sound of the front door opening, a clatter of voices as the line cooks pushed inside the café, laughing as they entered.

"I guess that's our cue." Jamie grinned, and I stepped down from the stage, aware that we were closer than ever before. "I'll email you a standard contract tonight. Have a lawyer look it over if you like, OK?" He was suddenly all business, and for the first time I could imagine him in a room with record execs in suits, reading through contracts and making deals.

Before I could answer, José, one of the cooks, yelled out, "Ava, you on tonight, mami? We're cooking up some carne asada. Gonna put some meat on those bones, girl." He cackled to himself before moving his considerable bulk through the swinging doors that led to the kitchen.

"I better go," Jamie said, picking up his messenger bag from the chair and slinging it over one shoulder. And with those words, my stomach sank, my pulse racing. I wasn't sure what I wanted, for him to leave and never come back or for him to never walk away at all. Something told me it was the latter, and Lexi's face flashed before my eyes, knowing and cold. I shivered in the sudden chill of the air-conditioning, which the cooks always cranked to full blast when they arrived each evening. Just as he reached the door, Jamie turned back for a moment, and I stood there, afraid to take so much as a step. He raised one hand, the door yawning wide, and then he was gone.

KAYLA

"Stand still, Lex. I can barely pin you with all this wriggling."

Lexi Mayhem stood on a pedestal in front of a full-length mirror, striking poses as though cameras were rolling somewhere in the hidden corners of the room. She looked impishly over one shoulder at her stylist, a woman in her midforties with a platinum crew cut, dressed head to toe in black. "Deal with it, Morgan. I had three espressos this morning."

Morgan just shook her head good-naturedly, clucking her tongue like a mother hen, and Lexi smiled, our eyes meeting in the mirror, her energy filling the room like helium. It was like nothing I'd ever felt before, potent, exhilarating, and exhausting all at once. After our initial meeting, my nerves had jangled manically, but I was also curiously drained.

As if I'd been bled dry by a succubus.

I'd never been inside anywhere as luxe as the Gucci flagship store on Fifth Avenue, and I'd been unprepared for the Cristal chilling in silver buckets, the private room lined with cream-colored modern sofas and gilt-legged chairs. The ornate chandelier hanging from the ceiling, crystals shimmering in the soft light. The air was ripe with the bloom of hothouse roses and woody sandalwood, with luxury itself. I wanted to wrap it around me like a cloak.

"What do you think, Kayla? It's for the cover of *Vanity Fair*."

Morgan placed the last pin and Lexi turned to face me, one hand on her hip, her platinum hair pulled back in a severe knot. Ivory satin pooled voluminously at her feet, the bodice strapless and boned, hugging her chiseled torso and offsetting the flight of tattoos covering one pale shoulder, delicate butterflies etched in black and gray. I'd been wading through a ton of early footage of her career, so there was no denying that my perspective was heavily skewed, but much like the dress she'd worn to the Emmys that Simone had so disparaged, this one also felt like an attempt to play it safe. It didn't parse at all with the woman I'd met in her bungalow at the Chateau with the bare, dirty feet and guileless expression. This look was more in line with her new career as the head of her own record label, and there was no denying that the dress *did* make a powerful statement. I just wasn't sure what exactly it was saying.

Or to whom.

"It's beautiful," I said, because it was true, but I couldn't mask the hint of hesitation in my voice.

"But?" she prompted, looking at me expectantly.

"No buts!" I said quickly, not wanting to annoy her this early into our second interview. "It's amazing. Full stop."

"I don't like bullshit, Kayla," she said evenly. "Tell me the truth."

"I mean . . . it's great. But . . ."

"But *what*?"

"It looks like something you'd wear to the Oscars. It feels . . . a little safe, maybe?"

There was a long pause, one in which I wondered if I'd just single-handedly killed the interview—along with my entire career. But then her lips parted in a slow smile, and she began nodding vigorously in approval.

"*Thank* you," she said in relief. "All I *want* is the truth. And it's the one thing no one ever wants to give me." She reached up and smoothed back an errant blonde strand of hair that had come undone. "I know you get it. I mean, you must be used to that in your line of work too."

"What's that?"

"People lying to you."

Our eyes met in the mirror. I nodded, curious where this was going. "It happens," I said carefully. "But most of the time, the truth comes out in the end."

I looked down at the open notebook in my lap. Written in red ink and circled three times was the word "AVA?" Since my visit to Staten Island, I hadn't been able to unhear the words Irina had spoken with so much fervor, so much pain. *My daughter was murdered.* I didn't know whether to write them off as the ravings of a grief-stricken mother, but I knew I wanted to learn more.

"I was watching some old footage of your early performances," I began, "and I was wondering . . . do you ever catch yourself in moments like this, in a ten-thousand-dollar dress, and think about how far you've come from the days of wearing a few rolls of electrical tape onstage? I was thinking of the costume you wore for your first gig at the Bitter End. That must have cost, what, like five dollars in materials?"

"If even that." She laughed. "Electrical tape and thigh-high leather boots. Man, that was forever ago. You know, I found those boots on St. Marks in the *trash*? They were just sitting there on top, barely worn, so I grabbed them. They were too small, but I knew I'd only wear them onstage for like an hour, so what did it matter?" She shrugged. "I've never thought that performing had anything to do with comfort anyway."

"But you've always seemed so at home onstage. Like you belong there," I mused, placing my notebook on the table in front of me.

"Well, I don't really experience stage fright. I'm lucky that way, I guess." She flashed me a smile, and I was again distracted by the sheer force of her personality. "So many singers do, and it can really kill their career." Her expression turned clouded for a moment, hazy, as if she had floated away momentarily. And then, just as quickly as it had descended, the fog lifted, and her features came back sharply into focus. "But I've never thought anything about a performance should be comfortable. Comfort equals complacency, and once you're complacent, you're done."

"So you're not interested in comfort?"

"In my personal life, sure. I like cashmere sweaters and warm baths and soft blankets as much as the next person. But onstage? I push boundaries."

Before I could respond, she turned back toward Morgan. "We good?" she asked, pointing at the folds of fabric hanging from her frame. The stylist nodded, reaching over to quickly unzip her. Suddenly, I was in a room with the most famous pop star in the world, clad in only a flesh-colored thong and an impossibly tall pair of silver heels. Her stomach was flat and muscular, her breasts round and full. There was something about Lexi Mayhem that made you unsure if you wanted to be her or sleep with her—or both.

"Throw me my dress?" she asked, kicking off the heels and pointing imperiously to a black pile of cashmere on the couch next to me. I scrambled to grab it, tossing it in the air. She caught it deftly, pulling the fine wool over her head. It swallowed her, hanging almost to her knees. She sat down on the podium, pulling on a pair of thigh-high black suede boots with ice-pick heels. Morgan bustled around her, hanging the satin dress on a padded satin hanger and thrusting it into a voluminous transparent bag.

"You've come a long way from boots you picked out of the trash," I said, pointing at the buttery suede she was pulling over her legs. "Speaking of which, I saw your friend Ava in some videos of your early performances. It's funny, though—I can't find any mention of her in any of your interviews."

Her head came up sharply, and she looked at me, her expression devoid of emotion. There was a long pause. "It was a long time ago," she finally said, bending to tug at the tops of her boots before standing to observe herself in the mirror once more. "And anyway," she said, "I barely knew her."

"It didn't look that way in the video."

"Well, it's the truth."

"Is it?" I asked lightly.

"Why are you so interested in this?" Her body tensed, her spine rigid, and I remembered how tenderly Lexi had brushed that tendril of hair from Ava's face in the video, her eyes soft as water. But the woman standing in front of me was anything but.

There was the sound of muffled footsteps, and then a man appeared in the doorway, wearing a crisp navy suit, and holding a take-out tray in one hand, filled with iced coffees. His dark hair was slightly receding and clipped short, so that the line of his skull shone through cleanly. His eyes were obscured by a pair of Ray-Bans, the lenses black and shiny as fresh paint.

"Ladies," he said smoothly, walking over to the low glass coffee table in front of me and depositing the drinks on top. "I hope I'm not interrupting. I just thought a little refreshment might be in order. Lex, I got your usual, a skinny caramel macchiato, of course."

He turned to me. "Ben Reynolds, Lexi's manager. You must be Kayla. Nice to meet you in the flesh." His handshake was firm, and he smelled of money, sharp and bracing.

"Great to meet you." I nodded, waiting for him to release my hand, which he finally did, but not before giving it a tiny squeeze.

Morgan glanced over, her arms full of fabric, and offered Ben a weak smile before looking away again. The tension in the room was thick and poisonous. There was no way that he couldn't feel it, like walking into a thunderstorm just before it began to rain, the wind howling like a lost child.

Ben's head swiveled to look at Lexi, then me, before he picked up one of the plastic cups from the table, the coffee a milky cream color, and held it out to her.

"I don't want any coffee," she said bluntly, her eyes still on me. "What are you doing here anyway?"

"Lexi, sweetheart," Ben cooed, seemingly unfazed by her tone. "Did we wake up on the wrong side of the bed this morning?"

Instead of responding, she ignored him, turning back toward her own reflection in the mirror.

"Everything OK?" Ben asked, removing his sunglasses and narrowing his eyes, which were the color of dark denim and only slightly bloodshot.

"We were just discussing the early days of Lexi's career," I said quickly, then turned my attention back to Lexi, who was staring at herself as if the glimmering surface were where all the answers were kept.

"Lexi," I said quietly, "where you came from and the people you knew back then are an important part of that story. I'm not trying to pry or upset you. I'm just trying to understand your background." I'd never had a subject go hostile on me so quickly. But her reaction told me I had touched a nerve, and that intrigued me.

"Hardly." She laughed, a short burst that sounded more like a bark, and Morgan reappeared, holding out a short black leather jacket for Lexi to slip her arms into, the soft hide covered with spikes and studs. "Some things are better off forgotten," she said, retrieving a pair of enormous black sunglasses from one pocket and sliding them over her face.

"Don't we have that press conference at three, Lex?" Ben said quietly, reaching over and resting a hand on her elbow.

She nodded once, curtly, shaking off his touch, and with her face half-hidden by those frames, it was impossible to know what she was feeling. If she was even feeling anything at all.

"Apologies, Kayla," Ben said with a smile that looked like he'd spent a few grand on professional whitening.

"I have to get going," Lexi snapped. "Can we pick this up another time?"

And with that, she swept out of the room, and I exhaled heavily, closing my notebook and turning off my recorder, shoving both back in my bag. As soon as Lexi was out of earshot, Morgan cleared her throat once, noisily, and then gave me a knowing look, as if we were coconspirators. And in a way, I supposed we were.

"She's a real piece of work, isn't she?"

"Comes with the job, I guess," I said, trying to make light of the situation, even though it was slightly embarrassing that I'd just been so effectively handled.

Somehow, she always ends up in control of the narrative, doesn't she?

"I've worked with a lot of celebrities over the years," Morgan said, picking up a silver dress from the floor and sliding it back on a hanger. She walked over to a freestanding rack in the corner, placing the dress on the metal bar. "And I bet you have too. So I don't need to tell you that they're all nuts in their own way. But with Lexi, you *really* never know what you're going to get. I mean, that's part of the fun of it, right? But it can also be frustrating as hell. Sometimes she's just impossible."

"Not impossible," I said, standing up and throwing my bag on my shoulder. "Challenging."

Morgan just shrugged and resumed picking up the clothes strewn across the floor in a patchwork of color. I walked through the store and out into the street, where the sweet smell of roasted nuts, almost cloying in its intensity, and the salt and smoke of hot pretzels permeated the air. I headed down Fifth Avenue, thinking about what Irina had said—*my Ava did not fall*—and the defensive look in Lexi's eyes when I'd mentioned Ava's name.

As I ducked into the subway, I couldn't shake the sinking feeling that not only was Lexi clearly sensitive about that time in her life and the people who played a part in it, but maybe it was even heavier, more clouded than that. The vision of Ava opening her arms filled my thoughts, Lexi stepping inside the shelter of them and holding on tight, Ava's expression, so tender and sweet, her eyes closed.

I barely knew her . . .

Bullshit.

She was lying. But why? My gut told me there was more to it, and when I'd had that feeling in the past, I'd hardly ever been wrong. *Some things are better off forgotten.* Astrid's pale face swam up in my vision, clouding it, and I shook my head to make it disappear. But still, it hung on, the feel of her warm hand in mine, the sharp, sweet scent of her strawberry body spray, and my stomach rolled with nausea.

The subway platform fell away, and suddenly I could feel the softness of the mattress on Astrid's narrow twin bed beneath me, how it dipped sharply in the center, could see her brow furrowed in concentration as she bent over the neat line of her splayed-out toes, carefully daubing each one with peacock polish. "I think he really noticed me today," she said as Lexi Mayhem's new album spun in the CD player, the disc flashing silver, Mayhem's voice a wild wailing. Something unhinged about her appealed to us, the life force that radiated from the songs and the music videos we watched on a loop. Listening to her music made it feel like everything was continually at stake. And it was. We just didn't know it yet.

"Who?" I said absentmindedly, though I already knew the answer as I rolled over onto my stomach, propping my chin beneath my hands.

"*Scott,*" she said, looking up impatiently, her eyes gemlike, slivers of topaz in her heart-shaped face. Her curtain of hair, crimson and burnished gold, fell across her eyes, and she reached up, pulling the weight of it back with one hand. "He smiled at me in the cafeteria. He's never *smiled* at me before."

I could see the hope alive in her face, naked and open, and I swallowed hard. I nodded, trying to rearrange my features into something resembling encouragement, or at the very least impartiality. But my stomach was in free fall. I opened my mouth to speak and then closed it again before words could come tumbling out. The things I could not say.

I liked him. I liked Scott too.

She had liked him before I did. And that somehow gave her the right. A right I didn't possess. But I wanted him nonetheless.

And it was beginning to be a problem.

Scott had always been just another boy we'd routinely pass on our walks home from school, dribbling a basketball in his driveway, nodding with a quick dip of his chin as we walked by. But when Astrid and I returned for our junior year, he had morphed, seemingly overnight, into the most popular boy at our high school. Tall, with buttery locks that fell disarmingly into his deep blue eyes, he sauntered through the halls with a newfound confidence. You could almost hear the intake of breath as he walked by, his leather varsity jacket wrapping his lean frame like a suit of armor. There had been a palpable shift. One that even I couldn't ignore.

"Hello!" Astrid's giggles infiltrated my thoughts, and I looked over to see her comically waggling her hands in front of her. "Earth to Kayla!"

And then she was gone, the train blazing down the rails on the other side of the platform, bringing with it a rush of hot air. I leaned against a pillar, taking deep breaths, and out on the tracks, a rat moved across the rails, its furry, bloated body moving slowly in the lights of the approaching train. I stood on the platform, the damp heat of the station making me sweat. But maybe it was more than that. My conversation with Lexi about Ava had unsettled me, and for more than just the mere fact that she'd dismissed it entirely.

Maybe Lexi and I had more in common than it appeared on the surface of things. As I stared into the dark void of the tunnel, I couldn't help but wonder if Lexi Mayhem was more than just your typically evasive, self-absorbed pop star.

Maybe she'd betrayed her best friend too.

AVA

Sequins, leather, and lace. Clouds of black tulle studded with stars. Pleather, a tar river flowing liquidly across my skin. Scents of church incense and clove cigarettes, a thick fog that enveloped every inch of the store. Trash & Vaudeville, an East Village boutique frequented by goths, punks, glam rockers, and heavy-metal aficionados. Two floors of spandex dresses and heavy silver jewelry. Jeans tattered at the knees, designed to slip down narrow hips. Racks of feather boas in a graduated rainbow of candy colors and every type of shoe, from combat boots to golden platform heels, lined the black-painted walls.

"What do you think?" Lexi asked, turning around, a pair of heart-shaped red sunglasses covering half her face. She struck a pose, one hand cocked jauntily on her hip.

"Did you suddenly change your name to Lolita?" I asked as she turned to vamp in the full-length mirror, her energy infectious. Even in a pair of faded black jeans and a long-sleeve white T-shirt, the image of the Sex Pistols defiantly silk-screened across the front, Lexi was undeniably glamorous. I looked down at my oversize sweatshirt, the neckline torn and jagged from the scissors I'd taken to it one night when I was bored, the black leggings that were part of my everyday uniform, the black down coat I'd found at the Salvation Army puddled on the floor. Jamie had said I had "it," whatever that meant. But standing next to Lexi, any uniqueness I possessed seemed to evaporate into thin air.

"I know." She sighed, throwing them on top of a glass display case full of jewelry. "But they're fun, right?"

The shine of silver caught my eye, and I pulled a dress from the rack, holding it up to my body. It wasn't my style, but I liked the way it shimmered against my pale skin. I moved this way and that, watching the sheen of the fabric shift under the lights.

"Hey, I *like* that!" Lexi reached out one hand to finger the material, rubbing it back and forth between her thumb and forefinger.

"I don't know," I said uncertainly, putting the dress back on the rack and shrugging.

"What don't you know?" Lexi said impatiently, grabbing the dress off the rack again and holding it out in front of us. "It would look great on you! And Jamie said you have some shows coming up, right? This would be perfect!"

"Don't remind me," I said, turning away and walking over to a rack of leather jackets, my hands sliding through the long row of them slick as oil. No matter what Jamie said, I knew I wasn't ready to step onstage in front of an audience yet. We'd met at the café a few times over the past few weeks, once for him to drop off the signed contract and twice more to work on a few songs. And as always, there was that sudden heat between us. A quickening I tried my best to ignore. With the show looming before me, it was a little easier to file those feelings away. Somehow, now that singing was actual work—the very act of writing songs, getting ready for gigs, or even just planning what to wear *onstage*—felt excruciating. I could sit on my bed with a pen and a notebook and write out lyrics for hours at a time when the idea of performing was nothing more than a faraway dream, shimmering somewhere in the distance, just out of reach.

But now it seemed all too real.

"Just get it!" Lexi said, grabbing my hand and pulling me through the racks of clothes and up the long flight of stairs.

"Lex, I'm broke," I whispered as we approached the register. I smiled weakly at the man standing behind it. Somewhere in his early forties, he was tall and lanky, wearing a black T-shirt with Marc Bolan's face on the front, and a pair of leather pants that looked glued on. His hair was platinum blond, artfully disheveled, and metal rings twined around his fingers like vines.

"Well, well," he said with a grin. "If it isn't the Freddie Mercury of the Lower East Side."

"Hardly." Lexi snorted, rolling her eyes. "Thanks for the compliment, though. This is my friend Ava," she said, jabbing her thumb in my direction. "This is Tommy."

"A sidekick." Tommy nodded. "I can dig it."

"Actually, Ava's a singer too. We're getting *this* for her first show." She threw the dress on the counter, and as she did so, the price tag, which I hadn't even glanced at yet, flipped over. Eighty-five dollars. Groceries for three weeks. I maybe had twenty in my account, at most.

"Hey," I hissed, pulling on her arm and leaning toward her, hoping Tommy couldn't hear. "I don't get paid again till next *week*. I can't afford this right now."

Lexi just ignored me, digging in her pocket with one hand and pulling out a wad of bills, tossing them onto the counter.

"Lexi, no!" I whispered, pulling on her arm again as if she were a misbehaving child.

"I want to," she said with a shrug. "You don't want it?" She raised one eyebrow, her expression impish.

"It's not that, but—"

"Consider it an early birthday present," Lexi said effusively.

"My birthday was in August," I mumbled. Not that she paid any attention.

August. Almost an entire month before Lexi and I had ever crossed paths. It seemed inconceivable now that I'd ever lived a life without her in it, that we'd never spent more than one New Year's Eve together, drunk on cheap champagne as we spun along the icy streets, her hand warm in my own.

"So, it makes perfect sense then!" Lexi crowed triumphantly. "Wrap it up, Tommy!" She gestured at the dress, the cash waiting patiently on the counter.

"Lexi," I said, tugging on her arm like a child, "you don't need to—"

"Sold!" Tommy interjected as he counted out the bills, shoving them in the register before throwing the dress in a hot-pink bag, one I took reluctantly, the store's logo plastered across the front in black lettering. "You see that review of your show last week at Max Fish?" he asked nonchalantly.

"What review?" There was a breathy excitement in her voice. A hunger. Lexi loved publicity more than anything else.

"In the *Village Voice*," Tommy said, reaching under the counter, pulling out a copy, and handing it over. "That critic. Keats something? What a wimp." He laughed. "Wouldn't know real music if he tripped over it."

But Lexi was already riffling through the newspaper, the pages rustling furiously before coming to a stop. As she began to read, her expression changed from excitement to fury in a matter of seconds. After a moment I heard her mutter the word "motherfucker" under her breath, and then without explanation, she ripped out the review with one hand, shoving the newspaper back onto the counter.

"This Keats guy? You know him? Seen him around?" she asked Tommy, her gaze like the edge of a knife. There was an energy, a buzzing, like the high-pitched whine of a chain saw.

"I've seen him up the street at Holiday Bar." Tommy shrugged. "But seriously, babe, who cares?" he said, his voice heavy with smoke. "The guy's a critic. What does he know about what it takes to get up onstage? Remember, the Sex Pistols got terrible reviews too," he remarked, pointing at her shirt. "All it means is that you got to this guy—you pissed him off. And that, my friend, is the measure of good art."

Not that Lexi was paying any attention. She shrugged on her wool coat, belting it tightly at the waist, and grabbed my arm, pulling me out of the store before anyone could say another word. "Thanks, Tommy," she called over her shoulder as we stepped outside, the review clenched tightly in her hand, her fingers white as ivy wood.

"Where are we going?" I asked as she pulled me along the street and through the crowd, her face set in determination, gritting her teeth against the cold. She didn't answer, just kept moving past the Japanese restaurant we'd been to a few times for sake and spicy tuna rolls, then down to the end of St. Marks, stopping in front of a bar with a red awning, multicolored strands of Christmas lights hanging festively above the door. She walked down a flight of concrete steps and pushed open the red-painted door, and then we were inside the bar.

I blinked furiously, my eyes adjusting to the darkened interior. When I could see again, I took in the colored Christmas lights hung from the ceiling, the red vinyl booths, silver duct tape covering long gashes from years of use. The place was mostly empty but for a few guys sitting on barstools and a woman hovering over the jukebox at the back of the room, cackling maniacally to herself, punching buttons as though they were her enemies. Then I saw him, a lone man sitting in one of the booths in the back. Late twenties, wearing an olive-green hoodie and jeans, dark hair grazing his shoulders. He was hunched over a laptop, a glass of beer in front of him, half-full.

Without missing a beat, Lexi strode to the back of the bar, and I followed until we were standing right in front of him. Lexi just stood there, waiting for him to look up and acknowledge her presence, daring him to challenge her.

"Can I help you?" he asked when he finally tore himself away from his screen. His eyes were as dark as his hair, which was glossy and well cared for. This was a man who possessed a certain amount of vanity. I got the sense just from looking at him that he might enjoy sparring with a tiny ball of energy like Lexi, who I knew from experience wouldn't even consider retreating until she got her way.

Without missing a beat, Lexi thrust the article at him, throwing it down on the table with a sharp smack.

"You write this?" Her voice was low and controlled but deadly.

He picked up the scrap of paper, peering at it curiously. "Yeah," he said after a long moment. "So?"

"So now that I'm standing right in front of you," Lexi began, crossing her arms over her chest, "why don't you say it to my *face?*"

There was an awkward silence, one the word "uncomfortable" didn't even begin to cover. My eyes darted between the two of them, and then almost as if he'd only just noticed me standing there, Keats looked over at me—for help, backup, who knew. Our eyes met for a split second before I quickly looked away. No way was I getting involved. Not because I thought Lexi was right. She wasn't. Bad reviews came with the territory. I knew I'd get my own soon enough. But as I stood there watching her confront him, I was suddenly flooded with envy. It crashed over me in a great green wave until I could barely focus on the scene in front of me.

I never stood up for myself, even when I knew I was right. And never to Ian, no matter how much I wanted to. So many nights I'd lain in bed, thinking of the things I should've said to him, what I could've done, if only I'd had the courage to open my mouth and speak. Lexi couldn't seem to live without speaking her mind, even when she was wrong. She was so sure of her talent, her opinions, of her absolute right to fame and fortune. It shone from her, as if she were already a star.

"Listen," he said apologetically, clearing his throat before speaking, holding his hands open before her as if he were pleading, "I'm just doing my job."

"If your job is to be a talentless *hack*, then you're really succeeding," Lexi hissed, bending down and resting her palms on the table. They were eye to eye now, and there was nowhere to hide.

"I know what I heard," he said quietly, a thin edge to his voice. "It wasn't your best night, Lexi. Not by a long shot."

"Maybe you should get your ears checked, then," she retorted. "Clean them maybe?"

At that, I couldn't help but laugh, and he looked over at me, our eyes meeting for a brief moment. I bit the inside of my cheek to quiet myself until drops of blood began to pool in my mouth.

"I'm playing the Bitter End next Friday," she said. She pulled a hot-pink flyer from the depths of the black leather bag slung over one shoulder and placed it on the table with a flourish, covering the offending review completely with a riot of pink. "You'll eat your words. I guarantee it."

He picked up the flyer, peering at it, then looked up, offering her a smile. "Fair enough," he said, nodding slowly.

She smiled back, a piranha grin, and for the first time it was like she remembered I was still standing there. "Let's go," she said, grabbing my hand and leading me to the bar. "Two shots of Cuervo," she called to the bartender, who had his back to us but waved a hand above his head to show he'd heard. She threw a twenty down on the wooden surface and turned to me, her green eyes glittering and alive, enveloping me in that crazy force she emitted. A certain pulsing.

"I guess you told *him*," I remarked as the bartender walked over with two shot glasses filled to the brim with clear liquid. As if on cue, we erupted into a fit of giggles. Lexi reached out and grabbed my arm to steady herself, her head thrown back in uncontrollable laughter. The bartender just shook his head and walked away, leaving us to our madness. When she laughed like that, all was right in the world. I savored these moments between us, squirreled them away like unexpected treasure, never knowing when it all might disappear.

"Let's get out of here," she said after we finally composed ourselves, throwing back the shot in front of her with one fluid movement. I picked up my glass and did the same, grimacing as the burn hit my throat. I put the glass down on the bar, and she grabbed my hand, her warm fingers closing around my own, and we ran out into the street, the late-afternoon sky darkening into a hazy blue twilight. It was us and the city, throwing its arms around us like an old friend. I leaned back into that comforting embrace, and we made our way through the streets of downtown until we were standing in front of Lexi's building, the stars just beginning to peep out from the sky, rhinestones sparkling against deep blue velvet.

I followed her into the building, and then just as we passed the fourth floor, where her apartment was located, instead of stopping, she kept moving, climbing up and up while I followed behind, breathing hard until we reached the top.

"I want to show you something," she said with a secret little smile as she pushed open the scarred metal door and let in the night. Then we were standing on a rooftop, the city stretched out before us. There were two battered beach chairs set up a few feet from the edge, and Lexi threw herself down in one, legs akimbo, hands cradled behind her head. I sat down gingerly in the other, the tar soft beneath my feet.

"This is where I come when I want to think," she said quietly, looking out over the expanse of the city, her cheeks ruddy from the cold. "When I'm not sure of anything anymore, when it all gets to be too much, I come up here and then I remember."

"Remember what?"

She turned to look at me, her face half in shadow, her eyes hooded, mascara smudged underneath like bruises. "Why I'm here."

I nodded, then looked out into the night, the skyline, the way the city always seemed so enormous with possibility and how Lexi and I were part of that possibility now. I felt a creeping pressure and then the weight of her hand in mine, and I let out a silent prayer to the universe, to whoever might be listening. *Please. Please let me keep this. Let it always stay the same.*

But the universe stayed quiet, giving nothing away at all, as the wail of an ambulance filled the night air, the sky deepening into blackness.

From: McCray, Kayla <kayla.mccray@rollingstone.
com>
Sent: Monday, April 29, 2019 9:06 AM
To: Ben Reynolds <b.reynolds@avantentertain-
ment.com>

Subject: Follow-Up Interview/Scheduling

Dear Ben,

I'd love to carve out some more time with Lexi
while she's still here in New York, if possible. Might
she have a free hour or two this week to continue
the interview? My schedule is completely flexible,
so please keep me informed on any possible gaps
in her schedule. I'd love to set something up ASAP!

Best,

Kayla

From: Ben Reynolds <b.reynolds@avantentertain-
ment.com>
Sent: Monday, April 29, 2019 12:32 PM
To: McCray, Kayla <kayla.mccray@rollingstone.
com>

Subject: RE: Follow-Up Interview/Scheduling

Kayla,

My sincere apologies. With the announcement of the label, along with the impending release of the new record, Lexi's trip is jam packed. I will do my best to fit you in, but unfortunately, I cannot firmly commit to anything at this time. Of course, Lexi is thrilled to be working with you, and will make herself completely available as soon as her schedule lightens.

Best regards,

Ben

From: McCray, Kayla <kayla.mccray@rollingstone.com>
Sent: Monday, April 29, 2019 12:46 PM
To: Ben Reynolds <b.reynolds@avantentertainment.com>

Subject: RERE: Follow-Up Interview/Scheduling

Hey Ben,

Thanks so much. It's been great to have some dedicated time to talk, to get to know Lexi and ask questions, but I'd really love to just see her in action, to be a fly on the wall, so to speak. Is there a day I might shadow her while she's working on the new label? I'd love to experience what Lexi Mayhem, record exec, looks like at this juncture of things. The upside, too, is that I will simply observe; she won't even know I'm there.

Best,

Kayla

From: Ben Reynolds <b.reynolds@avantentrtain-ment.com>
Sent: Tuesday, April 30, 2019 9:54 AM
To: McCray, Kayla <kayla.mccray@rollingstone.com>

Subject: RERERE: Follow-Up Interview/Scheduling

Trust me—she would.

But in the meantime, I'm enclosing Lexi's cell, which is to be used for scheduled interviews or emergencies ONLY, though I can't guarantee how long it will be good for, since she has the habit of changing it every few weeks. I'm sure you understand.

323.555.9057.

More soon.

Ben

[CAUTION] This email originated outside Avant
Entertainment.

KAYLA

2019

The storm pelted the rain-streaked windows of the wine bar, scarlet curtains framing the glass, turning the wet streets into a charming tableau of city life. Pedestrians hurried past, umbrellas in tow, children running in bright yellow slickers. When it stormed like this in Brooklyn, I could've been anywhere: Paris, Copenhagen. In its way, the language of spring was universal. I could feel the quickening of the buds on the trees, hear the flapping of wings. If summer was a kind of ripening on the edge of rottenness, spring was transformation. For that reason, I'd always waited for it with my breath held tightly in my throat. Maybe because the season itself was so fleeting.

A few weeks at most, and then the heat would fall like a hammer.

I took a sip of the glass of sauvignon blanc on the marble table in front of me, shifting in my seat, conscious of the fact that I'd dressed carefully for this meeting in a black knit dress and high black boots, dark hair twisted in a knot at the back of my neck, my lips a slash of red. The bun I'd tried to secure so carefully in place kept unraveling, and I reached up every few moments to tuck errant strands of hair away, glad to have somewhere to direct my nervous energy. I was too dressed up for a casual drink, but the last time we'd met, it had been raining, too, and I'd been soggy, disheveled, and self-conscious. I wanted today to be different—and that desire worried me.

When I'd called and impulsively invited him out for a drink, I did so knowing that if I couldn't get to Lexi, and Ben's emails had made it clear that she didn't want to talk to me right now, then my best bet was to seek out the people who'd known her—and Ava. Jamie was an obvious choice, and he'd agreed to the meeting immediately and without hesitation. Secretly I wondered if that had more to do with the prospect of seeing me than talking about the past. But I was also well aware of the fact that he was a source.

At least that's what I kept telling myself.

I heard the creak of the door opening, and there he was, shaking the rain from his caramel-colored hair, darkened with wetness. He smiled as soon as he saw me, heading over, carrying a black umbrella. He wore jeans and a thin gray sweater I wanted to bury my hands in, a waxed canvas jacket in deep charcoal thrown on top. He was one of those men who looked better with his jawline hidden in stubble. It sharpened his features, giving him structure.

"Am I late?" he asked, sitting down across from me at the small, round table and shrugging off his coat.

"Not at all," I said quickly. "I live close by. And I have the highly annoying habit of arriving anywhere at least fifteen minutes early—probably out of the paranoid fear I'll forget to show up entirely."

"Has that ever happened?"

"Nope," I said, taking a sip of my wine. "Not once. But, you see, at any moment? It *could*."

"Ah," he said with a grin. "Constant vigilance seems best, then. As a preemptive measure, of course."

"Exactly," I replied, placing my glass back down on the table. I was jittery, partly from the four cups of coffee I'd consumed earlier in the day and partly from the nearness of him.

"Do you want something?" I asked, looking back toward the bartender.

"What did you have in mind?" he asked, his eyes moving over my face, my dress, and just as I had in our first meeting, I felt that current running between us, electric and strange, and I felt myself thrown off-balance. "You look . . . different," he said, his eyes finally settling on my face.

"Different than what?"

"Then the last time we met."

"I'm wearing a dress," I said flatly.

"I can see that."

"I was hoping we could talk a little about Lexi's early years in New York—and that you might fill me in on what you know about Ava Petrova."

"What's the story about anyway?" he asked, running one hand through his damp hair. "Just the record label?"

"Do you want a drink?" I asked again, holding up my wineglass, the scarlet imprint of my lips marring the rim like a bloodstain.

"I'm good, thanks," he said lightly. "So if your story is about the label, then why do you want to talk about Ava? That's ancient history."

His eyes were the palest blue I'd ever seen, almost silver, but not insipid. The word "feral" came to mind, and I thought of Keats, of what he would think if he could see me now, flirting with a potential source. At best, he'd be disappointed. At worst?

I didn't even want to think about it.

"I'll level with you," I said firmly. "I'm not exactly sure what the story is yet. I was given one assignment, and it's kind of morphed into something else. Sometimes, the story finds itself. I'm just letting it lead the way right now."

"All right," he said slowly. "So, what do you want to know?"

"How would you describe the relationship between Ava and Lexi?"

"This is off the record, right?" he asked, furrowing his brow.

"I think it kind of has to be, don't you?"

"Why is that?" he asked, a playful smile tugging at the corners of his full lips. His hair was lightening as it dried, thin butterscotch ribbons cutting through the darkness.

"Can we focus, please?"

He let out a deep sigh before speaking again. "All right. Lexi and Ava were good friends."

"Define 'good.'"

"They were together constantly. Inseparable, really. To put it in the simplest terms, I rarely saw one of them without the other. They looked alike, dressed alike—hell, they were practically twins. At one point they were even talking about getting matching tattoos." He shook his head at the memory.

"How did they meet?"

"At the café. They worked together."

"Ava was a singer too?"

"Yeah," he said after a minute or so. "Well, more of a songwriter, really."

I turned the distinction over in my brain. "Wasn't Lexi also?"

He shifted in his seat, grimacing slightly, as if he'd suddenly sat on a pin. "Yeah, but Ava . . . Ava was in a whole other league." His expression was suddenly distant, and I could almost see the images flashing through his brain as he struggled to find the words. "Ava could write a whole song in ten minutes flat, like she was channeling it from some other dimension. It was more transcription than writing. For her, it was . . . effortless."

"She was really that good?"

"Man, I haven't thought about this in years," he said quietly. "It feels like it happened to someone else, you know?" He looked down at the floor, kicking at it with the toe of his boot as if he needed a distraction.

"I can imagine."

"And yeah," he said, looking up, his eyes meeting mine. "She was. One of the best I've ever seen. And I've worked with a lot of talented performers."

"You managed her *and* Lexi?"

There was a long pause.

"I did. For a while anyway."

"What was that like?"

He smiled, tracing a swirling pattern on the tabletop with an index finger. "Complicated," he finally said.

"Did Ava ever record anything? I searched online but couldn't find any info. Actually, I couldn't find much about Ava at *all*, really. I've seen some weird stuff over the years while researching a subject, but it almost seemed like the internet has been wiped clean of any mention of her."

Jamie nodded, then cleared his throat. "Well, remember, it was a long time ago. Not as much got archived online. There were no iPhones. Video was harder to upload. It's not that surprising, really. And then she was gone before she could break into the mainstream. There was a lot of interest in her. She was about to be signed to a major label right before she . . ." He looked over my shoulder at the long counter behind me, his words trailing away until they were lost in the chatter at the tables surrounding us, the sound of ice in a cocktail shaker, a rattling of bones.

"Did she ever write for anyone else?" I asked, wanting to move away from anything that might halt the conversation.

He looked back over, giving me a tight smile. "She helped Lexi with her own songs a little. But as far as I know, that was it."

"Lexi needed help?"

"Sure." He shrugged. "Everyone needs help sometimes, don't they? Even you."

"Is that what you're doing? Helping me?"

"You tell me."

There was another long silence, broken only by a rush of cool air as a woman in a red trench coat entered the bar, chattering away obliviously on her cell phone.

"Stop changing the subject," I said, leaning back in my chair and crossing one leg over the other. I pulled my skirt down as I did so, making sure my knees were covered, feeling his eyes on me the whole time.

"It didn't come naturally for Lexi back then. Not the way it did for Ava."

"But . . . I've seen the footage," I said, aware that I was protesting, almost sputtering. "Lexi was *amazing* onstage. A natural. She blew everyone away, night after night, like she was born for it."

"She did," he said quietly. "And she was. But writing wasn't Lexi's strong suit, at least not back then."

"Would you consider Ava a perfectionist?"

He laughed softly, looking down at the floor and then back at me again. "I'd say that would be putting it mildly. It was sometimes a struggle to get her onstage at all. If she wasn't feeling it for some reason, if she didn't think the songs were ready, she'd just shut down. Kind of like a kid having a tantrum, but instead of screaming and yelling? She'd practically lie down and refuse to move."

"Not literally, I take it."

"No. Not literally. But you get the idea. She could be very stubborn."

I shifted on the hard wooden chair. "So, in those moments, what would you do?"

"Calm her down." He leaned forward, resting one elbow on the table. "Tell her that I believed in her."

"Did Lexi ever have these kinds of problems?"

He laughed once again, his expression incredulous. "Lexi couldn't *wait* to get out in front of the audience, and she always had a somewhat inflated sense of her own talent. You couldn't convince her that she didn't deserve to be famous, even if you tried. She was so wholeheartedly focused on what she thought she deserved, and no one was going to knock her off course. She didn't believe in self sabotage."

"And Ava did?"

"Let's talk about something else," he said, his eyes lingering on my face, my lips.

"But we're here to talk about this."

"Are we?"

"I thought so." I shrugged, trying to lighten the tension. "It's not like this is a date or anything."

"Maybe we should fix that."

There was a long, uncomfortable pause.

"I don't think it's a good idea."

"Why not?"

My mind raced with thoughts, one reason stacking up on another like playing cards, too many to even calculate.

"Because I'm interviewing you for a story I'm writing for a national magazine that you've probably idolized since you were still listening to, I don't know, Smashing Pumpkins or whatever band was mildly cool back when you were a kid. It's completely unethical." I sat back, putting some distance between us.

"You always do the right thing, huh?" he said, but not unkindly. More as if he were taking it in. "I can't say I've always had that luxury."

"Doing what's right is a choice. Just like choosing not to."

"It's not always that easy, Kayla. And I think you know that. Or you wouldn't be here."

We stared at each other in silence for a moment, and the room seemed to stand still. There was a current in the air, much like the first time we'd met. I knew that if he so much as touched my hand, I'd be left defenseless.

"So you're a stickler for rules," he said, breaking the tension with a smile.

I uncrossed my arms, feeling my vulnerability creep up inside me like a prowler looking for an open window. I didn't want to have this reaction to him, but it was happening. It made me hyperaware of the fact that all that had once been solid was now unmoored as a boat drifting aimlessly out to sea. "When it comes to my career? Yeah. I am. It's not usually that difficult to pull off."

"But it is now?" he asked, his voice barely above a whisper.

I stared at him, unable to speak. The act of just looking at him was killing me. Being this close and not being able to touch him. There was something drawing us together like magnets, the grinding of metal on metal, making it difficult to stop myself from reaching over and pulling him to me. I'd never felt anything like it. Not with anyone. It destabilized me, that recklessness, a feeling I wasn't familiar with on any level. I wanted to push my hands under his shirt, feel his blood-warm skin against my palms. I could hear Keats in my head, that slightly chiding tone he always used when I disappointed him, his voice a warning.

You're on dangerous ground, Kayla. Better rein it in.

But his words had no effect, drifting past my ears as if they'd never existed. The room seemed to spin without moving, and I wanted to go to him, take his face between my palms, my mouth finding his, kissing him over and over until we could barely breathe. And in that moment, seeing what I was feeling mirrored on his face, I realized that there had never really been any choice at all. It was in his eyes. The way his legs were strewn apart under the table, his knee knocking against my own. How he was eating me up without even moving a muscle.

And then, like a dam breaking, I gave in.

"I live just around the corner," I said quietly, both of us refusing to look away now.

There was no need for words. For the first time in my professional life, they'd been rendered useless. He stood up, pushing back his chair in one rough movement, the legs scraping against the floor, and before I could take it back, second-guess myself, or say *stop, don't, we shouldn't,* we were out on the rain-washed street, his hand clenched firmly in my own.

AVA

We did everything together.

I'd grown up watching girls run in packs, sitting alongside one another in the cafeteria at school, leaning close to whisper their secrets in waiting ears. But I'd always sat alone in the courtyard, a dry, chalky ham sandwich in my lap, their laughter ringing through the air like church bells, a sermon I always missed. Every day was the same ritual of unwrapping the carefully folded tinfoil, peering inside, and hoping for something different, something I actually wanted to eat for a change. Irina didn't believe in condiments.

Mustard? Why? So you can get heartburn? American food is too spicy!

I'd throw the meat and bread in the trash, my stomach pinched with hunger, along with another feeling I couldn't quite identify. A chasm of emptiness. I was always alone in those days, left to my own thoughts. On the sidelines, watching as life passed by, leaving me behind. Most other girls my age looked right through me, discounting me with a nod of their head. *She's weird,* they'd hiss in my direction, covering their mouths with one hand to hide their laughter, shame coursing through me until I wanted to disappear into the ground.

But now, for the first time, I belonged to someone. It was different than with a man. With men, the energy was brash. Intense. They seemed to disrupt a room so that it vibrated with an almost painful twang, a guitar string woefully out of tune. But there was an intimacy between Lexi and me, a kind of sacred quiet. It was the way we refused to be separated, even in sleep. I would lie beside her, her foot lightly touching my own, our hands intertwined. When I woke in the early morning, light streaming through the large, southern-facing windows of her bedroom, she'd begin to recount her dreams in detail the minute I opened my eyes. *There was this bat, Ava, trapped in the bathroom, hideously black against the white tile, almost furry. What do you think it means?* Most of the time, we didn't even have to talk. A glance was enough, a look. I could read her emotions, sense her mood from a foot away.

Her apartment was a refuge from the dirty concrete outside, the men crowded in doorways, bottles covered in brown paper sacks tucked between their feet. The rooms spartan, almost bare, but for a queen-size bed tucked in one corner and a few half-busted chairs she'd picked up off the street. White-painted wood floors, always scuffed, but the lightness imparting the space with the charm of a country house. She was high up enough that her windows framed the few lone trees lining her street, bare branches covered in snow in winter, a rustling riot of green in summer. Candles burned on nearly every surface, even the windowsills, scented rivulets of red and white beeswax that puddled on the floor as they cooled. On our days off, I'd curl up in a patch of sunlight, music running through my brain as I hurried to get it all down on paper before it disappeared, the songs arriving like unwanted guests, one after another. She would watch me as if I were an exotic beast, her mouth half-open.

"What's your greatest fear?" she whispered one night in bed, the full moon illuminating the room till it glowed like Saturn. Snow had fallen earlier that evening, dusting the city in a fine layer of sugary white powder, making everything seem clean and new again.

"I don't know," I demurred, hoping she'd let it go. But as always, with Lexi that wasn't really an option.

"Tell me," she urged, her voice an insistent whisper. She wanted to know everything about me. I wasn't used to it, that kind of attention. Even Ian had wanted me as only a prize, something won at a carnival and paraded around for everyone to admire.

"Failure, probably," I said after a moment of silence. "What's yours?"

Her eyes were wide as dinner plates in the moonlight, her face exquisitely shadowed.

"Being forgotten," she said quietly, the words themselves a breath. And as I watched, a lone tear made its way down her cheek, disappearing into the folds of her neck.

"That will never happen," I said, reaching over and brushing her hair back from her face. In that moment, I longed to tell her about Jamie, how it felt to be near him, the way my heart quickened in his presence, the feeling of need that sprang up in my chest whenever I caught so much as a glimpse of his face. But before I could say a word, or think better of it entirely, she smiled, closing her eyes, and then sleep came like a thief in the night.

———

A few days later, I was at the café, my hands filled with cash, the paper greasy and soft against my fingers. I placed the bills one by one in the register, counting under my breath. I knew when I finished restocking the register that my hands and fingers would be black with grime, dark as the soot lining the buildings of the city. There was nothing in this world dirtier than money. It was just before opening, and there was the rich scent of short ribs braising, the rustling of ice, and the intermittent pop of a cork.

I'd been working with Jamie on some of my songs that week, and each time we met, the tension between us grew. Once, at the rehearsal space he rented out from time to time, we'd sat together at the piano, so close that I could hear him breathing, felt the pulse and heat of him moving toward me. As I'd tentatively played a few chords, he'd reached out, covering my hand with his own, and for a moment, time stopped entirely. I sat motionless, afraid to even breathe. Was I breathing? *I am, I am.* But I knew that if I turned and looked at him, saw those arctic eyes staring into mine, there'd be no turning back. And so I refrained, and like all moments, eventually he drew back his hand from mine and it passed.

Nothing had happened. Not really.

But I knew I would never be the same.

The phone rang behind the bar, a shrill sound that cut through my thoughts, and I reached over to answer it. "Cornelia Street Café," I said, hearing an intake of breath on the other end of the line, and then a familiar voice began to speak.

"Ava? That is you?"

I felt my stomach drop at the sound of my name in her mouth.

"Yes, it's me, Irina," I said, leaning my hip against the counter, feeling it cut into my skin.

"How are you, my darling?" she asked, her voice a low purr. But before I could answer, she went on. "Ian has been trying to reach you." I heard a *tsk-tsk* noise, a clicking of her tongue. "He says you haven't been returning his calls. Now why is that?"

"You know why," I muttered under my breath, knowing she'd heard me anyway. I picked up a glass and began polishing it with a rag. Anything to distract myself from what was currently happening.

"He wants to visit you," she went on, as if I hadn't said a word, "but I don't even have an *address*. Imagine that. A mother not knowing the whereabouts of her only child."

My anger suddenly ignited, brittle paper engulfed in flame. "I told you," I said, "no matter how nice he acts, that's all it is, Mom—an act. We're broken up. I don't want to see him or talk to him, and I don't want him visiting me."

"But, Ava," she began, her voice warming with that tone that had always lured me back in for so many years, always convinced me to do as she asked, "you must reconsider! He said that he only wants—"

"I can't talk about this now. I have to go." My voice broke sharply, and I closed my eyes, squeezing them shut so tightly that I saw stars. My anger had always hovered so treacherously close to my tears, and it made me feel helpless. *Be gone,* I thought to myself like a mantra, and before she could say another word, I opened my eyes and hung up the phone, placing it back in the cradle.

"What was that all about?"

I turned to see Lexi behind me, her face creased with worry.

"My ex is looking for me," I said, letting out a long sigh. "And my mother doesn't understand why I won't see him."

"So why won't you?" She leaned back against the bar. The room was starting to hum with adrenaline. In just a few minutes, the doors would open, and the crowds would descend, putting us on our feet for hours. This was the last moment of calm before the storm swallowed us for the duration, the last moment I had to tell her anything at all.

"Because he scares me," I answered without even thinking. And that was the truth of it. Ian scared me so much that I could hardly even think of him anymore without a cold sweat breaking out on my skin. "We broke up when I left. But he's never really let go of me. Not in any way that lets me be free for too long."

124

"He sounds delightful." Lexi snorted. "Why does your mom even *care* if you talk to this dreamboat ever again?"

"His family owns an auto body shop," I said flatly. "It'll be his someday. She thinks he's a catch. That I should be grateful to end up with him. She doesn't see what he's really like."

She nodded, crossing her arms over her chest. "Oh, trust me," she said, "I get it. I dated this guy last year who treated me like a princess in public. But behind closed doors, he was kind of manipulative. It was never that serious." She shrugged. "But he just didn't want to let go. Even now I'll randomly get a string of texts or calls from him, like nothing ever happened. It's bizarre."

"What happened between you?"

"Same thing that usually happens." She laughed, shaking her head at it all. She was always so willing to laugh at the absurdity and chaos of her own life. It was one of my favorite things about her. "I got bored with it." She walked over to the prep station behind the bar, making sure the small bins of lemon and lime wedges were already filled.

"Why didn't you tell me about him? Before now, I mean." There was a note of hurt in my voice, betraying my emotions. I'd thought we were so close that there was no room for even the smallest shred of a secret between us. But I hadn't told her about Jamie either. No matter how much I might have wanted to, I hadn't been able to say the words. Mostly because I knew that if I did, everything would change.

"It doesn't matter now." She looked over at me, a half smile on her lips, before refilling the crimson vat of maraschino cherries. "I've got my eye on someone else. And I think it's going to work out this time."

Before I could say another word, the front door opened, letting in a blast of wintry air, and there was Jamie, brushing the snow from his black wool coat. Lexi looked up, raising one hand in greeting, her excitement palpable. I felt my heart sink in my chest as if it had been suddenly disconnected from my body, spurting vital fluid into nothingness.

"He's here!" she whispered, smoothing her mane of hair back from her face, her cheeks glowing like apples. I forced myself to smile as he walked toward us, knowing already what Lexi had failed to understand.

He had come for me.

KAYLA

All police stations, regardless of their location, looked exactly the same. In that way, they reminded me of hospitals, so blandly antiseptic in nature that they were almost indistinguishable from one another—and the one I was currently standing in was no exception. When I stepped inside the Lower East Side precinct on East Fifth Street, the interior was even less memorable than the exterior, if that were even possible. The walls were a beige so clouded and yellow that it was hard to tell if the color choice was deliberate or if the paint was just coated in years of grime.

I suspected the latter.

Not that it mattered much. I could've been on the moon—that's how much location counted anymore. Wherever I was, the subway, walking along the streets of the city, on a bus, Jamie's face would suddenly appear in my vision, the way he'd pulled me to him as soon as we were inside the door of my apartment, his mouth on mine, hot and feverish, our clothes falling away piece by piece, curling on the floor like drying rose petals. Then there was only his mouth on my flesh, greedy and insistent.

The next morning, I watched him dress, already half in love with the way he moved, the scent of his skin, like fresh pencil shavings and sandalwood. *This is trouble,* I told myself. But I didn't know how to stop it. Or if I even wanted to. As he walked out my front door, pulling it closed softly behind him, I knew that I'd see him again if he asked.

I looked around the room, which bustled with cops and civilians alike. Along one wall was a wooden bench where a few men sat handcuffed, looking bored and miserable. Over the last two weeks, I'd sent multiple emails requesting access to Ava's case file but had heard nothing back. I called the precinct, getting rerouted, shuffled around, and put on endless holds while listening to the syrupy fog of elevator music for what felt like hours at a time until I finally gave up. But a day later, an unknown number illuminated the screen of my phone, and when I picked up, a gruff voice asked me to come down to the station. I still didn't know what I hoped to glean from Ava's file, but I knew instinctually that there was a story there. And chasing it was certainly a better use of my time than filing a few thousand bland words on Lexi Mayhem that simply repeated whatever generic drivel her suit of a manager might approve.

"I'm here to see Detective Diaz," I informed the harried-looking woman behind the front desk, the phone clasped beneath her chin.

She pointed with nails filed into neat red ovals. "Down the hall, third door on the right," she said, then turned her attention back to whoever was on the other end of the line.

The hallway was painted an institutional green, which wasn't much better than the dirty beige of the waiting area. I knocked on the door, two short raps with my knuckles, and then, hearing a voice inside, pushed it open. I had to yank hard at it to open it, but once it gave, I found myself in a windowless room, a table smack in the middle of it with two stools on either side, all bolted to the floor. A stout, darkhaired man in his fifties was seated on one, what was left of his hairline receding badly, and I immediately felt confused by the fact that he was wearing not a tweed polyester suit like a *NYPD Blue* character but a crisp blue button-down.

"You must be Kayla," he said, standing up, reaching for my hand with a wide smile. "Detective Diaz." His teeth were shockingly white against his deep-olive skin, and he was built like a whiskey barrel, his bulk filling the room, but not in an intimidating way. Instead, everything about him radiated friendliness and warmth.

"Hey there," I said, shaking his hand. "Thanks for making the time to meet with me."

"Not at all," he said, sitting back down. I noticed a manila folder resting on top, the words PETROVA, A written on the tab. "I'm sorry you had such a hard time getting ahold of me. It can be nuts around here," he said apologetically. "And I was working on a case up in Morningside Heights, so I was a bit MIA."

"I'm just glad to have the chance to connect with you now," I said, sitting down across from him. I hated how infantilizing stools were, the way they made me feel like I was back in a high chair.

"So," he said, clasping his hands together in front of him on the table, "you wanted to discuss the Petrova case?"

"I'd like to see the incident report and anything else that was in the case file. But really, I'd just like to hear what you remember, if anything. I know it was a long time ago."

He nodded. "Yeah. But the funny thing is I never forgot it. It stayed with me for some reason." He shrugged. "A young, beautiful girl hurling herself off a roof like that? Talented? Full of promise? It just didn't make a lot of sense. But you never really know what's going on in people's heads, right?" He went on before I could comment or even agree. "I've seen stranger things over the years. But this one unsettled me."

"Is there anything strange or special that you remember about that night?" I asked, pulling out my recorder. "OK if I turn this on?"

"Sure," he said, giving it a cursory glance. "But keep me on background if you can, OK?"

"No problem."

The lightweight navy wool coat I wore bunched uncomfortably around my middle, and I unbuttoned it, waiting for him to continue.

"Something was off that night," he began slowly. "I couldn't put my finger on it, but I could feel it."

I nodded, pulling my arms out of the sleeves, laying the coat across my lap.

"You want me to hang that up for you?" he asked.

"I'm good," I said quickly, not wanting to lose the thread of the conversation just as it was starting. "What do you mean by 'off'?"

"I mean, at first glance it looked like your typical suicide. There were no security cameras. No signs of forced entry, no clear evidence to suggest it *wasn't* what it seemed. The neighbors heard arguing that night, but that didn't pan out to anything."

"Arguing?"

"Yeah. A woman shouting. But when we looked into it, we came up dry. And the other girl we found on the scene was passed out cold."

"Lexi Gennaro?"

"The Mayhem chick. I've never seen anyone that out of it who wasn't dead or on their way there. When the paramedics arrived, I think they said her pulse was in the forties? She was obliterated. Honestly, at first glance I thought she *was* dead."

"Did she give a statement?"

"Yep," he said, opening the folder, pulling out a piece of paper, and handing it to me.

We'd been at Balthazar with Christian Vane and some other label execs. During the meal I began to feel unwell, and Ava offered to take me home. I remember telling her that I needed air, and we climbed up to the roof, the way we always did after a night out. I fell into one of the chairs I had up there—I felt the slap of the plastic against my legs, and that's the last thing I remember. The next day I woke up in my bed and my manager was there waiting for me to wake up. He told me about Ava. That she was gone. I could see his lips moving, but I stopped hearing the words. And then every-thing stopped. The world. The noise of the city. And it felt like my heart stopped too, right along with hers.

Some things are better off forgotten, she'd said when I'd asked about her past. But in this statement, it didn't seem like Lexi was even remotely capable of erasing Ava—or her death. So what had changed?

I looked up at Detective Diaz, who was waiting expectantly. "If Lexi was out cold," I began slowly, "and no one else was there, *and* it appeared that Ava had no good reason to jump . . . then how do you reconcile that? Did you consider Lexi as a suspect despite the condition she was in?"

"She was a suspect in the sense that she was *there*, but that's about it." He shrugged again. "I've seen people do crazy things when they're on the verge of an OD—hell, even *while* they're OD'ing—but that's exclusive to stimulants. We once pulled a guy down off the side of the Empire State Building who was out of his mind on meth, convinced he was Superman. He died en route to the ER. But with booze? There's a point of no return that's really just that—you drink enough to be *that* out? You aren't doing anything. And the Petrova girl? She had drugs in her system. Per the toxicology report." He reached into the file again and drew out another slip of paper, looking it over. "Ketamine. It was a popular party drug back in the day," he said. "Special K, they call it. There was a little fentanyl in her blood too. Not a lot. But it was there."

All I knew about ketamine was that it was an animal tranquil-izer and hallucinogen. In its heyday, it had enjoyed massive popularity among the rave and club-kid set. By the time the drug trickled down to the suburbs, news stories were flooded with reports of packs of delin-quent teenagers stealing the drug from veterinarians' offices, looking for a high. And fentanyl? My only reference for that particular narcotic was that it was the drug responsible for killing Prince, who'd met his demise in an elevator. A purple one, at that, if legend holds true.

"So where do you land with it, then?" I asked, handing him back the reports. "Not in terms of what's in the incident report or what the coroner ultimately determined as the cause of death, but how do you explain what happened that night? If Ava didn't seem like someone who'd jump, and Lexi was incapable of pushing her?"

He leaned back a little on his stool, and for a moment I thought he might topple over completely, but at the last minute he righted himself, grabbing on to the edge of the table with one hand.

"It's a tough one, and I've thought about it a lot—especially back then. Maybe she tripped, maybe it was a freak accident? I mean, she was inebriated, so it wouldn't have taken much. I guess someone could've pushed her? But who? The only person on scene was practically coma-tose." He sighed, letting out a long breath. "I really can't say. That's the thing, and really this is one of the hardest things about being a cop: sometimes you just don't know; there just isn't enough evidence to say *definitively* what happened. That girl . . ." His blue eyes turned cloudy with memory. "Even . . . dead, she still looked so alive. Like she could wake up at any moment. It stayed with me all these years for some reason. The waste of it all."

He looked down at the table, clearing his throat. "This is for you," he said, grabbing the manila folder and handing it to me. "I hope it's of some use."

"Thank you," I said, tucking it into my tote. "I really appreciate it."

"I wish I could be of more help," he said, stepping down from the stool and standing up, "but that's all there is."

"You've been great," I said, taking this as my cue to leave. I fumbled with my recorder, switching it off before standing, throwing my bag over one shoulder, and pulling strands of hair out of the collar of my coat. I headed for the door, but then a thought froze me in place, and I turned back around so quickly that I almost knocked into him.

"If you were to reopen the case," I asked, choosing my words carefully, "where might you look first?"

"The boyfriend," he said without hesitation. "I got a bad vibe when we brought him in for questioning. Ultimately, there was nothing linking him to the scene, so we had to let him go. But I didn't like the guy at all. He was shifty. A con artist."

"He had an alibi, I take it?"

"Yeah." He snorted, shoving his hands into the pockets of his trousers. "Said he'd gotten drunk at a bar and was too wrecked to drive home. Fell asleep in his car. We talked to the bar manager, who confirmed he'd been there."

"So it checked out."

"On paper, there was nothing we could nab him on. But between you and me?" He leaned a bit closer, dropping his voice. "There was something off about that guy. His story may have checked out, but it never sat right with me."

I nodded. "Good to know."

"Let me know what you find out," he said with a smile. "If anything."

I shut the door behind me, my brain already turning with possibilities. As I exited the precinct, stepping onto the street, a surge of energy shot through me and I raised my hand, hailing a passing yellow cab, which screeched to a stop in front of me, then idled at the curb.

As I climbed into the back seat, I felt the insistent buzzing of my phone, and when I pulled it from my coat pocket, Jamie's name stared back at me, daring me to pick up. I looked at the glowing screen, wanting to answer, but as much as every cell in my body wanted to see him again, to touch him, something was holding me back. The story. Ava. Usually chasing down a lead would've distracted me enough that nothing would've even remotely tempted me to push my reporting aside. So why wasn't it working this time?

Focus, dammit, I admonished myself as I pressed "Decline," letting the call go to voice mail. I sat back in my seat as the cab began to lurch its way through traffic and back over the bridge toward Brooklyn, crossing the water, crossing the limits of everything, and as my phone rang once again, I wondered how many of my own had been breached.

This time, before I could stop myself, I answered.

AVA

My heart wouldn't slow. It rocketed away in my chest like a horse trying to bolt, rearing up rebelliously. I forced myself to look in the lit mirror backstage at the café and take a series of deep breaths, filling my lungs with air, then releasing it. Somehow it helped a little, and I felt my pulse descend by a few beats. I leaned closer to the glass, drawing a thick black line on my upper eyelid, then moving to the lower, outlining it until the jade of my irises popped, a trick I'd learned from Lexi.

You can do this, I told the girl in the mirror, unfamiliar and strange. A doppelgänger. She stared back at me uncertainly, her face white with fear. I still couldn't bring myself to wear the silver dress Lexi had bought me, so I'd borrowed her leather pants, pairing them with a jet T-shirt patterned with metal grommets I'd bought for five dollars on St. Marks Place.

But no matter what I wore, I still felt like an impostor.

"You're going to be great," a voice behind me said, and I whirled around, startled.

Jamie smiled, walking over and standing behind the chair I sat in, placing his hands on my shoulders. The warmth of them on my bare skin made it impossible to think, to remember even why I was sitting backstage, waiting to perform in public for the first time ever. The realization made me start to panic all over again, and I smiled weakly at him in the mirror, hoping he wouldn't notice the fear that was all over me, a strange and deadly perfume.

"I'm not sure," I began, my eyes drifting away from his, "that I can do this."

It felt like an admission of guilt. Like confessing a murder. But the only thing I was killing was my own career. His hands left my shoulders, and my skin felt momentarily cold in their absence as he moved around to face me.

"Listen to me," he said, crouching down so he was at my level. His eyes were such a pale, almost colorless, blue that I felt suddenly weak, as if I'd been hypnotized. The bones of his face were so fine that they should've been hung on the walls of a museum or studied in a classroom. "You can *do* this," he said insistently. "You're comfortable here, so it's low stress. Just focus on me, OK? I'll be down front."

"Are there . . ." I cleared my throat, forcing the words from my lips. "Are there a lot of people out there?"

"Full house," he said brusquely, and I felt the fear rise in me again. "But remember, you got this, OK?"

I nodded, hoping he was right, the feeling of dread creeping over me so intense that I felt compelled to lie down on the floor until it passed. But I forced myself to stand up and walk to the wings, where I waited in darkness for the sound of my own name.

"Remember," Jamie whispered, his voice so close to my ear that I shivered, his lips grazing my skin. "Just look at me."

I heard him walk away, and I was alone again, more alone than I'd been in my life. Everything was moving too fast, the lights, the faces of the audience a blur as I heard my name and forced my feet to take one step, then another, until I was standing in the glare, the microphone in front of me. I searched the crowd for Jamie's face, scanning the sea of bodies until I found him, standing off to the left. He nodded at me, his face full of hope, and I heard the music swell behind me, the musicians beginning what we'd rehearsed, the first song I'd written when I moved to New York, the one we'd been practicing for weeks now. The twang of the guitar filled my senses, and I closed my eyes, a feeling sweeping over me that was unfamiliar, one of belonging, of destiny even, the stars aligning over my head just so, and when I opened my mouth to sing, I knew somewhere deep inside me that everything would be all right.

That this time I couldn't miss.

When the applause came, I opened my eyes, a smile breaking across my face. I turned toward the guitarist, giving him a quick nod, the signal to begin the next song. Somehow twenty minutes went by seamlessly, as if time itself had shifted, and when it was over, I was sorry to leave. The stage felt warm now, protective, and I was coated in sweat, my face and arms sheened with it. It felt phosphorescent, like I was aglow in the dark, and when the lights came up, Jamie's was the first face I saw as I stepped offstage and walked toward the bar.

"You did it," he said, leaning in to hug me, sweaty limbs and all.

"Thanks to you," I murmured in his ear, and he took a step back to look at me.

"No way," he said firmly, his hands gripping me tightly. "You did it, Ava. *You.* No one else."

I nodded slowly, because I knew he was right, even if that knowing was uncomfortable, like wearing someone else's shoes. But for the first time I sensed that the feeling of strangeness might dissipate in time, evaporating slowly as smoke clearing the air. But what would it be replaced with? I wondered. The kind of innate confidence that Lexi radiated so effortlessly? Or something else entirely?

"Oh my god, you were amazing!" In a rush of air, frantic heat, and light, Lexi was at my back, and I turned and hugged her, breaking free from Jamie's grip. "You blew everyone away!" She radiated such joy that I couldn't help but laugh, the tension of the past hour falling away, and then she threw her arms around me. I leaned into her warmth and closed my eyes, taking in her familiar scent of lilies and musk, mixed with the acrid bite of her sweat.

"We need to celebrate," Lexi said after she pulled back, "but I'm working until close. Tomorrow, OK?"

I nodded happily, and she threw Jamie a seductive glance, looking at him from under the fringe of her lashes, spiky with multiple coats of mascara. "And *we* need to *talk*," she said pointedly. It sounded like a threat. But maybe an enjoyable one.

"Sure thing," he said, a touch too jovially, his eyes moving uncertainly between us. "Give me a ring tomorrow." And with that she was gone, a bird who flew in the window, stretching her wings, only to make her immediate escape.

"So," he said once she was out of earshot. "Just because Lexi is indisposed doesn't mean we can't celebrate, right? Just us? Want to grab a drink somewhere?" His tone was casual, almost deliberately so, and thoughts crowded my head in rapid succession. I couldn't forget how Lexi had looked up from the bar the other night when Jamie had shown up to meet me, or her words. *I've got my eye on someone else . . .*

But before I could answer, a young guy sidled up to Jamie, a bashful expression on his face. He wore a dark zip-up hoodie and the thick glasses of a computer nerd, the black trucker hat on his head clearly an attempt at looking cool that was failing miserably. Despite all this or maybe because of it, he had an endearing quality, even at first glance.

"Hey," he said, high-fiving Jamie before turning his attention in my direction. "Wow," he said admiringly, "you were super great up there."

"Wasn't she?" Jamie agreed.

"No doubt," the young man said, smiling broadly.

"Ava, this is my assistant—"

There was a sudden crash of cymbals as the next act took the stage, the lights fading into darkness. Although I hadn't heard his name, I nodded at him as if I had. "We're going to grab a drink," Jamie yelled in his direction. "I'll see you at the office tomorrow."

He gave a thumbs-up as Jamie reached down and took my hand, leading me through the serpentine crowd that twisted their bodies along with the music, the pounding bass, the electric hum of the guitar, the singer's voice a plaintive wail in the dark. I looked back at Jamie's assistant, but his attention was already focused on the stage, nodding his head to the beat.

On the street, Jamie's hand in mine, shy glances between us in the neon glow, icy pavement underfoot. We ducked into the dive bar around the corner, falling into a vault as he led me through the crush of bodies to a table in the back. Heavy metal coming through the speakers above, screech of guitar. I sat down across from him, his hand raised to flag down a passing waitress, ordering two beers. I was parched, my tongue sticking to the roof of my mouth. I would've drunk gasoline if he had offered it.

When the waitress reappeared with two bottles of beer, unceremoniously plunking down two water glasses beside them so the liquid sloshed over the sides, I reached for a glass without thinking, draining its contents in a series of long swallows, a stream of water escaping the side of my mouth. I brought a hand up, wiping my face as I lowered the empty glass to the table.

"Guess you were thirsty," Jamie said, his eyes on my lips. Those wolf eyes taking me in. Even in the dimness of the bar, I felt my cheeks flush, and I looked away, then back at him.

"Does it get easier?" I asked, leaning forward so that he could hear me over the music.

"Performing? Yeah. With time," Jamie said. I could feel his breath on my cheek, a warning, and I sat back quickly.

"Once I was up there," I said, reaching for a bottle of beer, pulling it toward me, "I forgot about everything. It was like the whole room disappeared. It was just me and the music." I brought the bottle to my lips, my mouth filling with the bitter perfume of hops.

Jamie nodded. "I could see it. That's how I know you're the real thing."

"What do you mean?"

"I get goose bumps when you sing," he said, leaning toward me so that our faces were millimeters apart again. "I can feel it everywhere—my head, my heart."

"But I don't have any training . . . ," I stammered. "Lexi studied for—"

"You can't buy what you have, Ava. It's God-given. You can't compare it to anything else."

"OK," I said slowly, still not ready to accept it. "But if you know what it looks like, why aren't you up there doing it yourself?"

"I can't sing worth a damn, for starters. I played guitar in a band for a while in high school, but it never went anywhere, so—"

"Were you guys any good?" I interrupted.

He laughed, picking up his beer, draining it in a series of long swallows. "God no. We were awful." There was a long pause, broken only by the sound of shouting coming from the very back of the room, where a group of college girls huddled around a dartboard. "But what I was saying before I was so rudely interrupted is that not only do you know how to write songs, Ava, but now we know that you can perform them too. That ability you have, it's innate. It comes from deep inside you."

"Why do you believe in me so much?" I said quietly, looking away, tears inexplicably clouding my vision. My emotions had always been too close to my skin, if only someone cared enough to access them, to let me know it was safe to feel anything at all.

"Hey," he said softly, leaning forward so only the smallest distance hung between us. "Because you're that good. You just don't know it yet."

When I looked up, our eyes were so close, our expressions mirroring one another, longing and desire mixed with understanding, a feeling

I'd never had with anyone before. The kind I knew was dangerous. Because what if I got used to it? Started to depend on it? I knew what would happen—it would all fall away, crumbling into nothingness, leaving me wondering if love was nothing more than an illusion, a story we tell to make life bearable.

But before I could begin to say any of this, his lips were on mine, the sounds of the bar suddenly muffled and distant. I breathed inside his mouth, feeling his hands on either side of my face, warm and sure. I kissed him back, unable to stop myself, unable to think at all. All I knew was the pressure of his lips, his tongue snaking in as he pulled me closer, his hands moving in my hair, the weight of it tangling in his fingers.

"Ava," he breathed when we finally broke apart.

Just one word. My name. The same name I'd always had.

But now? Everything was different.

———

When we exited the bar, arms wrapped around each other's waists, there was a humming beneath my skin, in the city itself, a feeling of possibility. He turned to me, brushing back a strand of hair that had caught at the corner of my mouth in the sudden breeze, his fingers gentle on my skin. The way he looked at me made the bottom fall out of everything. But as he leaned in to kiss me, a feeling of trepidation came over me, my skin prickling not with excitement but fear, the unmistakable sensation of being watched. And then I saw him. Across the street, standing in the doorway of a bodega, waiting for me.

Ian.

My eyes widened, and I watched as his lips curled into that smug smile I knew so well. And then, without warning, the silver flash of a bus flew by, stopping in front of the bodega and obscuring him from view. I went rigid in Jamie's arms, my muscles tensing as if before a fall.

"What is it?" I heard him ask, but his voice was down a long tunnel, a place I could not reach. I held my breath as the bus began to move again, leaving a cloud of exhaust hanging in the air as it made its way down the street. When I looked again, there was only the red neon sign, blinking frantically.

Maybe it wasn't really him, a voice inside me said hopefully. *Maybe you're just tired.*

But I knew. I could feel it in my body, the sneaking sense of fear bordering on revulsion that Ian always incited in me. It was unmistakable. It had been him.

And I knew he'd be back.

KAYLA

The rain pattered against the window in a rhythmic beat, and I turned over in bed, moving closer to the heat of Jamie's body. I rested my head on his chest, listening to his heart beating slowly against my cheek, then reached up, twining my arms around his neck, pulling him in for a kiss. He'd been in my bed every night for a week now, and I was almost getting used to it. His warm presence, the way he'd throw one leg over mine as we drifted off to sleep.

When I'd finally picked up the phone on the way home from the police station, my breath caught in my throat as I heard the low tremor of his voice. *Do you want me to come over?* he'd asked, and I'd nodded first, shaking my head uselessly before agreeing, my voice barely above a whisper.

I'd been hypervigilant with anticipation, my senses attuned to every sound in the street outside until I heard the ring of the buzzer. He'd bent to my body as if in prayer, sliding his mouth along every inch of my skin, and when he slipped inside me, he'd stopped and stared down at me, a questioning look in those pale eyes, one I didn't know how to answer. I'd pulled him to me, crushing his body against my own until he moaned aloud, burying his face in my neck. I raised my head, breaking our connection, a sleepy grin on his face as he stretched his arms overhead and groaned.

"Want to grab dinner tonight?" he asked, stifling a yawn.

"Can't," I said, sitting up and running a hand through my hair, which was hopelessly tangled.

"Why not?"

"I'm working." I grabbed my phone from the bedside table, checking the time. "Damn," I muttered under my breath as I sat up and scrambled out of bed, walking over to the closet.

"C'mon, Kayla. It's Friday night."

"Your point being?" I looked over, raising an eyebrow, as he picked up the black T-shirt from the foot of the bed—the very one I'd peeled off him last night—balled it up in one hand, and tossed it at me, missing my head by an inch.

"Has anyone ever introduced you to the concept of 'the weekend'?" he asked as I bent down, grabbing the warm cotton from the floor, and lobbing it back at him.

"Yeah . . . ," I said slowly. "He's dating Bella Hadid now, right?"

"You're impossible, you know that?"

"So I've been told," I said lightly as I turned to survey the contents of my closet.

"OK, then I'll order in," he said with a shrug. "You like Mexican?"

"What did I say?" I laughed as I grabbed a pair of jeans and a white top with ample, flowing sleeves, the metal hangers chiming noisily. "I'm serious, Jamie. I've got to work tonight. I'm way behind."

"Kayla," he said, and the tone of his voice was suddenly somber and direct enough to halt me in my tracks. I stood there motionless, clutching the soft pile of fabric I held to my chest, as if stanching a bullet wound. "I want to get to know you better. Spend real time with you."

"I thought that was what we were doing," I said softly.

He was quiet now as I walked over to the oak dresser I'd bought on Craigslist for fifty dollars, my eyes meeting my reflection in the antique mirror I'd propped on top, the pewter tarnished to a dull shine. My bangs needed a trim, and my long bob didn't look as razor sharp as it had a few months ago, but my skin was clear and flushed, as if I'd just finished a five-mile run. I looked . . . happy.

Happy was dangerous.

I turned my back on that reflection before it could take hold.

"You headed into the office?" he asked, switching gears.

"Nope. Out to Staten Island."

"Jesus, why?" He laughed, sitting up in bed. He reached for his own phone and scrolled through his email.

"I want to talk to Ava's ex," I said, pulling the shirt over my head.

"Isn't this a story about Lexi?" Jamie asked, looking up from the screen, his face blanketed in confusion. "How does he fit in?"

"Something doesn't add up," I said as I stepped into the jeans, pulling the denim over my hips. "About her death. I can't shake it."

Jamie should've been focusing on the way my nipples hardened in the cool morning air, but instead, his eyes fixed on the expanse of sky outside the window, the green leaves of the trees shaking in the wind. "Just be careful," he said quietly. "That guy was always bad news."

I walked over and stood in front of him, and he drew me close, his head resting on my stomach, his arms wrapped around my waist. "I don't like the idea of you going out there," I heard him say, and just the vibration of his mouth on my skin made my eyes flutter shut for a moment.

"I'll be *fine*. I'm not some delicate flower, you know," I said with a snort. And with that, he raised his head and looked up at me, arching one eyebrow as a challenge, and pulled me down in the tangle of bedsheets.

———

I wasn't sure where I'd been expecting the formerly menacing ex-boy-friend of a dead almost pop star to reside—a seedy hovel near the train tracks, perhaps. But the carefully tended home on a rain-washed, tree-lined street was the direct opposite of any grim scenario I could've imagined. The high-pitched squeal of children's voices rang through the air, and everything, from the neatly trimmed bushes flanking the walk to the newly painted exterior to the lawn mower parked in the driveway next to a shiny red tricycle, told me that whoever lived here valued not only appearances but family too. A green garden hose lay curled tightly near the flower beds beneath the bay window in the front, and the cheerful yellow faces of daffodils were just beginning to peep through the earth in a neat line. The garage doors were open, revealing two shiny white BMWs parked inside. "His" read the license plate of one, while "Hers" graced the other.

The house was a reminder that some people weren't comfortable anywhere but the same familiar streets they'd walked their entire lives. As soon as I could, I'd fled to New York, leaving Minnesota and its endless winters behind, shedding layers of coats and scarves I no longer needed. There was familiarity and comfort in going home but also a sense of suffocation. Every time I stepped off the plane and into the frigid air, a cloud seemed to descend from the overcast sky, heavy and thick, wrapping itself around my shoulders. A panic rose up inside me, and I'd immediately want to turn around and reboard the plane. Astrid's presence hovered, trailing my every move, though for all I knew, she was long gone herself. Her blue bathing suit dotted with cherries. Her autumn-gold hair like corn silk in my hands. That night at the party, her tear-streaked face in the moonlight, mascara in pools beneath her eyes, shadowing them, making her into something older, knowing.

Shattered.

After a visit, I was always glad to return home to Brooklyn, to the haven of my apartment, to the city itself, where I was accountable to no one and nothing. There was only the sound of trucks rumbling past along the street outside, the anonymous faces in the subway, belying the proximity of our bodies. Blank stares and ears stopped with headphones. But Jamie's entrance into my life threatened to change all that.

As I rang the doorbell, the rain stopped, and a sliver of sun peeped through the clouds. I could hear the thump of tiny feet padding around inside the house. There was a rustling, and then the door opened and a petite blonde woman in her early thirties stood there wearing jeans and a white T-shirt. Her hair was pulled into a messy bun atop her head, and her feet were bare, her toenails painted a light, unobtrusive pink. While she appeared harried, her blue eyes, as she looked at me hesitantly, were kind.

"Can I help you?" she asked.

"I'm looking for Ian Strickler." I smiled in a way that I hoped was reassuring. "I'm a reporter from *Rolling Stone* magazine, and I'd like to ask him a few questions."

"*Rolling Stone?*" she said, frowning. "Why would you want to—"

"Jenna? What's going on?" a deep voice called from inside the house, and then a man appeared in the doorway, clad in a pair of gray sweatpants and a black hoodie, a pair of crisp white Nikes on his feet. He was in his forties, dark-haired and handsome, clean-shaven, his biceps straining against the thick material of his sweatshirt. His eyes, black as onyx, flitted over my frame, sizing me up.

I heard the clatter of small steps again, and before I could speak, a little girl, no more than two, her hair a tousled mass of blonde waves, ran up to her father, throwing her arms around his legs and staring up at me solemnly, pushing a thumb into her mouth.

"Hey there," he said to me with a friendly smile, reaching down to rest a hand atop her head before extricating himself and walking outside. "How can I help you?"

"You're Ian Strickler?" I asked as the little girl's face cracked into a grin, exposing a row of tiny teeth.

"Last I checked," he said with a dry chuckle. "And you are?"

"Kayla McCray," I began, reaching into the inside pocket of my tote and pulling out a business card. He took it, turning the slick white paper over in his hands. "I'm a reporter from *Rolling Stone* magazine. I was hoping you might be able to answer a few questions about Ava Petrova."

His head came up sharply. "Ava?" he asked, his voice full of disbelief.

"It'll just take five minutes," I said, acutely aware I was still hovering in the doorway.

"Hang on a sec," he said distractedly as he stepped out on the porch, pulling the door shut behind him. He walked out onto the driveway and turned to face me, his pleasant expression sliding away. He narrowed his eyes, crossing his arms over his chest. It was as if a wall had suddenly gone up, obscuring the friendliness he'd exhibited only moments before.

"What's this all about?"

"Well," I said awkwardly, "I'm writing a story on Lexi Mayhem. You've heard of her?"

"Who hasn't?" he snapped, crumpling my business card in one fist, then shoving it in the front pocket of his hoodie in a way that felt like a threat.

"I was researching Lexi's early career, and Ava's name came up. I'm just trying to track down a few sources who might be able to give me some background on her."

The question was reasonable enough, or so I thought, but from the way he stiffened at the very mention of Ava's name, it was clearly not one he wanted to entertain in any capacity.

"Listen," he said, taking a step toward me until we were standing so close that I could see the dark beads of stubble along his jawline, the flat sheen of his eyes. "My life is different now. *I'm different.* I don't want all that crap getting dredged up. I worked hard for the life I have now. I love my family," he said fiercely. "Whatever happened back then? It's long gone. And that's the way I want it."

"I understand," I said calmly, taking a step back. Even if he had nothing to do with Ava's death, Jamie had been right—this was not a man to be trifled with.

"Back then, I was the primary suspect," he said, spitting out the words like bits of shrapnel. "Did you know that? Everybody thought I did it. People thought I was a monster *for years.* Moved their kids away from me in the goddamn grocery store! You know what that's like?"

"I can imagine," I said quickly, wanting to get as many answers out of him as possible before he stomped back into the house. "But the way that she died . . . it just doesn't make a whole lot of sense. By all accounts, she was incredibly talented, on the verge of making it in the music business. There doesn't seem to be a good reason why she'd take her own life."

"Well, you didn't know her," he said authoritatively. "I *did.* She was talented, but she was also incredibly insecure. Anyone tell you that? She was an endless fucking *sea* of self-doubt. She wasn't cut out for it, I'll tell you that much."

"Cut out for what?"

"Any of it!" he yelled, throwing his hands in the air. "The pressure, people expecting her to actually produce on demand. Performing? It terrified her."

"Did you see Ava the night she died?"

He blanched at the question. "No," he said, looking away. "I was with someone else. I was pissed off, OK?"

"You told the police you'd been to a bar the night Ava died."

"I *was* at a bar," he said, as if I were impossibly dense. "That's where I met her. The girl."

"Why didn't you just tell the police you'd gone home with someone that night? It would've taken you right out of the running as a suspect."

"Because it was none of their business. It had been over between Ava and me for a while, but I still didn't want her family thinking I was a piece of shit."

"Over for her," I said, guessing now. "But not for you?"

He met my eyes, and there was anger there, but also a smattering of deep pain.

"What's over," he said through gritted teeth, "is this conversation. But if you want to know the truth?" He took another step toward me again, and this time I forced myself to stand my ground. "The only thing I was guilty of was loving that girl too much."

There was a pause, filled only by the sound of a Mister Softee truck making its way down the street, emitting its familiar tinkling melody.

"We're done here," he said flatly. "And if you know what's good for you? You won't come back." The veiled threat hung between us for a moment before he turned away, leaving me standing there as he walked inside the house, shutting the door tightly behind him.

I stood awkwardly on the curb, punching buttons on my phone until my Uber arrived, then climbed gratefully into the back seat, sure he was watching me from the windows. As soon as I leaned back against the car's black vinyl seats, I exhaled heavily, not sure what to make of what I'd just heard. I knew from stories I'd worked on in my early days reporting hard news that the guiltier the suspect, the more they tended to erupt in anger when questioned. And there was also the fact that Ian's alibi didn't exactly corroborate what he'd told Detective Diaz. But even so, he couldn't be traced back to Lexi's building that night or the rooftop where Ava had died. And anyone would be sensitive about having an ex-girlfriend who'd allegedly killed herself.

If that's what had really happened. I watched the ranch houses roll past, thinking of the other square-jawed Ians who lived inside them. It was clear that whatever had happened between the two of them, he'd loved Ava once, and despite his assertions that he'd long since moved on, maybe he even still did. But didn't we always hurt the people we claimed to love the most? The thought made something sink inside me, and the streets flashed by outside the window, the city looming ahead, glittering with promise.

AVA

2006

"I *knew* that dress was perfect," Lexi proclaimed as she stood behind me in the full-length mirror, nodding approvingly.

"I'm still not sure," I said as I pulled the silver spandex down over my thighs, where it immediately sprang up again, like an evil jack-in-the-box.

"Don't second-guess it," she said, standing back to admire her handiwork. I balanced on the ice-pick heels of stiletto ankle boots, my newly blonde hair gleaming under the lights. Lexi had bleached it the night before as I'd sat on the rim of her bathtub, my scalp tingling dangerously. Later, she'd stood behind me, scissors flashing as she snipped at the wet, almost translucent strands till they stopped at my shoulders in a neat line.

"Breathe," she said as piles of hair littered the tile, tickling my bare feet. "You're releasing old energy, Ava. That's what hair is. Dead energy from the past. Let it go."

I took a deep breath, then released it, and as I did, I felt something shift inside me, molecules rearranging themselves into new shapes and patterns. A spiral. A dahlia, violet petals unfurling. Some monumental weight was lifted from my being, not just the mere heaviness of my hair. Afterward, I felt light as a dancer, toes balanced on blocks of wood stuffed into satin slippers.

"You look like a rock star," Lexi said, her voice jolting me back to the present.

"I don't *feel* like one."

"Well, that's ridiculous." She was impatient now, brushing me off. "Listen, I took the night off to come see you. You better bring it out there."

"No pressure, though, right?" I joked. But the words felt hollow to me. A nest of birds had taken up residence in my stomach, flipping and turning, their claws scratching against my flesh. Nesting. Settling in.

"Be right back!" she said excitedly, walking out the backstage door, which hung ajar, and over toward the velvet curtains the color of dark blood that lined the stage of the Bitter End. She pulled them apart slightly, peering at the audience waiting just beyond. The birds flapped their wings again, and I felt my heart flip-flop in response.

"There's a scout out there!" Lexi said as she rushed back in, her excitement filling the room, the tattered jeans she wore slipping down to expose her taut navel, a ring winking in the center, her cropped black cardigan glittering with jet beads. "From Epic Records! He's in the back standing near Jamie."

Jamie.

Don't think about his hands or his touch or how he whispered into your hair, his breath making your flesh dimple. Don't think about his eyes, seeking your own.

Don't think.

"What?" I stared at her in disbelief. "How do you know?"

"Because I met him once before at some sleazy industry event," she said, clearly exasperated with my questions. "Ava, this is it! Your big break!"

I swallowed hard and forced a smile. "It's only my second show," I said, pointing out the obvious. "It can hardly be my big break."

Lexi ignored me, walking back over to the mirror, pulling out a tube of lipstick from her back pocket and swiping it carefully over her mouth. She pouted at her reflection, then blew herself a kiss. "Stranger things have happened, you know. Not everyone pays their dues."

"You do," I pointed out distractedly. "You are."

Her expression darkened for a moment as she looked at me, and for the first time, I saw a flicker of contempt in her eyes. She opened her mouth to speak, but before she could utter even one syllable, Jamie appeared.

"Sorry to interrupt," he said apologetically. "But Ava's up."

Could I vomit feathers? It seemed a distinct possibility as I walked to the stage, waiting in the darkness of the wings. I could sense Lexi and Jamie behind me, hear the murmur of their voices as they spoke, but it was in another language entirely. There were only the bright lights of the stage, now that the curtain was drawn back, revealing the audience, pressed body to body on the floor.

There was a moment of sheer panic as I walked onstage, a smile pasted to my lips, then the sound of the guitar and the beating of drums. The room whirled away, and I was shot into space, surrounded by the soft pinpricks of constellations, the music swelling to a crescendo as I leaned into the microphone and parted my lips. The birds in my belly quieted as my voice rose higher, filling the cavernous space with song. After a few moments, I felt safe enough to open my eyes, and when I made eye contact with the audience, there was a whooping that reverberated off the walls, their joy infectious. I felt my lips curve into a grin, and I took the microphone from its stand, holding it close as I began to move across the stage, swaying my hips to the beat.

The audience swirled in my vision, melting together until one familiar face stopped me in my tracks. He was dead center in the audience, standing motionless, his arms crossed over his chest in that belligerent stance I knew so well. The music drifted along without me, and the melody stopped short, a car skidding off onto the side of an icy road. Ian tilted his head to the side in that menacing way I'd become accustomed to over the years, and all at once the panic sprang up, a living thing, my heart beating wildly out of rhythm.

Run, a voice inside me urged. *Run now.*

My feet carried me, swift and sure even in my stiletto boots, as I bolted offstage, the sound of the audience at my back, moaning their disappointment. But I didn't care. I had to get away. Away from Ian and everything that had the power to hurt me. I grabbed my jacket from the metal folding chair I'd thrown it over before heading to the exit door, the neon above it promising escape, safety. I'd blown it, I knew. Blown it all. I was done with the past. But the past was oblivious. It crept back, insistent and pleading.

I leaned against the wall in the back alley, and a cat flickered past in the darkness, a flash of white scuttling by my feet, then there was only the noise of the nighttime city, the rumble of a garbage truck, the hiss of a bus closing its doors. It was still winter, but you could feel spring just below the surface, the molecules in the air shifting ever so slightly. I moved away from the wall and began to pace, unable to think clearly, my heels clicking on concrete.

There was the sound of footsteps, and Ian appeared, his dark eyes boring into me the way they always did. Even his stance was a form of provocation. He was as alarmingly handsome as ever, his dark hair combed back from his face, his lean body lightly rippled with muscle in the worn jeans and Aerosmith T-shirt he wore. The leather jacket that stretched against his wide shoulders.

"So here you are," he said with a nod. "Big shot in the big city, huh?"

"Hardly," I said, crossing my arms over my chest to protect myself.

"Yeah, you really fucked up out there," he said with a snort.

"Thanks a lot," I said, tears springing to my eyes. Ian was nothing if not blunt. But I knew he was right. I'd let my fears control me once again. With disastrous consequences.

"You don't belong here, baby," he crooned, his tone softening, catching me off guard. He took a step forward, reaching out and grabbing my arm. "You belong back home," he said, insistent now, "with me."

"Don't touch me," I spat, the words like flames, every part of me trembling. All at once it came rushing back. The way he'd turn off his phone for days at a time, only to return to police my every move. His voice in my head. *You'll never be more than I say you are.* Telling me what I could wear, where I could go, who I could be friends with. But what friends? Ian had never allowed me any. And I'd gone along with it because I thought it was all I deserved. That it was all I was worth. That it was his right alone to dictate my value. But not now. Not anymore. And looking at him, I could see that he knew it. He had lost control.

And it was killing him.

"Ava," he said, a flash of anger moving across his face, "you *have* to listen. I just want to—"

"What's going on here?"

Lexi, materializing as if by magic, her voice glacier cold. She stepped between Ian and me, severing his grip and pulling me behind her, her body a shield.

"We're *talking*," he sneered, his eyes flashing in the dimness. "Mind your own business, why don't you?"

"This *is* my business," Lexi snapped, taking a step toward him, and I watched with satisfaction as Ian stepped back, almost a stumble, a look of confusion washing over his face. "Why don't you get the hell out of here before I call the police?"

"You'd like that, wouldn't you?" He leered, regaining some of his footing.

Lexi just stared at him, unblinking. The seconds ticked by like hours.

"Don't show your face here again," she said when she finally spoke, her tone a warning.

"I'm going," he said finally. "But this isn't over." He looked directly at me, and I forced myself to return his gaze, holding it. "Not by a long shot." He shoved his hands into his jacket pockets, his shoulders hunched, a figure retreating into the darkness of the alley until he disappeared entirely.

"What the hell was *that* all about?" Lexi asked, searching my face for answers.

"I saw him out there," I said haltingly, "and I panicked. Oh god." A cry escaped my lips, and I put a hand over my mouth to stifle it, turning away so that she couldn't see my face. I didn't know what I was more ashamed of, what had happened onstage or the fact that Ian could still have that kind of effect on me. That he stepped back into my life whenever he felt like it, just to destroy what little peace I'd managed to create.

"He was in the club?" she asked, her voice high and thin. I nodded, not wanting to face her. But then the tears overcame me, and I let them spill, covering my cheeks in wetness. I felt the gentle pressure of her hands on my shoulders, and she turned me around to face her. I looked at the ground, refusing to meet her eyes.

"Maybe he's right," I whispered, shivering in the night air in that slip of a dress. "Maybe I don't belong here."

"What?" Lexi's voice was like ice cracking, and I looked up almost involuntarily. "Right?" she said in disbelief, her green eyes widening. "He's *not* right. He's a piece-of-shit narcissist who wants to bully you into giving up. Don't let him. There will be other shows."

"But the scout. He was out there and I—"

"There will be *other* scouts," Lexi said as if it were obvious. "Other *nights*. He ruined this one," she went on, her voice measured and sure. "Don't let him do it again."

Tears made their way hotly down my cheeks. I nodded, but inside I wasn't sure of anything. But if Lexi believed in me, it had to mean something. She was so fierce in her convictions, so sure of everything. And if someone like that thought I was something, anything, then maybe I could learn to think of myself that way too.

"You've got this," she murmured, her voice hypnotic as a lullaby. "Don't let anyone take it from you. Especially not some guy who wouldn't make it anywhere off the island." She slung an arm around my shoulders, and I wiped the tears from my face and tried to smile.

"Let's get a drink, rock star," she said, smiling as she opened the door with one hand and stepped inside. And I followed. I would have followed her anywhere back then, searching the first snow for her tracks, light-footed, quick as a fox. I knew I'd pursue her until I was limp with exhaustion, follow her down every twisting, narrow path, no matter where it led.

Even to hell itself.

KAYLA

Waking in the morning light, I reached for him, half-asleep, only to find the bed empty, the sheets cool and smooth beneath my hand. My eyes fluttered open, squinting in the rays of sunlight illuminating the large windows of his loft. I sat up, pulling the blanket around me, shielding my nakedness from the morning air. My skin felt well used, languid, my muscles still quivering after the night we'd shared, one where I'd barely slept, his hands roaming obsessively over my flesh each time I threatened to drift off.

No sleep, he'd murmured in my ear. *Not yet. I can't stop touching you.*

But strangely, I didn't feel tired.

I stepped out of the bed, my feet sinking into the thick ivory shag rug underfoot and grabbed his T-shirt from the end of the bed, pulling it over my head and inhaling deeply, my stomach dipping at his scent. Only a few days had passed since my trip to Staten Island, but with each passing hour, Jamie and I drew closer to each other. Whatever was happening between us felt inevitable. But like everything else, maybe that was a story I'd concocted to justify my own actions.

I smoothed the shirt down over my body, the fabric hanging almost to my knees, and walked out into the living area, which was basically one huge room bisected by a few columns. His kitchen was an assault of stainless steel and looked as though it had never been used. Jamie had never left the Lower East Side. He'd mentioned the night before, his voice a whisper in the dark, that his current space was only blocks away from the dilapidated loft on Twelfth Street where he'd spent the majority of his twenties.

"Jamie?" I called out tentatively, sniffing the air for the smell of coffee, but there was no response. The silence told me that I was alone, but I looked around, hoping for a glimpse of him anyway. I wandered around the room, taking in the long couch in the shape of an L, leather the burnished hue of a worn saddle, the simple wooden coffee table, and the navy-and-gold woolen rug beneath it. I walked over to the long marble kitchen island, on which rested a single sheet of paper.

Out for provisions.

Back soon.

—J

I smiled, momentarily relieved, though I hadn't really been worried. I busied myself in the kitchen, rummaging through the cabinets, looking for a glass, which I filled at the sink, gulping down the water greedily, as if I'd been swallowing sand. As soon as it was empty, I filled the glass again, this time carrying it with me as I looked around his apartment.

A long bookshelf completely covered one wall, and I ran my hands along the rainbow-hued spines, letting my fingers trail aimlessly down the rows until a glossy red jacket caught my eye, and I pulled the book from the shelf. Neruda's *Love Poems*. I'd always loved their sparseness, the way the letters pulsed on the page. Since we'd met, everything seemed heightened, including words. Colors seemed sharper. Scents richer. The world shone a bit brighter, as if it had been tinted with a fluorescence only he and I could see.

There was the metallic sound of a key in the lock, and I shoved the book back onto the shelf. The door opened and there he was, wearing the same beat-up pair of jeans he'd answered the door in the night before and a wrinkled white button-down shirt. He held a brown paper bag in one hand and a carryout container holding two cups of coffee in the other.

"Hey," he said, placing the food and drinks on the dining room table before walking over and folding me into his arms. "Good morning."

"It is now," I said, reaching up to kiss him. His lips lingered on mine, drinking me in.

"I'll get some plates," he said, releasing me and walking into the kitchen. "I got some bagels. I didn't know what you liked, so I went a little nuts." He laughed. "So how was Staten Island?"

I sighed, walking over to the table as Jamie piled the bagels on a plate in a formidable tower. "It was . . . troubling," I said as I pulled a chair out and sat down. "You were right about that guy."

"What do you mean?" he asked, plucking a sesame bagel from the plate. "Toasted?" he said, holding the bread in the air like a prize.

"No self-respecting New Yorker toasts their bagel."

"Well, this New Yorker does," he shot back, walking over to the kitchen counter.

"I have a hunch about him," I admitted hesitantly.

"Ian? What kind of hunch?" He looked up from the cutting board, a knife in one hand. "And shouldn't you be focusing on Lexi?"

"Yep. That's exactly what my boss would say too. But I can't shake the feeling that there's more here. In *Ava's* story."

"And what does Strickler have to do with it?" he asked, picking up the neatly halved bagel and placing it in the silver toaster perched on his kitchen counter.

"I think it's possible he killed her. Or at the very least, he knows a hell of a lot more than he's letting on."

Jamie halted his movements and was silent for a long moment. When he finally turned to face me, for the first time his expression was vacant. Unreadable. "What makes you think Ava was killed?" he said slowly. "It was suicide, Kayla. She jumped off the roof of Lexi's building."

"What if she didn't?"

"Let's entertain that for a minute. Even if that's the case, you think *Ian* is responsible? C'mon, Kayla. That guy couldn't find his way out of a paper bag, much less commit murder."

"You sure about that?"

"Jesus, why are you digging all of this up anyway? For a story on Lexi Mayhem and her new label? What's the point, Kayla?"

"Why do you care," I shot back, "*what* I write?"

"Because I loved her, OK?" he shouted, and I stood up, the chair scraping against the wood floor. We stared at each other, and for the first time in my life, words eluded me. There was a flash of anger in his eyes but also the hollow echo of regret, a deep, permanent sadness. A wound that wouldn't heal.

I knew better than anyone what that felt like.

"You . . . and Ava?" I asked, my voice suddenly a hoarse whisper. "Why didn't you tell me?"

"I'm telling you now," he said quietly. "I don't even like to think about it. Much less talk about it." He walked over to the couch and sat down heavily, looking at his knees, as if it were too difficult to face me—or himself. I moved across the room, sitting down on the coffee table across from him, suddenly conscious of the knots in my hair; my bare, unshaven legs; the mascara smeared beneath my eyes. I tried to pull the shirt down over my knees, waiting for him to explain.

"What happened between you two?" I was afraid to know the answer, but I had to ask. For the story, yes. But also for myself.

"We . . ." His voice trailed off for a moment, almost helplessly. "It was a long time ago, Kayla. But it was all my fault." He stood up, pushing past me, and began pacing around the living room as if he needed to get away. But there was nowhere to go.

"What do you mean?" I asked as fear crept in, stealing over me in a dark wave.

"We fought that night. The night she died."

I saw the naked pain in his face, the open wound of it, and I went to him, reaching for his hand. But before I could touch him, he drew it away, my fingers coming up empty.

"Talk to me," I whispered, pleading with him now, but he wouldn't look at me. "You said yourself it was *suicide*, Jamie, right? If that's true, then it was nobody's fault."

"I destroy everything I touch," he said, finally looking up. "You shouldn't be with me, Kayla." His gaze was blank and disaffected, and any feeling he'd had for me seemed to be frozen in time. "Do you know what it's like to have you digging this all up? It's like watching her die *twice*. For fuck's sake, just let it lie."

"You know I can't do that," I said softly.

He just stared at me, then shook his head in disgust. "You should go," he said brusquely, walking into the kitchen and pulling his phone from his pocket, scrolling through it as if I weren't even there.

I nodded, then made my way to his bedroom, dressing fast, my fingers fumbling with buttons and snaps, remembering how easily our clothes had fallen away the night before. It never ceased to amaze me how things could change so quickly, so sharply, that the world seemed to spin out of sync.

When I walked to the front door, I stopped, one hand on the knob, and looked back at him. He was standing in the kitchen looking out the window and drinking one of the cups of coffee he'd bought, staring out into the sun-washed city, his face a blank page.

Turn around, I willed him. *Please.*

I waited a beat, then two. But he didn't move. I wanted to say something, anything to change what was happening, but my words were stuck in my throat, immovable. Left with no other choice, I turned the knob and walked out, pulling the door shut behind me.

———

The office was the only place where I could calm the tumult of my mind. There was something about the hum of the coffee maker in the break room, the bustle of bodies rushing past, the clicking of keystrokes and rows of cubicles that made me feel grounded and safe. It was almost like halting time, being in this huge, windowless space, like crawling into the deepest recesses of my own brain. But Jamie's face still haunted me, how he wouldn't look directly at me, as if the very sight pained him.

I walked toward the ladies' room, pushing open the door, the scent of soap enveloping me. The bathroom was blessedly empty, the subway tile bland and shiny. I stood in front of the row of porcelain sinks, taking deep breaths and avoiding my reflection in the mirror, which I knew would stare back at me, pale and uncertain. The watery blast of a flushing toilet made me jump, and Simone emerged from a stall, her slim frame draped in a black wrap dress, her braids ending in rows of gold and silver beads that clicked as she moved. She blinked at me from behind her black glasses as she came and stood beside me at the sinks, running her hands beneath a stream of water and lathering them in pink soap.

"You look like shit," she said without looking up.

"Thanks." I laughed, turning on the tap in front of me and mindlessly washing my hands, for something to do as much as anything else. When I looked up at myself in the mirror, my hair looked stringier than usual, my cheeks devoid of color.

"Did the story tank or something?"

I sighed, reaching over for a towel from the dispenser on the wall, rubbing my hands with the coarse paper.

"I wish," I muttered, balling it up and throwing it in the trash.

"Can't be that bad," she said, peering into the mirror and removing her glasses to swipe at a corner of one eye with an index finger. "Never is."

"I feel like you've never screwed up a story in your life," I said, a short laugh escaping my throat.

"That's where you're wrong."

She glanced over, giving me the side-eye, vaguely amused. Which for Simone meant that her expression changed only by maybe a millimeter. But it was enough.

"I'm chasing ghosts. Which is exactly what I'm sure Keats is going to tell me in mere minutes."

"You're psyching yourself out," she said coolly. "Just focus on the story—not how you feel about it. Quit trying to make the narrative fit whatever ideas you've got in your head. Stick to what you know."

"That's the problem. I'm not sure what that is anymore. Just when it seems like I have a grip on the story, it slides away."

Simone just stared at me. I wondered what she was thinking, and if her pulse ever climbed above sixty. Maybe at the gym—if she even bothered with that kind of thing. I couldn't imagine Simone participating in anything as banal and potentially time-wasting as exercise.

"Give me your phone," she commanded, holding out one hand expectantly.

"What?" I said distractedly, turning to face her.

"Phone," she repeated as if I were dense. "Hand it over."

I reached into my jacket pocket, retrieving the hunk of glass and plastic. I unlocked it, passing it over without protest, and her fingers tapped the screen expertly, her nails painted a glossy lavender.

"My number," she said as she handed it back. "To be used in emergencies only—if you get *really* stuck. Right now, you're just doubting yourself. Your talent. The story itself. But that's life, baby. Not a four-alarm fire."

"Oh," I said, suddenly flustered, my cheeks flushed. "Thank you. I mean, I'd love to bounce some ideas off you if you're game and—"

"Emergencies," she said, cutting me off and walking toward the door, yanking it open with one hand. *"Only,"* she stressed. "I'm getting some damn lunch." She walked out without a backward glance.

Back at my desk, I stared at the screen of my laptop, the cursor blinking at me aggressively. All my research had come to a dead end. Jamie was right. What did I really have except a hunch, one that hadn't even remotely panned out? In all likelihood, Ava was just another tragic suicide, a talented young woman who couldn't handle the pressure and chose to take her own life. It was an old story, and not one worth repeating. And worse yet, in trying to make it into something it wasn't, I'd hurt Jamie, bringing up something he didn't want to remember. Still, the fact that he hadn't told me about Ava before I practically dragged it out of him nagged at me. Even if it was hard to talk about, he knew the story I was reporting, knew that at the very least, it was relevant information. How long would he have hidden it from me?

"How's it going?"

Keats's voice at my back made me jump, and I swiveled around in my chair, startled, one hand on my heart. "Jesus," I said with a grin. "You scared me."

He pushed his glasses up on his nose with a wry grin. Today I noticed that he was wearing his favorite cream linen blazer paired with fawn-colored trousers, a square of beige silk peeking from his jacket pocket. I'd always thought the ensemble made him look a bit like a nerdy Gatsby. "Look around, McCray," he said, pointing at the crowded office, the constantly ringing phones, the low drone of conversation. "It's not exactly quiet in here."

"True," I agreed. "But sneaking up behind anyone who didn't see you coming would scare the crap out of most people."

"I didn't think you were most people," he said calmly.

"Touché," I answered, silently praying that I could somehow exit this conversation without him asking about the story.

"How's the Mayhem piece coming along?" he asked, taking a sip from his ever-present Starbucks venti.

I cringed as the words left his lips. But I knew I'd have to answer.

"I thought I had a scoop. But it turned out to be a dead end."

"I hate to say this," he began, his voice low but firm, "but you're not supposed to be breaking any news here, Kayla. This is a fluff piece disguised as a business story, and it's mainly going to sell copies based on whatever scantily clad photo of Mayhem we put on the cover. That might be tough to hear, and I know this is your first cover and you're just trying to do right by it, but don't go all Carl Bernstein on me right now—we don't have enough time before the close to reel this back in."

I nodded, swallowing hard. He was right. I'd veered so off course that I wasn't even sure what I was covering anymore. And that was a dangerous place to be. I'd become so focused on Ava that I'd forgotten what the story was really about: Lexi Mayhem and her transformation from pop star to record executive.

"Do I need to assign this to someone else?"

"Of course not," I said, clearing my throat. "I'll pull it together. It's not a problem."

"I hope not," Keats said, regarding me warily. "I'd hate to have to reassign this at the eleventh hour."

"You won't have to," I said quickly. "I'm on it. Don't worry."

Keats nodded, appeased for the moment. "Glad to hear it," he said before he began walking away. But before he took more than a few steps, he stopped and looked back at me. "Everyone wants to break the big story, Kayla," he said, tossing his cup into the trash can a few feet from my desk. I'd bet money on the fact that it was at least half-full. "But sometimes you need to start with the stuff that just sells copies."

He strode back to his office, closing the door behind him. As soon as he was out of sight, I exhaled heavily, turning back to my computer. *Just start writing,* I told myself. *This is no different from any other piece. Just get it done.* But even I knew that wasn't really true. There was something that drew me to Ava's story, something that tugged at me, urging me to learn more. Why couldn't I just let it go, when I knew it was in my own best interest to? "It's *a* story," I reminded myself, mumbling under my breath. "But it's not *the* story."

Before I could change my mind, I shoved my AirPods in my ears and turned on my recorder. I bent over the keys and started typing, the sounds of the office disappearing as my fingers flew across the keyboard, drowning out the chorus of voices in my head.

AVA

Christian Vane sat back in the red booth, tilting his chin up and sur-
veying the glamorous crowd as if he alone had created it. He was sun-
bronzed fake tan. A halo of sun-streaked curls. A sudden baring of white
teeth. Aviators he wore indoors, the green or turquoise lenses hiding his
eyes. A smile that swung between practiced and predatory. He was rum-
pled suits and the silky leather seats of a new car. He was straight mezcal
and champagne kirs, the black currant liqueur like a rose imploding.

"You been here before?" he asked in his lazy California drawl, craning his neck to take in the room, possessing it, as if it belonged to him
alone. A server moved silently toward us, depositing another bucket of
champagne tableside, the ice bucket dewy and cold.

"I haven't," Lexi replied, her lips outlined in a bright crimson stain.
She wore a long black lace dress I'd never seen before. It swirled around
her legs, fluid as a dancer. The back of the dress was cut open all the way
down to her waist, exposing the bones of her back, her spine a ladder
of secrets. Her mass of dark hair was piled atop her head and secured
with a clip, tendrils falling on either side of her face, her neck delicate
as a swan's. It was a far cry from the shredded jeans and the scrap of

a pleather top she'd worn onstage at the Knitting Factory earlier that evening. She was refined now, elegant, as she toyed with the champagne flute on the table in front of her, bringing it slowly to her lips.

I shifted uncomfortably, glaringly aware that I was still dressed in the clothes I'd worn when I'd exited the stage a few hours ago: a loose white skirt that fell to my ankles and a white tank, my worn leather jacket cradling me like a lover. I played with the row of bangles on my wrist, a feeling of awkwardness engulfing me. It was the school cafeteria again, but this time the stakes were higher.

So high I could barely breathe.

There were two other men in the booth, "associates," Christian had called them when he'd introduced us after the show. When the notes of the last song faded into silence and the lights dimmed, I'd stepped offstage sweating and exhilarated, making my way through the crowd. Jamie had been right—this time it *was* easier. There had been only one real moment of panic when I'd stepped into the stage lights, stunned by the ferocity of the glare, my eyes watering uncontrollably. But when the music swelled around me and I parted my lips to sing, my nerves quieted, the room blurring along the edges. The songs ticked by, one after another, until applause filled the room with a rush of energy.

As I walked to the bar, Jamie sidled up beside me, whispering in my ear, his breath warm and slightly damp against my skin, making me shiver.

Christian Vane is here—from Phoenix Records. He wants to meet you. Lexi too.

Suddenly he was propelling me over to the far end of the bar, where Christian held court, surrounded by a group of doe-eyed young women who gazed at him adoringly, pouting around the long red straws buried in the ice of their drinks. But when Jamie and I approached, Christian shooed his harem away with a wave of his hand. He reeked of money, even in the dimness of the club, and his eyes were hidden by a pair of dark glasses that made it impossible to know what, if anything, he was actually thinking.

"You were incredible," he said, leaning in to kiss me on both cheeks, the pressure of his mouth lingering a second too long on each side. I pulled back, smiling woodenly. "Such power, such *presence*," he said admiringly, gesturing fluidly in the air with one hand, a gold signet ring gleaming on one finger. "You must be hungry."

"Famished," Lexi said, suddenly at my elbow, staring straight at Christian, who removed his glasses to examine her more closely. She'd already changed her clothes, and yards of black lace frothed around her, dripping to the floor. I shifted my weight self-consciously. She had known Christian was in the audience tonight. And she hadn't told me. That was the only explanation I could find for what was currently happening.

I touched her arm lightly with the tips of my fingers, but she wouldn't look at me, so I dropped my hand down at my side as Jamie placed a hand on my back, ushering me toward the exit. A long white limousine idled at the curb, but when Jamie tried to climb inside, Christian stopped him with one raised hand. "Just the ladies tonight. We'll meet up tomorrow to talk business."

Before he could answer, Christian was already inside the car, Lexi following close behind. Jamie turned to face me. "You'll be fine," he said declaratively, as if it were himself who he needed to convince. I nodded, wordless, and he squeezed my hand in his own before letting go entirely. I stepped from the curb into the limo and the darkness waiting within.

The lights of the city flashed by outside the tinted windows in a watercolor blur. Lexi sat next to Christian, bending close, then throwing her head back in peals of laughter, the sound fake and hollow. It was like no laugh from her I'd ever heard, and the sound made my skin crawl. I stared out the window, feeling small on the slick leather seats, like I might disappear into them entirely.

At Pastis, the leather booths were a bloodred that perfectly matched Lexi's lipstick, the napkin in my lap snow white, awaiting the press of my mouth. The server appeared, placing a wooden platter of steak frites before me, a green salad at Lexi's elbow. Just looking at the seared meat, the crisped potatoes, steam rising off the plate, wafting toward me, my stomach rumbled. I picked up my knife and fork and dug in hungrily. I hadn't eaten all day, and I fell to the plate like a starving dog. The first few bites made me close my eyes, the room evaporating in the rush of pleasure that overtook me.

When I came to, my meal was half-gone, and I looked around the table as if I'd been in a trance. Lexi toyed with the leaves of her salad, piercing them with a fork but never consuming them. Instead, she laughed at Christian's jokes, then put the fork down, her dinner all but forgotten.

"Lexi," I said, trying to get her attention. "Is that all you're having?"

She looked over at me, her face impassive. "I had a late lunch."

That was a lie. We'd worked a full shift at the café, then gone straight to the show. Neither one of us had eaten since breakfast, which was generally a cup of bodega coffee. I had the sneaking feeling again that there was a game being played here, the rules of which I didn't understand.

"You were both incredible tonight," Christian said, smoke billowing in a cloud around his head. "Do you have any vocal training?" He looked expectantly from one of us to the other.

"I studied for *years* at Tisch," Lexi said confidently, toying with the crystal salt and pepper shakers. "Voice, music, dance. And before that I worked privately with a vocal coach."

He looked at me expectantly, and I clenched my napkin under the table in a tight fist, conscious of his eyes on me. The two other men at the table were deep in conversation, their heads turned toward each other. It was just Christian, Lexi, and me. And I was in the hot seat.

"I . . . ," I started, my voice swallowed by the din of the restaurant. "I really haven't had any training. Not really at all."

"She's self-taught," Lexi broke in, kicking me sharply beneath the table with the toe of her boot. "Right, Ava?"

"Right," I said gratefully, turning back to face them both, trying to smile.

"A natural," Christian said, nodding thoughtfully. "You seemed so self-possessed onstage tonight. It is hard to believe you have no formal training."

"It was only her third show," Lexi said, her voice like steel. Our eyes met across the table, her face blank and hard, but no less beautiful for that.

"Really?" Christian said, picking at his plate of salmon with one gold-dipped fork so that the flesh of the fish showed, apricot pink against the white china. The sight of it turned my stomach, and I pushed my plate away.

"I've been performing all over the Lower East Side for two years." Lexi picked up her glass and drained the last of the champagne in one long swallow. "*And* I'm recording. Jamie's booked me some studio time next week."

I blinked, as if coming into sudden light. That was news to me. I wondered why Jamie hadn't mentioned it. Or Lexi. We spent practically every day together, working side by side at the café, in her apartment, walking down the street, her hand in mine. That uneasy feeling crept over me again, my stomach swelling like a balloon filling too rapidly with air, and I clutched the edge of the table with bloodless fingers.

"I take it you are familiar with my work?" Christian asked slyly, feigning modesty.

"Oh my god, yes," Lexi began excitedly. "I worshipped the last Arabella Sanchez record. I know you signed her when she was just—"

"You have good taste," he said with a self-satisfied smile.

Arabella Sanchez. I racked my brain, looking for the reference and coming up empty. I didn't even listen to the radio. I lived in a kind of vacuum, alone with the music tumbling around inside my head, the melodies that kept me up at night, weaving themselves around me like a blanket. But now, I was beginning to see that my ignorance put me at a disadvantage.

"And signing the Autocrats when they were still in high school was a stroke of genius," Lexi said, her tone bordering on reverence. Christian, like a preening bird fluffing its feathers, puffed out his chest a bit, nodding in agreement. He refilled his glass with the dewy bottle, then sipped at it greedily.

"They were young but so . . . ripe for stardom." He gave us a sly smile, and I felt my stomach dip again, turning sharply. "I'm always looking for that certain something in a performer." He glanced over at Lexi, his eyes traveling to the vee of her dress, the bare skin exposed in twin mounds of flesh.

"I think you're a visionary," Lexi breathed. "Working with you would be beyond my wildest *dreams*. What you did on the last Justine Diamond album—the production alone," she gushed, her words toppling over one another, "blew me away."

A sinking feeling came over me, the same feeling of helplessness that had stolen over me the moment I'd seen Ian's face in the audience at the Bitter End, staring at me as if I were already his. There was no room to enter the conversation, nothing for me to say. I knew next to nothing about pop music and, it seemed, little else of any importance.

"Well," Christian said, dabbing his lips with a napkin, "there's no doubt that you're both talented. But I don't need two more female singers on my roster."

"Why *not*?" Lexi blurted out indignantly.

Christian shrugged. "I simply don't have room for both of you."

"We do very different—"

"Not different enough," he said sharply.

The server cleared the table, Lexi's salad mostly untouched, the remains of Christian's fish strewn across his plate haphazardly, the flesh pink and gutted. I had to look away, my stomach churning. Then, beneath the table, I felt the subtle pressure of Christian's leg pressing against my own. For a split second I sat there in disbelief, and before I could stop myself, I pulled away quickly, my body reacting before my brain had time to catch up. I could tell by the dour look that crossed his face that he was far from pleased, and I smiled apologetically, but he refused to look at me. In that moment, I disappeared entirely, my chair suddenly vacant. I was as insubstantial as a specter hovering over the table. Only Lexi remained, and Christian turned to her with interest, ignoring me entirely.

"You see, it all depends," Christian said, leaning forward, resting his elbows on the table so that he and Lexi were inches apart. "On how badly you want it."

"Oh, I definitely want it," she murmured, their eyes locked.

At that moment I stood up, knocking over my water glass with the sudden movement. Lexi looked over in annoyance as the water spread across the tablecloth, the ice in a small puddle. My heart was beating too fast, the world out of sync. A song played off-key. This was Lexi. And for the first time, she was unrecognizable to me.

"I should go," I said, throwing on my jacket so quickly that one hand caught in the lining of the sleeve, tearing it. "Thank you for dinner."

Christian looked over at me, a faint hint of triumph in his eyes. "I'll be in touch," he said dismissively before turning his attention back to Lexi as though I'd somehow become what I was at the café: a server. There to do his bidding. As I walked out of the restaurant, the smell of fresh flowers and roasted meat enveloping me, I turned and looked back only once. Lexi and Christian were sitting closer together now, talking intently, and before I looked away, he bent to whisper something in her ear, his lips moving soundlessly against her skin.

KAYLA

After I'd recommitted to the story I was being paid to write, I'd begun researching Lexi's ascension to pop stardom in earnest, which was probably what I should've done in the first place. I began, as Keats had suggested, at the beginning, delving into the history of Lexi's first label—Phoenix Records, headed up by Christian Vane, whose reputation for finding undiscovered talent in the early aughts and spinning it into gold and platinum records was the stuff of legends.

Lexi had stayed with Christian for more than ten years, so the relationship must've been profitable all around. But as I searched through myriad links detailing the history of the label, I stumbled on a Reddit thread among the glossy profiles and MTV interviews—a list of the Top Ten Shittiest Men in Music. Lists like these had been all the rage for the last few years, ever since the Weinstein case broke wide open, exposing his predatory behavior. And there, buried among comments flat out accusing one top-tier music exec after another, was this thinly veiled riddle:

What music mogul with a label named after the act of rising from the ashes enjoys drugging and assaulting his female assistants, pulling them down in the dirt?

The allusion was obvious: Phoenix Records.

As I stared at the screen, my first interview with Lexi at the Chateau came rushing back to me, her assertion that it was commonplace in the music industry for suits to make advances toward talent or expect sexual favors that went well beyond "business." And then I remembered the statement Lexi had given the police, that she and Ava had dinner with Christian the night Ava died. It was probably just coincidence, but now I couldn't help but wonder if there was more to the story. I screenshotted the comment immediately, leaned forward in my chair, and began to dig.

The user, BelleJar89, had a Tumblr under the same name, and after poking around her social media, it didn't take long to find an email address. To my surprise, she wrote back almost immediately and, after a bit of back-and-forth, eventually agreed to meet for coffee. I suggested the most nonthreatening place I could think of—a Starbucks in Midtown. I knew from experience that it would be busy and banal, a combination that had proven effective at quieting the nerves of a skittish subject.

On the day of our meeting, I grabbed my keys and headed for the subway, wondering how much she'd really tell me once we were sitting down together. It was totally possible that she'd balk once I started asking about Christian or just ghost me completely. I hoped this conversation would open more doors into the connection between Ava and Christian, but as I swiped my card through the turnstile, the train thundering below me, I wondered if I was just chasing something as ineffable as the smoke that rose from the manhole covers dotting the city streets.

"I wasn't sure if I should meet you," Bella Sloane said, her eyes darting nervously around the room. "But I googled you pretty exhaustively, and you seem to be legit."

I leaned forward to hear her more clearly, my open notebook balanced on my knees. The murmur of voices surrounded us, along with the buzzing and ringing of cell phones and the tyranny of pinging notifications. And above it all rose the intermittent hiss of the espresso machine, the nasal twang of the barista as he shouted out orders.

Bella smiled tightly, her tortoiseshell hair falling to her shoulders, eclipsing her face each time she bent forward. Something about her scrubbed complexion, her milky skin and ruddy cheeks, free of paint or artifice, her nondescript, baggy clothing, told me she preferred it that way. Even though she was in her early thirties, she seemed much younger, clutching the sky-blue leather tote in her lap as if it might escape.

"I'm really grateful that you came," I said warmly, trying to put her at ease. "So, you were Christian Vane's assistant?" I looked down at the legal pad in my lap, checking my notes. "From 2014 to 2016?"

She bit her lower lip, her teeth sinking into the soft flesh. "I didn't name him in that post," she said, the smooth skin of her forehead creased with worry. "I didn't say who it *was*."

"It's OK," I said quickly, trying to reassure her. "Right now, we're just talking—nothing about your experience specifically will get back to him if you don't want it to. This is deep background. But the thing is, Bella, no matter how rich he is or how protected, if what you say is accurate, eventually others will start coming forward too. It's really only a matter of time."

"I'm not sure that's true," she said bitterly, bringing the cup to her lips. "Guys like him never get what they deserve."

Astrid's voice floated back to me, cutting through the noise of the room, and a sudden surge of anger rushed through me.

Nothing will happen to him, Kayla! No one will believe me.

"I was his assistant for two years," she said with a grimace, as if the milk had gone bad or the memory itself had soured her. "It was my first job out of college. I thought I'd won the lottery." She laughed softly under her breath. "It seems crazy now. But at first, he was totally professional. I'd heard some things, but after a few months, I didn't think I had anything to worry about."

"What had you heard?"

She shrugged, placing her cup back on the table. "That he'd been a little too . . . close with his former assistants. And some of the talent too."

"Did you ever confront him about those rumors?"

"God no." She shook her head vehemently. "I mean, we barely even talked about the weather before . . . that night. It was always 'Bella, call for my driver.' Or 'Bella, make a reservation at Nobu for Friday.' Most of the time it felt like he barely even noticed me—and I was fine with that. But then everything changed." She fidgeted in her seat, looking away.

"Do you want to tell me what happened?" I asked gently.

"We'd been to an industry benefit," she said after a minute, taking a deep breath and meeting my gaze again before continuing. "Red carpet, media coverage, a lot of hand shaking and schmoozing. I was expected to attend those kinds of functions with him. He liked to drink, and he needed someone there to remember who he'd talked to, what he'd promised them."

"Was he often inebriated?"

"At the office, never. But when we went out, he liked to party. Most of these guys do. But the worst part is that the drunker he got, the more he'd pull me into things. Ask me to go up to women and tell them he wanted to buy them a drink or join him in the VIP area. I hated doing it, but I didn't know how to say no. I was afraid he'd fire me, and at that point I still wanted the job."

I took a sip of my coffee, still too hot, wincing as the liquid incinerated the skin on the roof of my mouth.

"Anyway," she said with a sigh, "that night, instead of flirting with every woman in sight, he was glued to my side, which I guess should've tipped me off, but honestly, it had been a long week and I was exhausted. All I could think about was going home, putting on my pajamas, and getting into bed with a glass of wine and some Netflix. So when he asked me to come up to his room at the Plaza to debrief—he keeps a suite here when he's not in LA—I was a little annoyed, but I didn't think twice about it. In hindsight, I probably should've."

"Had he ever asked you to accompany him to his room before?"

She began fidgeting with a small gold ring on her index finger. "Not at night, no. Only during the day to drop off paperwork. I was hoping we'd talk for a few minutes, then I'd leave. But . . . when we got in the room, he started immediately insisting that we have one last drink. Like I said, I was exhausted, so I tried to beg off. But he wasn't having it. 'C'mon,' he kept saying, 'we need a nightcap after that horror show.' Finally, just to get him to shut up more than anything else, I agreed, and he opened a bottle of champagne. I drank a glass fast, hoping that would be the end of it. But then things got . . . weird."

"How so?"

She hesitated, a look of sadness veiling her eyes. "I started to feel . . . strange. Light-headed. Christian was sitting next to me on the couch and watching me curiously, sipping at his drink. Things felt like they were tilting, like I was falling, even though I knew somehow that I was still upright. I remember telling him that I didn't feel well and him suggesting that I lie down for a few minutes. Next thing I knew I was in the bed, and he was leaning over me. He was running a hand up and down my arm, but it was weird because at the same time I couldn't really feel anything at all. I'd gone numb. Then things went dark."

She took a breath, placing her drink down on the table. "When I came to, I was undressed, cold, on top of the comforter, and Christian was beside me, completely passed out. It hurt"—her voice stopped in her throat—"inside me, and I knew something had happened. My head was pounding, and I just wanted to get away from him. I dressed as fast as I could and left. When I got outside of the hotel, a bout of nausea stopped me in my tracks, and I bent over and vomited. It felt like my guts were spilling onto the pavement. The doorman kept saying, 'Miss? Miss, are you all right?' 'Hospital,' I managed to get out, and he hailed a cab in seconds, depositing me in the back seat. By this time, I was shivering violently. I puked twice more in the cab, which didn't exactly endear me to the driver, but what could I do? He took me to New York-Presbyterian."

"Did they do a rape kit?" I asked quietly.

"No," she said, shaking her head. "I didn't tell them . . . about that. Just that I didn't feel well."

"Did they run any tests?"

"Blood work. It came back positive for narcotics."

"Do you have a record of that?"

"At home," she said, crossing one leg over the other and finally releasing her death grip on her tote so that color rushed back into her fingers.

"Would you be willing to share it with me?"

She bit her bottom lip, and I could tell she was weighing the idea in her mind.

"Yeah," she said finally. "I can email it to you. But it needs to end there, OK?"

"Of course," I agreed, already wondering if I'd ever get that email. Not because I thought she was lying but because it was clear she was still frightened. Not that anyone could blame her. "Did you ever confront him?" I asked, already knowing the answer.

She shook her head, her eyes glassy. "He sent a few emails, asking when I'd be back. And then a week or two later, his new assistant called, asking for my passwords for his files on the office computer. That was the last contact I had with him."

"You never saw him again?"

A man in a red backpack passed behind her chair, knocking into her sharply. She drew back as if she had been burned. "Sorry," the guy mumbled before heading off toward the restrooms. I reached out a hand as if to steady her—a hand she flinched from.

"I'm OK," she said, brushing off my concern, but her guarded expression told me she was anything but. "And to answer your question, no, I never saw him again. And I hope to god I never do. I like to believe in karma, you know?" she said, the pain in her eyes so vast and deep that it made me ache for her. "That people eventually get what they deserve. But some people never get what's coming to them. Not in this lifetime, anyway."

———

Later that night, I was sitting at my computer when an email arrived, hitting my inbox with a sharp ping, Bella's name in the address line, the subject in all caps: DO NOT SHARE. "Thank you," I breathed, clicking on the attachment. When the lab results appeared on the screen, I stared at them in disbelief, the letters and numbers spinning before my eyes. The drugs detected in Bella's bloodstream the night Christian had allegedly attacked her? Ketamine and fentanyl.

The very same drugs found in Ava Petrova's system the night she died.

AVA

2006

The streets swam in front of me, yellow cabs swarming the hive of the city, the xylophone ping of steel drums in my ears. The spring air caressed my skin like a lover, green buds in the trees and the scent of rain-washed blossoms in the air. The buildings looming above were no longer protective, but predatory now, as if they might reach down and snatch me from the sidewalk. There was only the metronome of my boots on the pavement as I walked, a steady clicking that was usually reassuring but tonight offered no solace at all. It was now meaningless noise, like so much of what swirled around me as I followed the crowds uptown, the dinner with Christian and Lexi replaying itself in my mind like the reels of a terrible film. Lexi's face, the hardness in her eyes, as if she'd been suddenly split in two. The person I knew and loved—and the mannequin. A plastic doll in a lace dress who nodded and smiled and said all the right things.

There was only one place to go, and when I arrived, I stood in front of the building for a moment before pressing the buzzer once, hard. And there was Jamie's voice, full of happy surprise. I walked up the three flights like pushing through rough water, and when I reached his floor, he was waiting in the doorway, his eyes full of questions I didn't want to answer.

I'd been to Jamie's apartment only once, just for a moment to drop off my contract. But this was the first time I'd made it past the front door. I looked around hesitantly, expecting the worst. Ian's place had been a bachelor's den of half-eaten cartons of Chinese food littering the kitchen counters, the coffee table strewn with rows of empty beer bottles like sleeping soldiers. There was always a yeasty tang in the air, the product of windows left closed too long and blinds drawn.

But Jamie's apartment was neat and orderly. One large room with huge windows and a king-size bed dominating the space. Overhead there were exposed beams and the silver gleam of pipes snaking across the ceiling, as if it had once been a factory of some kind. There was a marble kitchen island with barstools drawn up to it but nowhere else to sit other than the bed. I tried not to think about that and looked at him instead. He was wearing the clothes he'd had on earlier, a pair of indigo jeans and a crisp white T-shirt. His face was scruffy, and his eyes shone blue as the lightest sea glass, half-buried on the stones of a rocky beach.

"How was it?" he asked, closing the front door and locking it behind me. "You OK?" He came over, placing his hands on my shoulders. "He can be kind of a letch. Did he try anything?"

The feeling of Christian's leg pressed against mine, that insistent heat, came rushing back. The way he and Lexi leaned close together, his lips at her ear. That look in her eyes as I was leaving. Like I was unknowable. Inconsequential.

A stranger.

"You knew about that?" I asked.

"His reputation kind of precedes him," Jamie said grimly. "He's handsy but mostly harmless. Anyway, I figured you'd be fine with Lexi and the other A&R guys there."

"He said he can only sign one of us." My voice sounded hollow and wooden. Even in the safety of Jamie's apartment, nothing felt real.

"What?" Jamie said, releasing me and stepping back. "Why?"

"He said we weren't different enough."

"That's bullshit," he replied, incredulous now.

"Well, that's what he said."

"I know it's what he *said*." Jamie walked over to the kitchen counter, grabbing a bottle of whiskey and pouring two shots into empty glasses. "But he's wrong. You couldn't be more different from one another. If it were my label—and someday it will be—I wouldn't think twice about signing you both." He put one glass down on the island and pushed it toward me. I walked over and drained it in one swallow, the whiskey burning my throat.

"And Lexi . . . ," I began, my words trailing off into nothingness.

"What about her?" Jamie tossed his shot back as though it were water and refilled our glasses.

"She was so . . . different." That hard gaze. The practiced lines she gave him, so smooth. Where had she learned all of it? I thought of the way she had turned toward Christian, as if I'd evaporated completely, leaving behind no trace. I shook my hair from my face, as if to release the memory.

"Different how?" Jamie walked over and sat on the barstool next to me. I stood there awkwardly, wanting to sit but afraid of how close that would put us to one another. As it was, I couldn't seem to be in the same space without wanting to touch him, to take his hand in mine, just to feel the warmth of it against my skin. Instead, I picked up my glass and drained it again, barely wincing this time.

"It was like I wasn't even there," I said quietly. "She was out for herself. I've never seen her act like that before. It was like she became another person entirely."

"I hope she knows what she's doing with him. I think she's out of her depth." He frowned, his face marked with concern. "But frankly, I'm not surprised. Lexi does whatever it takes to get what she wants."

"I guess I don't," I mumbled, tracing the intricate patterns in the marble with one fingertip. There were constellations in there and mica that sparkled like stars. My eyes filled with tears again, and I fought them back, not wanting to give Lexi the satisfaction of winning. When had this become a game? *But she did win. At least tonight,* a voice inside me said.

She will always win.

"Hey." Jamie reached out, pulling me toward him, and I let him. I let myself go, my limbs folding seamlessly into his own. He held me to his chest, and I breathed in the woodsy scent of him and closed my eyes. I knew I needed to leave, but something deep inside me didn't want to. "You are *you*," he said softly. "And it's more than enough."

"I thought Lexi and I would make it together," I whispered, fighting back my tears. "I didn't know it was a competition."

"I don't think she did either," he murmured into my neck. "Maybe not until tonight. But now you need to look out for you. Understand?"

I nodded silently, tears finally spilling over my cheeks, hot as his breath on my skin. He tilted my chin up to meet his eyes, and the world fell away again as his lips touched mine. I pulled him closer, and my lips opened under his own, and I couldn't stop myself. I was moaning into his mouth, and he pulled at my clothes, running his hands beneath the skirt I wore, and I gasped when he touched me, holding on tighter. He stood up, and we kissed all the way over to the bed, our mouths ravenous.

He laid me down gently, so gently that I felt as if I were floating. I pulled at his shirt, and he at mine until we were pressed skin to skin, hot and electric. For the first time that night, I didn't think of Lexi or Christian. There was only Jamie. His hands on my skin, his breath in my ear, and in the moment where he slid inside me, pulling back to brush my hair from my face, something in his eyes that looked like fate.

KAYLA

2019

As I entered the Midtown office of Christian Vane, I found myself momentarily disoriented, squinting against the glare. Everything from the snowy shag rug underfoot to the modern furnishings that were either entirely without pigment or fashioned from shiny chrome made me feel as if I'd landed on the moon. There was a vaguely seventies vibe to the decor—a futuristic egg-shaped chair sat in the corner, a crimson cushion nestled inside. A chandelier glowed overhead, each one of its curved chrome arms punctuated by a cluster of large globes, the glass frosted and opaque.

Christian stood up as I entered, walking around the Lucite desk to greet me with a smile. He wore a black suit, a white T-shirt beneath, and his eyes were small and narrow up close but friendly enough. His nimbus of blond curls shot through with gray, the strands glimmering like buried treasure. His trademark sunglasses, I noticed, were absent.

"A pleasure to meet you," he said, shaking my hand. His grip was limp, like holding a dying animal in my palm.

He strode back over to the desk, gesturing to the white leather arm-chair beside it, the silver legs shining in the sunlight. I sat down, placing my tote on the floor beside me, glad I'd dressed a little more formally than usual in a white scoop-neck bodysuit, black blazer, and a pair of black wide-legged pants. My dark hair was pulled back in a low pony-tail, and I pushed my bangs out of my eyes as I reached into my tote for my voice recorder. "This OK?" I asked, holding it up in one hand.

"Oh, I don't think so." He leaned back in his chair as if he were about to take a nap. "As I said over email, I'm not sure how much help I'll be—but what I *will* tell you is strictly off the record." He held his hands together in front of him, pressing his fingertips against each other, as if in prayer.

"OK then, off the record," I agreed, slipping the recorder back into my bag. "As I mentioned, I'm writing a cover story on Lexi Mayhem, and I was hoping to ask a few questions about her early career."

"Lexi and I were quite the team for a while." He laughed softly to himself, as if the notion were amusing. "I had the clout and the con-nections. She had the moxie. And the combination shot her to super-stardom. Under my tutelage, she became a pop legend. Which is all she ever wanted anyway."

"What is it that you taught her, exactly?"

"The game, of course."

"The game?"

"Everything is a game, Ms. McCray. Don't you agree?" Before I could answer, he went on, lost in thought. "Especially in this business. It's all who you know, which palms you'll grease to get ahead. Lexi had good instincts, I'll give her that, but I taught her the practicalities of it all—which DJs to court during interviews. How to conduct herself on camera. What questions to dodge in print."

"How did Lexi feel about all of this?"

"She was an apt pupil." He smiled as he picked up a small gold paperweight on his desk, turning it over in one hand. "She wanted it so badly—the attention. The fame. The flashbulbs each time she exited a limo. There wasn't much she wouldn't do to get it."

Bella's face flashed through my mind, her pained smile.

Some people never get what's coming to them.

I sat back in my chair, crossing one leg over the other before advancing again. "I was researching Lexi's early performances, and I came across your name more than once in connection with another up-and-coming singer."

"And who might that be?"

"Ava Petrova? She performed under the name Ava Arcana. By all accounts, she and Lexi were inseparable."

A look of incredulity passed over his face. *"Ava?"* he said slowly. "Now there's a name I haven't heard in ages."

"Is it true that you'd been interested in signing her back then?"

"She was certainly talented enough," he said as he picked up a pencil and began hitting it against the desktop in a sharp staccato beat, "but she was a bit of a tight-ass. She could've benefited from some loosening up."

I had the sudden urge to reach across the desk, grab the pencil, and stab him with it. Somehow, I managed to restrain myself.

"Benefited how?" I asked lightly.

Christian let out a sigh, leaning forward in his chair. "That's a pretty naive question, don't you think, Kayla?"

"Is it?"

He stared at me with a smug condescension. "The music business can't be that much different than the magazine world."

I frowned. "I'm not quite sure what you mean by that, Christian."

Without responding, he reached forward, pressing a few buttons on the intercom on his desk. A woman's voice entered the room, even and pleasant with a slight British accent. I pictured her dressed in a fifties cardigan and a pencil skirt, her blonde hair set in careful finger waves.

"Yes, Mr. Vane?"

"Marcy, can I get an Americano?" He paused, looking up at me. "Would you care for anything?"

189

"Maybe just a water," I said, if only to clear the bad taste from my mouth.

"Right away, Mr. Vane," the voice said crisply, and then there was silence.

"Sorry," he said with a smile, "but I haven't quite reached my target heart rate for the day. Where were we?"

"You were asking me if I thought journalism was much different than the music industry."

"There's a certain amount of quid pro quo in *any* industry, don't you think?" Christian said, sitting back and crossing one leg over the other. "You scratch my back and I'll scratch yours."

"What are you saying?"

"I thought I made that clear, Ms. McCray: I'm not *saying* anything," Christian replied tersely just as the door opened and a young woman entered, carrying a tray holding a coffee cup and a bottle of water. She was dressed entirely in black, her ebony hair shorn in a severe, triangulated bob, her face devoid of makeup. Heavy silver rings hung from her ears, and a diamond stud shone in one nostril. She placed the tray down on the desk in front of Christian, who nodded at her in thanks, and then slipped out the door noiselessly, exiting as quickly as she'd arrived.

"The night Ava died," I said, changing the subject, "you had dinner at Balthazar with both Ava and Lexi. Did anything with Ava seem . . . off that night?"

"I'm not sure what you mean by 'off,'" he said, picking up the coffee and bringing it to his lips. "And are you seriously questioning me about some insignificant event that took place more than a decade ago?"

"I suppose I am," I said evenly. "Did you see anyone leave with them that night?"

"We'd been *drinking*," he said as if I were dense. "And even under the most sober of circumstances, it was still thirteen years ago. I can barely remember the events of last week, Ms. McCray."

I took a swallow of water, tilting the bottle a little too quickly, and a rivulet ran over my chin. I reached up and swiped at my face with one hand, hoping he hadn't noticed. But when our eyes met again, he gave me a sly smile. Christian Vane was the kind of man who noticed everything. Especially one's weaknesses.

I cleared my throat and began again. "When I was investigating Ava's death, I came across the toxicology report. There was ketamine in her system. And fentanyl. One of your former assistants claims that you drugged her with this exact same cocktail one night after an industry function. I've seen a toxicology report. It checks out."

"Two young women happen to ingest the same drugs and it's some big conspiracy?" he said nonchalantly. "Coincidence is more like it."

"If that's so, it's quite the coincidence."

He stared at me, his upper lip twitching as if he were trying his best not to sneer, and I felt the molecules in the room shift ever so slightly. It was almost imperceptible, but I'd been trained to look for tells like these for my entire career.

"Who exactly," he began icily, leaning forward in his chair, "do you think you are? Coming in here on your high horse and accusing me—of what?"

"I'm not accusing anyone of anything," I said calmly. "I'm asking you a question."

"Aren't you here to interview me for a story on Lexi Mayhem?" he asked, his voice rife with indignation. I could sense his rage simmering just below the surface, and I wondered what it looked like when it was unleashed. I remembered the terrified look on Bella's face as she described the night in that hotel room, the drugs making the world tilted and unfamiliar as a fun-house mirror, Christian looming over her, and I knew that I didn't want to find out.

"What could you possibly be getting at with this kind of innuendo?" he went on. "Do I need to inform your boss of your impudence?

It only takes a phone call," he said, as if he could do anything and get away with it. And maybe he could. Maybe he *had*.

Wasn't that why I was there?

"In my experience," I said, "someone who responds with threats when they're confronted with sensitive information usually has something to hide."

"We all have something to hide." He glared at me with undisguised contempt. "You, me. Even Lexi Mayhem. But if you're asking me if I had something to do with Ava Petrova's death, the answer is no. Now get the fuck out of my office."

I stood up sharply, my face hot with anger. I managed to hold my tongue as I picked up my bag and headed for the door, opening it and filling the room with harried footsteps and ringing phones. Before I could say something I'd regret, I closed it behind me and headed to the elevator.

In the lobby, I pushed through the crowd to exit the building, walking briskly through the glass-ceilinged atrium full of plants and through the revolving doors to the street. But what Christian had said about Ava kept nagging at me. *She could've benefited from some loosening up.* What had really happened between them? After all, if Christian crossed the line with every female in his path, then why would Ava have been any different? Or Lexi? At best, Lexi had tolerated Christian's advances in exchange for fame and fortune, which wasn't exactly a breaking news story—or any kind of shocking cover-up either.

But maybe it wasn't just that Lexi had turned a blind eye—a strange choice for the head of a feminist record label—but that *everyone* did. They'd excused Christian's abuse for years, simply because of his reputation as a hitmaker. The songs climbed the charts, and the girls were laid down on beds in opulent suites, their lifeless bodies shining in the lamplight as the clothes came off, one hand over their mouths to stifle their screams.

He hurt me, Kayla.

Astrid's voice penetrated my thoughts, and my eyes instantly stung with salt, tears that I wiped away as fast as they appeared, my breath coming quickly. I couldn't even remember the last time I'd cried, and if I started, I knew I might never stop. I took a breath, willing myself to let the memory go. But I couldn't. Because now, just as I was then, I was silent, the memory trapped inside me like carbon embedded in quartz, a black haze dulling the clear shine.

I walked down Broadway, the spring air lifting the hair from the back of my neck. I could almost feel Jamie's hands on my skin, and I had to fight myself not to reach for my cell and call him before I could talk myself out of it; we hadn't spoken since the day he'd asked me to leave, but I missed him with an ache that surprised me. Instead, I ducked into the subway, the humid air hitting me in the face along with a mildewy, rank smell I couldn't quite identify mixed with the acrid sting of urine. I stepped over a large, unidentifiable puddle, swiped my MetroCard, and walked down to the platform, every step taking me farther into the bowels of the city.

What really happened on that rooftop? I wondered as I stood on the platform, craning my neck in search of the rush of wind that would signal the oncoming train. I could almost see Ava standing on the roof, the tar beneath her bare feet, the moonlight bleaching her hair white as bone, her face in profile as she perched on the edge, staring out into the night, the lights of the city shining like pinpricks of stars, oblivious to what might lurk in the shadows.

AVA

2006

In the studio, it was always three a.m., the red lights in the booth reminding me of New Orleans. The stately houses of the garden district, moss creeping on stone walls, elaborately carved marble angels in cemeteries, stuck in time, the days slipping by like so much brackish water. *We'll go there together one day,* Lexi had said one night as we teetered on the edge of sleep, the windows cracked to let in the patter of spring rain. *We'll eat beignets until our teeth ache at Café du Monde and drink Hurricanes at the bars on Bourbon Street.*

There was something about the studio, the sanctity of the space itself, dark, reserved, and private. It made me want to make questionable decisions, to spill my secrets like so much ripe fruit into willing hands. Everything was moving at a quicksilver pace now, and at each show, there were more scouts, more label execs. I could feel them circling like hyenas, following the scent of blood in the air. A few weeks ago, I'd never even heard of a showcase, and now I was preparing to sing for a group of men who could, with the stroke of a pen, change the course of my life forever.

And Lexi's too.

"It's a private performance for the suits," Lexi had explained patiently as we'd restocked the bar in the early evening, my hands filled with bottles of cherries, their red eyes winking in amber syrup. "A kind of audition. A chance for them to see you in action. And it's at Webster Hall!" she said excitedly. "The big time!"

She took the jars from my grasp, opening the lids in a manner so practiced, it made my heart ache. Lexi belonged not behind the bar but onstage, her ears drowning in the rush of applause. "I can't believe it's all finally happening," she said, the sweat on her brow glinting in the light. But unlike Lexi, all I wanted was for time to slow to a crawl, just so we might keep these small moments before the wave arched majestically in the distance.

Before it crashed on the shore.

I looked down at the yellow pad in my lap, the scrawl of words filling the page, and then over at Lexi's pad, which was almost blank. Lexi sighed heavily, bringing the pen to her lips and placing one end between her teeth, biting down on the hard plastic. I could feel her anxiety, an invisible signal like a dog whistle. I was already finished while Lexi was still struggling to find the words. She tore the page off the pad, crumpled it between her palms, and then threw it across the room with a frustrated cry.

"It's OK, Lex," I said carefully, knowing how sensitive she was about her writing. "It'll come. Just relax. Everybody gets stuck sometimes."

She shot me a murderous look, jumped to her feet, then began pacing around the booth as if she were looking for a way out. "I'm not everyone else, though," she snapped. "I'm Lexi *fucking* Mayhem. And *you* don't," she said, stopping in place and pointing at me with the pen as if it were a sword.

"I don't . . . what?" I asked, not wanting to hear the answer.

"You don't get *stuck*," she said, stopping to look at me, an edge creeping into her voice. "You could write a song in your *sleep*. I'd be surprised if you haven't already."

"Lexi, you OK in there? You want to run the track again?"

The voice of Simon, the recording engineer, came over the intercom, startling me. Lexi turned and smiled at him. Sharp incisors and stardust. That ineffable sheen she could turn on and off at will. It was only a little after ten p.m., but Simon already looked exhausted, burrowed deep in a gray hoodie, a black ball cap pulled over his eyes.

"I'm good right now," she called back before slumping down on the floor beside me.

"Let me see," I said, getting up and walking over to the corner where she'd thrown her lyrics, uncurling the crumpled paper and smoothing it out.

"Noooo," she moaned again, lying on her back and staring up at the ceiling. My boots were soundless on the thick carpeting as I made my way back over to her.

"There are some great lines here. *You use the little girls, break all the little girls, take all the little girls?* That's really good!" I said encouragingly.

"It's shit," she replied, sitting up and making a grab for my pad. "Lemme see yours."

"It's not really finished," I protested as she peered down at the paper, then up at me again, her expression quizzical.

"Do I thrill in your spine, no breath, a dying song, your lips on mine?" She read it aloud, the words making the blood rise in my face, pinkening it. "Pretty juicy stuff. Who's that about anyway? Surely not Ian!" She cackled mischievously, shoving the pad at me.

Jamie. It's about Jamie. And the way I wonder if he thinks about me when we're apart the way I think about him. But there is no way to tell you, Lex. No way at all.

Not that won't cause you pain.

"It's not about anyone," I said quickly. "I made it up." My face twisted with the effort. I hated lying—especially to Lexi. With every untruth that dropped from my lips, I pulled another brick out of the wall of our friendship. Soon there would be only dust.

The studio door opened, and there was Jamie, his pale eyes warming at the sight of me. He wore the leather jacket I loved, and just the thought of his naked body beneath the jeans and sky-blue shirt he wore made me feel like I'd been punched. His assistant trailed two steps behind him, a soft black hat crushed down on his head, a phone pressed to one ear.

"How's it going, ladies?" Jamie asked, waving at Simon before turning his attention to us.

"Horrible!" Lexi moaned, letting out a sigh so enormous, I wondered if she'd been holding it in all night long. "Ava's already done, if you can believe that." She scowled, and I stuck my tongue out at her, making her laugh. I could always make her laugh.

"You'll get it, Lex," Jamie said soothingly, coming over and pulling her to her feet. "You always do, right?"

"I guess so," she said grudgingly, but I could tell she wasn't entirely convinced.

"You got this," Jamie said again firmly, and a pang of jealousy shot through me. It was what he always said to me, right before I went onstage. For the first time I let myself wonder what else Lexi and I shared with him. She smiled softly, reaching out and punching his arm lightly.

"You little *punk*," she said, her tongue caressing the word almost lovingly. "Some help you are, arriving at practically the last minute."

"I'm sure you survived just fine." Jamie laughed.

"I'm running to the ladies' room," Lexi announced, walking to the door, "and when I get back, I want to run the track again," she declared, the excitement creeping back into her voice. "So Jamie can hear it."

"You got it," Jamie said as she opened the door that led to the hallway, the bathroom that waited just down the corridor, and vanished behind it. Jamie's assistant finally hung up, smiling at me apologetically, and walked into the engineering booth, where Simon turned dials on the mixing board. I could see them both through the glass, the sight of their silent laughter sending an eerie shiver through me.

"Hey," Jamie said, standing before me. "You OK?"

"I'm good," I said quickly, fighting my need to reach out and touch him, to pull him toward me. He looked at me curiously, taking in the way I bit my lower lip, the nervous look in my eyes.

"No," he said, taking a step closer. "You aren't. What's going on?" His face was filled with concern, and I knew that if he touched me, I'd crumble. I stared over Jamie's left shoulder and into the booth, where Simon and Jamie's assistant were still chatting away obliviously.

"I don't feel right about it."

"About what?"

I didn't answer, just looked down at my boots. Anywhere but his eyes.

"About *what*, Ava?" he asked insistently, and this time I looked up.

"About *this*." I gestured at the space between us. "About *us*. It's not right."

"That's bullshit," he said calmly. "'Right' is literally the *only* word that describes us. And you know it."

"That's not what I meant," I said hurriedly, unable to keep the edge of frustration from my voice. "It doesn't feel right to hide it from Lexi anymore. Honestly, it never did. Not to me. She's my friend. My *best* friend, Jamie. And I'm lying to her every day."

Just saying the words out loud made me feel the intensity of the shame I routinely buried now, along with the pang of fear that somehow, I'd become my worst self. The kind of woman who betrayed a friendship for the oldest and most pathetic reason in the book.

A man.

"Listen," he said, taking my hands in his and squeezing them reassuringly. "We're going to tell her eventually, right? Let's just wait until the dust settles a bit, OK?"

I nodded, but inside I was screaming. *What dust? What settling?* Even so, I nodded and agreed, though every cell in my body told me it was wrong. I did what I had always done. Even though I knew that I was signing my own death warrant. But instead of my head, it was our friendship on the chopping block.

I glanced over at the engineering booth, and behind the wall of thick glass, Jamie's assistant peered at us curiously. His posture was rigid, as if he were watching us intently. Then, as our eyes met, his placid expression morphed, became knowing, maybe even a bit smug. It was like a veil falling. He nodded at me once, a smile on his thin lips before turning away and resuming his conversation with Simon.

A pang of fear shot through me as Lexi entered with a bang and a clatter, laughing as she shut the door behind her, leaving only an uneasy feeling in my gut. *Nothing happened,* I told myself as Lexi walked into the booth, throwing her head back with laughter at something Jamie's assistant said. I knew that despite the return of her humor, we were running out of time, the clock counting down to whatever denouement awaited us all. And when the explosion came, how could it not decimate all we had shared?

How could it not blow everything to bits?

I wrapped my arms around myself and held on, wondering if I could weather the storm.

KAYLA

2019

It had been two weeks since that awful day at Jamie's apartment, the silence stretching between us like a fraying rope. There were no more arms pulling me close. No hot breath in my ear. No eager hands exploring the curves of my skin. My phone had never seemed so dead, so defiantly useless. Each time it pinged with an incoming text, my heart leaped in my chest, and I would grab at it with hopeful fingers. But when I stared at the glowing screen, my stomach inevitably sank in disappointment. It was never him.

Until one morning, it was.

Can we talk? Coffee maybe?

A quick one, I'd written back, suddenly wide awake, before I head into the office.

I'd then promptly fallen into a black hole of Yelp reviews looking for the perfect neutral spot near my hood but not *in* it. All I needed was for him to end up back in my bed. I was determined to keep things on the level this time, at least until I knew where we stood. After all, the last time we'd seen each other, he'd practically ordered me out of his apartment—and his life.

We sat awkwardly across from one another at a small, wobbly table placed just outside the front door of the coffee joint I'd chosen in Bed-Stuy. The place was full of hipsters and their laptops, and the barista, although covered in tattoos, looked like he was fresh out of high school. I'd dressed in my favorite faded jeans and a loose white shirt, my black leather jacket thrown over it all, despite the mild weather, trying to look as though I didn't care. And when he approached me, dressed nearly identically, we couldn't help but laugh out loud.

"Great minds and all," he'd said, leaning in to kiss me on the cheek, and I closed my eyes at the delicious nearness of him. There was no explaining or accounting for his effect on me. It was like a panther had just strolled down the street and into my arms. Seductive and feline, sharp with musk.

"I didn't know if you'd even want to see me," he said a few minutes later, raising a paper cup to his lips. "But I figured it was worth a shot."

"Well," I replied, fidgeting with the straw in my iced coffee, "I'm here, aren't I?"

"I'm sorry about what happened," he began hesitantly. "And that it's taken me this long to reach out. I needed some time to cool off and think things through. But I wanted to apologize for shutting down on you."

"It's OK," I said, as if his dismissal hadn't sliced right through me.

"No, it isn't," he said intently, and as always, it was as if he could see past the thin covering of my skin and into the core of my being. Had he looked at Ava the same way? A pang of jealousy shot through me. I didn't want to know. "I'm still not over her death, and I don't know if I ever really will be. It's not the easiest thing for me to talk about."

"I get that," I said woodenly, the jealousy still thick in my chest, a virus contaminating everything. Turning it rotten.

"So . . . where does this leave us?" he asked.

"I'm not sure," I admitted. "It probably shouldn't have happened in the first place."

"But it did," he said, his voice softer now. "And I'd like to give it another try."

Everything in me wanted to pull him to me and fall into his arms. The feeling was so strong that it almost toppled me. I didn't answer, just looked down into my coffee, unsure of what to say.

"I'm not sure what happened the night Ava died." He leaned forward, pushing his cup to the side and resting his arms on the table. "But I'll tell you what little I know."

"That didn't work out so well last time," I pointed out.

"Try me," he said, leaning back in his chair and crossing his arms over his chest.

"What was going on between Lexi and Ava?" I asked, trying my best to refocus my attention. "You mentioned that they were best friends."

"That would be putting it mildly." He ran one hand over the scruff on his chin, the blond hairs glinting in the sunlight. I could hear the rasp they made against his palm, and it pulled at me like a song. "They were inseparable. Until the suits started sniffing around and it became a competition."

"Why compete at all?" I asked, frowning as I picked up my cup, the condensation on the plastic dampening my hands.

Jamie nodded. "I always thought they were so different as musicians. But I guess not everyone agreed. Especially Christian Vane."

"He was interested in signing them, right?"

"Only one of them," he said as he uncrossed his arms and grabbed his cup, cradling it between his hands. "He was hitting on them both, playing them against one another. He has a bit of a reputation, as I'm sure you've heard." A look of disdain crossed his face. "And things between them just imploded."

"I had a friend like that once," I found myself saying aloud, more to myself than Jamie. "A long time ago." The trees swirled around me in a shower of green, the small steel tables lining the sidewalk slowly fading from view, and just like that, I was sixteen again, walking the hallway outside the science lab, that stretch of corridor that reappeared without warning in my dreams, the walls a dusty, faded turquoise.

We were arm in arm, Astrid and I, as Scott strolled down the hall toward us, a half smile on his lips. As we passed, his eyes slid over Astrid's expectant face—and locked on mine. I felt my cheeks burn, and I stopped where I stood, watching him pass by, disappearing around the corner. It was like being hypnotized, as if some invisible force drew me to him, my mouth dry with wanting. *Magnets,* I thought, my brain dense and cloudy with lust.

Fire.

"What was *that?*" Astrid pulled on my arm, her face masked in confusion. "Why were you staring at him?" There was no answer except what I couldn't say, not even to myself. That I wanted him for myself. I wanted him the way she did.

Maybe even more.

"I-I didn't," I finally managed to sputter. "I just—" But before I could finish, her eyes narrowed, and she turned her back on me, walking quickly down the hall as if she couldn't wait to get away from me. The thought made my stomach churn, and I stood there, unable to move forward, wanting only to go back.

"Kayla?" I jerked my head up, flashing Jamie an apologetic smile. How long had I been down that rabbit hole? Seconds? A minute? Time had lost all meaning. "You still here?" He peered at me cautiously, as if at any moment I might crack.

"Sorry," I said with a little laugh, hoping it sounded carefree, not the cackle one exudes before plunging headfirst into the abyss.

"You were saying something about a friend?"

"Yeah," I said, clearing my throat and wrapping my fingers around the damp plastic cup as if it could steady me. Or make what I needed to say next any easier. "Astrid. We were best friends for . . ." My voice trailed off as I tried to think of a time when my life hadn't included her. "Forever, really." I shrugged. "At least that's how it felt."

"What happened?"

I could feel the limitations of words as I struggled to find my own, how unless they were written down on paper, you were never sure they'd come out exactly right. I could rewrite an article over and over, moving slowly toward a kind of perfection—or at the very least, completion—but talking felt like diving headfirst onto a minefield.

"What you've said about Ava and Lexi? What happened between Astrid and me wasn't dissimilar," I said finally. "But it wasn't music that split us apart."

"What, then?"

"The most predictable thing," I said as I tried to smile, but the skin on my face felt unnaturally tight, as if I'd been sealed under a layer of plastic wrap. "A guy."

Jamie nodded, and I looked over at the street at the cars driving past, the joggers sprinting by. Anything to stay in the moment and keep talking. Because all at once I knew that I wanted to tell him what I'd never breathed a word of to anyone else. About Astrid and me—and what happened that night at the party. But something inside me pulled me back from the edge, placing a soft hand on my shoulder and whispering, *Wait. Not now.*

Not yet.

I remembered the coldness in Astrid's eyes, once so warm and guileless when they'd looked my way, and I shivered, hard. I could see the roof in my mind's eye, Lexi and Ava standing at the edge, the city lights in the distance. Had they been arguing that night? Was there a moment when Lexi reached out a hand, resting it on Ava's shoulder? It wouldn't have taken much. Ava's hair blowing in the wind, the pale strands obscuring her vision before she pushed them away with one hand, Lexi moving toward her determinedly . . .

"Do you think there's any possibility," I began slowly, "that Ava didn't just fall that night? That Lexi could've pushed her?"

"Lexi was unconscious. Completely blotto. By all accounts, she could barely walk, much less commit murder."

"What I asked," I said, refusing to let it go, "is if you think it's *possible*."

Jamie was quiet for a moment, looking down at the table. A breeze ruffled his hair, and my drink sat in front of me, shards of ice melting into the caramel-colored liquid. There was the sound of laughter from the table of twentysomething girls seated across from us, and their clear voices in the humid air, the herbal scent of their clove cigarettes reminding me of Astrid, of Lexi and Ava, of all that had been lost.

"I think," he said quietly, looking up to face me, "Lexi Mayhem is capable of just about anything."

AVA

2006

We walked the streets of the Lower East Side, his hands at my waist, stopping every few feet and trading sidelong glances at each other, the same look of wonder in my eyes mirrored in his own. It was one of those days where the sun makes everything new, and there was a humming in the air, the sky a sparkling cobalt blue. It had been a week of waking in his bed, the damp sheets cradling our bodies, late-night phone calls, the sound of his breath in my ear making my blood run fast with desire. I was all longing, heat, and wanting.

I couldn't get enough of him.

I didn't want to.

We were suddenly in front of my building, and I blinked up at the stone facade in amazement. Time seemed to disappear when we were together, folding in on itself like a magic trick. "Come up?" I asked, not wanting to let go of him just yet.

"Can't," Jamie said. "I have to stop by the office for a sec." He squeezed my hand in his own, then let it go. "Gotta pick up some paperwork. But I'll be by later, OK?"

"OK." I grinned as he leaned in for a quick kiss, then made his way down the block.

Inside my apartment, take-out containers littered the kitchen counter, and there were piles of discarded clothes on the floor by the bed. Over the past week, I'd been too preoccupied with work and Jamie to do much cleaning, and I immediately marched into the kitchen, turning on the faucet and covering the dishes in the sink in a layer of bubbles. I threw the windows in the one large room wide open, the white sheets I'd tacked up as curtains moving gently in the breeze. Once upon a time, Lexi had helped me tack those sheets, teetering on a chair, one foot dangling in midair, her hands moving deftly, capably, and a frisson of anxiety shot through me at the memory. Would she still be my friend when she found out about Jamie and me?

As I finished stripping the bed, balling the sheets up in my arms, there was a sudden knock at the door, and I smiled, tossing the sheets back onto the bare mattress, ringed with mysterious stains. I walked to the door, throwing it open wide, fully expecting to see Jamie's smiling face looking back at me.

But it was Lexi who stood there on my doorstep, as if I'd unknowingly broken whatever hex had kept us apart, wearing a black denim miniskirt, a scarlet silk shirt knotted just above her navel, the studs on her leather jacket the gunmetal gray of ammunition. Her dark hair was pulled into two low pigtails that spilled over her shoulders, her ears lined with rows of silver hoops. I remembered how she squeezed my hand so hard when the needle pierced her flesh, the hollow pop of cartilage making me flinch. We might have been strangers now, and I felt the smile slide from my face, replaced by what I knew was a stricken look. Panic.

"Lexi," I blurted out, "what are you doing here?"

I wanted to snatch back the words the moment I uttered them. She just stood there, staring at me. Daring me to tell her to leave. But I couldn't. Would never. And she knew that too.

"Aren't you going to ask me in?"

Without hesitation, I opened the door wide, and she stepped inside, a space she'd been to so many times before. But now the air was charged with a dangerous friction, and everything between us was different. I followed her inside, closing the door behind me, and she turned to face me as if preparing for battle.

"Expecting someone?" she said, looking around the room as if there might be a figure lurking in the corner. "Someone besides me, that is."

"I was just . . . ," I said, aware that my voice sounded weak and apologetic. That I felt like prey. Beneath my arms was damp with sweat already, and I could feel my body beginning to shake, like a tree in a sudden wind. Lexi could bend me any way she wanted. And she knew it. "Cleaning up," I finished.

"You're good at that, aren't you," she said. "Cleaning up the little messes you make?" The way she looked at me. As if I were no one she knew, no one she had ever known. It tore me in two. "Do you think I'm an idiot?"

"What do you mean?" I asked, even though I knew. I knew before she spoke even one more syllable.

"You and Jamie." She took a step toward me, dropping her arms to her sides. The room was warm, despite the open windows, and I wondered if she was sweating the way I was. "I know you've been screwing him behind my back."

I felt as if someone had shut a door quickly, catching the ends of my fingers in its hinges. I winced and took a step back, as if to guard myself from her words. She looked at me mockingly, a slow burn in her green gaze.

She's jealous. She's jealous of me. Of Jamie and me.
Of everything.

"Lexi," I said when I could speak again. "It's not like that. What happened between Jamie and me . . ." My voice trailed off. The easy

208

banter between Lexi and myself was gone now. Every word, every sentence, drove us further apart.

"So it's some big love story? Is that it?" She reached up and adjusted one of her pigtails, rings glinting on her long fingers.

"I should've told you," I said, bowing my head, the shame overtaking me. "I'm sorry. It was wrong." She moved closer, so close that I could see the tiny pores on her face, the black liner smeared beneath her eyes in the midday heat. A tiny pimple along her jawline, angry and inflamed.

"It's all so easy for you, isn't it, Ava?" I could feel her shaking with rage, a high whine that set my teeth on edge. She looked me up and down, an overflowing dumpster filled with rats and rusty cans, empty bottles, stray cats whining along the perimeter, and I felt myself shrinking down as I saw myself through her eyes. "You come here, and within a few weeks you have a career and a manager—a manager I *gave* you. I got you a job, hooked you up with Jamie, gave you a *name*, and this is how you repay me? You stab me in the back."

"Lexi, it's not like that. You're my friend. My best friend," I whispered, afraid to say the words, no matter how true they were. Even if she didn't believe them anymore.

"Some *best friend*," she sneered. "You don't care about me at all. I was just too blind to see it—until now."

She stared at me contemptuously, tiny beads of sweat dotting her upper lip, and for a moment I wondered if I could somehow be the traitor she claimed. But whether I was or not, I knew that whatever I did or said didn't matter now. Once Lexi was done with someone, she was finished, and there was nothing that would change her mind. Our friendship was gone, blown away in the storm as if it had been as insubstantial and weightless as cellophane.

"It's clear where your priorities lie, little Ava—and Jamie's too," she said, turning away and walking to the door, yanking it open before I could respond. "You two deserve each other," she said as she stood in the doorway, her back to me.

Don't go, I thought but didn't dare say the words aloud. *Not like this.*

I stood there hoping that she'd turn around, say she was only kidding. That she had a new song she was dying to sing for me. That she was starving, and we needed pad thai right now. *C'mon,* she'd laugh before linking her arm through mine again, pulling me down the long flights of stairs to the street below. And when the sun dipped in the sky, I'd fall asleep with her hand in mine, her drowsy, soft weight pinning me to the bed.

I counted to five, praying under my breath that she wouldn't let it end this way.

Please.

I closed my eyes, holding my breath, and as I did so, I heard the door slam shut. It was only then that I finally let my tears fall, my heart splintering in my chest. I went to the window, watching as she exited the building, her long legs moving fast, propelling her away from me as if I'd never existed.

As if I'd never been a part of her world at all.

KAYLA

2019

The office was always quiet in the lull right after lunch, a meal I was ignoring so Keats could fit me into his already packed schedule. In the bullpen, reporters lolled at their desks, and a cluster of bodies formed at the front of the room near the coffee machines, counting on a burst of caffeinated energy to get through the remainder of the day. When I'd called that morning and requested a few moments to discuss the Mayhem story, his tone conveyed all he didn't need to say out loud: *This had better be good, Kayla.*

The walls of his office were lined with framed *Rolling Stone* covers, and Tina Turner, the Beatles, and Kesha stared down at me as if in silent judgment. Keats sat behind his desk, which was clutter-free, the blond wood gleaming as if he'd just polished it moments before I'd walked in. And knowing Keats? He probably had.

I took a deep breath, waiting for him to quit typing and acknowledge my presence. As usual, he was nattily turned out in gray tweed, a red silk square protruding from the pocket of his blazer, his wavy dark hair brushed neatly, the temples sprinkled with gray. In contrast, the navy yoga pants and Michigan State sweatshirt I wore made me look like I'd just rolled out of bed.

"Done," Keats said, tapping a few more keys before closing his laptop and blinking at me curiously from behind his spectacles. "Get me up to speed."

"I wanted to update you on the Av—on the Mayhem story," I said, catching Ava's name before it slipped out of my mouth.

"I'm listening," he replied, setting the pencil down on the desk.

"In the process of researching Lexi Mayhem's early career, I came across some archived footage of one of her early shows. In the video, I saw Lexi with a young woman who could've been her sister, the resemblance was that uncanny."

Keats nodded. "Go on."

I uncurled my legs, placing them flat on the floor before continuing. "Her name was Ava Petrova. She was on the brink of pop stardom when she allegedly jumped off the roof . . . of Lexi Mayhem's building. I tracked down Ava's mother out on Staten Island, and she gave me complete access to Ava's remaining belongings. I'm still going through them, but it's clear that Ava was massively talented. Would've been a huge star."

"And before that could happen, she killed herself?" Keats frowned.

"Allegedly. But I spoke to the detective who handled the case, and I got the feeling he didn't buy it. Her mother didn't either . . . It's why I started looking into it to begin with. I mean, on paper it's an open-and-shut suicide. Lexi was apparently on the roof at the time of Ava's death but so inebriated that she was practically comatose. But it seems that even so, there's more to it. Christian Vane was making a play for them back then, wanting to sign one of them to Phoenix—but not the pair."

"He ended up signing Lexi, didn't he? I seem to remember Phoenix being her first major label deal."

"He did, but only after Ava died. I've been wondering if Christian—and maybe even Lexi—might've played a bigger part in Ava's death."

"What do you mean?"

"I tracked down Vane's former assistant, who claims that he drugged and assaulted her one night after an industry function—with the same drugs that were found in Ava's system the night she died. And if that's his pattern, his track record, it's probably been going on a long time. Maybe he tried something with Ava? Maybe he even had something to do with her death."

"Hmm," Keats mused, bringing a hand up to his chin and stroking a nonexistent beard, the way he always did when lost in thought. "Interesting. But it's a real stretch. A murder? A cover-up? This is real life, Kayla. Not a Netflix series."

"OK, but even if it is, there's a *story* here, Keats," I said, holding my hands out in the air. "Even if it's not Christian, something happened up on the roof that night. Something nobody knows about. Granted, it's not the feature you asked me to write, but I can't shake it. I'm asking you to give me a few more days to see where it leads."

Keats nodded slowly. I could see the wheels spinning in his brain as he turned over every possible angle in consideration. Because that was Keats and the way he operated. There was never a simple yes-or-no answer. He sat back in his chair and smiled, his thin lips stretched taut.

"Did you know that when I was twenty-five years old, I fucking hated Lexi Mayhem?" he said airily, as if he'd just told me he was headed out to pick up his dry cleaning. "She went out of her way to make my life miserable for a while."

I sat there, dumbfounded.

"You . . . *hated* Lexi?"

"I was freelancing for *Village Voice* back then, covering live music. I panned one of Lexi's early performances—and she literally hunted me down. Demanded that I give her another listen. I did what she wanted because it was clear she was never going to give up otherwise—and that second show was *still* awful. So I ended up giving her *another* bad review. And that was it: I was on her shit list for years. And trust me,"

Keats said, suddenly serious now, "once you make an enemy of Lexi, she never forgets. And she'll make sure you don't either."

We sat there in silence for a moment, every muscle in my body tense, as if bracing for impact. And then Keats spoke again.

"Listen, it's a great story, Kayla. I'll grant you that," he said, reaching over and grabbing his cell phone and scrolling through it distractedly. Keats could never go more than ten minutes without checking his email or returning a text. "But the question is, can you prove any of it? Even if you could, we'd be tied up with legal for years."

"I know," I admitted. "It's a long shot. But I want to try. Can't you understand that?"

"Of course," he said, putting his phone back down. "I sat where you're sitting once, too, you know." He gestured to my chair with one hand. "But these are powerful people you're dealing with, Kayla. And I can only protect you to a certain extent."

"Protect me from *what*?"

"You don't want to find out what happens when you start poking around in a story someone *really* doesn't want told," Keats said quietly. I nodded, but inside I knew I was well on my way to doing that already. "But I still want you to follow your instincts. Just move quickly, tread carefully, and share what you've got with me before you accuse anyone of things we can't take back. I'll give you a few more days to follow this. But that's it. And I want you to keep working on the story you've been assigned simultaneously, so that we have something to run if your theories don't pan out. You'll need to work overtime if you want to do both," he finished, shooting me a weary glance as he opened his laptop again and began typing, which was the usual sign to get the hell out of his office, pronto. Keats would never do anything as direct or banal as actually tell you to leave.

I stood up, hovering in front of his desk, waiting for him to look up. "Thanks," I said when he finally did, looking at me as if he were surprised I was still there.

"You're welcome. Just don't go too far down the rabbit hole, OK?" He stared at me for a moment, then looked away and began typing once again.

I turned and walked out the door and into the bullpen, the cacophony of constant chatter and the clacking of keys slightly comforting. I stopped by my desk to answer a few emails and jot down some notes, Simone nowhere to be found, and by the time I looked up again, the room was mostly empty. I stretched my arms overhead, the muscles in my back unclenching, thoughts of the gym forgotten as my stomach began to growl noisily. I'd consumed nothing but a half-eaten bagel that morning, and suddenly I was craving a plate of spicy Thai noodles. A curry maybe? Lime wedges on the side, a tall glass of golden beer. I grabbed my things and headed out.

By the time I exited the building, that hazy blue twilight was beginning to fade, darkness overtaking it. As I walked down Sixth Avenue, I wrestled with my bag, pulling out my AirPods and shoving them in my ears, drowning out the noise of the city. It was only a few blocks to the subway, but I was starving now, impatient. My couch and takeout, the afghan my mother had knitted years ago in her "crafty" phase thrown over my feet, sounded like the definition of heaven.

But I'd barely made it a block down when a strange feeling came over me. My skin began to crawl, bit by bit, the back of my neck tingling with the unmistakable feeling of being watched. I whirled around suddenly, causing a teenager walking directly behind me, silver headphones atop her head, to bump into me, a grimace on her face. "Watch it," she mumbled as she hurried past. My eyes scanned the perimeter, noticing nothing out of the ordinary at first. I craned my neck, looking around from one direction to another, but there was nothing but the crowds hustling past, the sound of belligerent horns.

But then, maybe a half a block down, I spotted him. A man in a black bomber jacket, his eyes hidden behind a pair of dark sunglasses, the brim of the black baseball hat he wore pulled down low. I squinted, trying to get a closer look, and as I did, he stopped dead in his tracks, hovering on the pavement as if he were almost levitating. At that moment instinct overtook me, and I knew I had to run, but my feet were weighed down by invisible steel girders. A sudden gust of wind blew my hair into my eyes, and I pushed it away frantically. And then he took a step toward me. Just one step. But there was something in that small movement that threw me into action.

I sprinted into the street, a bus whizzing dangerously close, so close that I could smell the chemical haze of exhaust, feel the wind generated from the behemoth of metal, its sheer size and speed, and I moved out of the way at the last second. I looked around frantically for a taxi, dashing to the other side of the street and throwing my hand in the air, waving desperately until a cab pulled up in front of me. I yanked the door open and tumbled into the back seat, slamming the door behind me.

"Where to?" the driver asked, turning on the meter.

"Just go," I said anxiously through the glass partition that separated us. "Go *now.*"

"Jesus, lady," he muttered. "You think you're in a movie or something?" Despite the flippancy of his words, he pulled out into traffic and sped down Sixth, merging into incoming traffic so quickly that I was thrown back against the seat. I pulled the seat belt across my chest, snapping it into place, then swiveled my head around to look out the back window as we stopped at the first light. But I saw nothing.

You're losing it, I told myself as the streets sped by, lights changing from red to green as if choreographed by some higher power. But I knew, despite the logic that my rational brain insisted on to survive, my body knew better—and it never lied. It knew that I was being followed. But why? And by whom?

"You gonna tell me where we're goin' now?" The cabbie's voice cut into my thoughts, and he reached over and turned on the radio, the car filling with a lilting Caribbean beat.

"Downtown," I said, peering out the back window again, my nerves on high alert. "But just drive for a few minutes first, OK?"

He shrugged. "It's your dime."

I settled back in the seat, willing my heart to slow as the realization dawned on me. Could this be about the *story*? The thought made my heart speed up again, skipping beats, a sick feeling rushing through me, obliterating the wild hunger I'd felt only moments earlier. I reached for my cell, and when Jamie answered, the sound of his voice, the familiar, deep timbre of it, made my panic begin to recede, the needle moving out of the red, and I forced myself to fill my lungs with air.

"It's me," I said, exhaling as the numbered streets counted down and we moved into the belly of the city. "I need to see you."

AVA

2006

The box arrived by messenger. The length of my arms and stark white, a glossy black bow circling the perimeter, the words "Yves Saint Laurent" printed on the ribbon in white. There were layers of snowy tissue paper inside, and I pawed through them, my hands touching fabric as smooth as water, heavy as iron. A dress made of a swath of pristine cream-colored leather, the smell intoxicating and fierce, as if an animal had entered the room without warning. And perched on top, a thick black card, tarnished with silver ink.

Compliments of Christian Vane.

I walked to the full-length mirror I'd propped up on one wall of my apartment, a mirror Lexi and I had found in the trash piled on the street months ago and lugged up five flights, sweating rivers and stopping to laugh at every landing before collapsing in triumph at the top.

The memory hit me like a dart. A quick sting.

It seemed like forever ago now.

Ever since our fight, she'd avoided me. At first, she simply pushed past me at work, her eyes barely meeting mine, flitting over my face as if it held no interest. And even when they did register my presence before her, it was with a tight smile, as if I were a cipher. Her absence was a hole gouged out of my heart, a chasm not even Jamie could bridge. There were no more after-work dinners, sharing a plate of steaming pancakes, fragrant with scallions and ginger. No whispering into the stillness of the night, the warmth of her foot on mine as I sank deeper into the softness of her bed. No more texts and calls, my phone silent as a stone. No milkshakes at Ray's Candy Store, standing out front as boys sauntered by in packs whispering, *Hey, mami,* Lexi's chin tilted to the heavens as they looked her up and down, lingering on her taut flesh.

Let them look, she'd hiss, a faint smile on her lips. *Someday people will pay for the privilege.*

I didn't doubt it.

Then, after a few days, she vanished from my world completely. It was as if I'd conjured her up to begin with, so swift and immediate was her disappearance. She'd either quit the café outright or changed her shifts so that we never once ran into each other. I was afraid to ask which.

Afraid to know the truth.

I could tell that Jamie was doing his best to juggle the both of us, like spinning twin pianos in the air. In the days leading up to the showcase, he had coached me relentlessly, pushing me onstage at the café over and over until I felt not even the faintest twinge of fear. But there were nights he was gone too. Nights I knew he was working with Lexi. And no matter how attentive he was after he showed back up at my apartment, how deeply he kissed me, his tongue searching my mouth, I couldn't stop the torrent of jealousy from rising in my throat.

But I also missed her. Missed what we had been to each other. *Let her be signed,* I thought to myself as I forced myself through my shifts at work, the time dragging on endlessly. *Let me be signed too.* Because only then would we be on equal footing again. And then maybe what had happened between us would cease to matter. She would get what she'd always wanted, and everything in the past would fade away.

Even my betrayal.

I held the dress to my body, could see how it would hug my flesh tightly, a perfect fit. I stripped naked and stepped in, the coolness of the leather against my bare skin making me shiver. As I zipped up the back, a woman I didn't know stared back at me. Edgy and confident. Untouchable. I moved closer to the glass. No matter what I felt about Christian Vane, it was clear that his instincts were impeccable. This was the dress I'd perform in at tonight's showcase, the armor I hadn't known I needed.

By the time I made it to the Webster Hall, my nervousness was threatening to careen out of control, despite the alcohol. I stepped through the red velvet curtains flanking the doorway, pulled back with glittering tassels. A long wooden bar ran along one wall, and the room was packed with industry execs in suits, talking into their cell phones and looking bored, gold watches shining on their wrists. I teetered on my black ankle boots and walked to the bar to steady myself, leaning against its solid weight.

I made eye contact with the bartender, who walked over lazily, his mass of wavy, dark hair just grazing his collarbone.

"What do you need?" he asked, leaning slightly toward me.

"Shot of mezcal," I shouted over the music, his hands moving swiftly as he poured the liquor into a glass, the coiled worm at the bottom of the bottle winking with one clouded dark eye.

I threw it back in one gulp, tossing a ten onto the bar, and took a deep breath, walking into the crowd, my eyes scanning the room for Jamie, for Lexi, and then the crush of bodies parted, and she was standing in front of me, my mirror image, my twin. The black leather dress she wore hugged her curves as if it had been sewn directly onto her, the very same dress that graced my skin. Her hair was dark, mine platinum, a reverse image, a tintype, a direct exposure on metal, light and dark intermingling until there was no separation between them.

Christian Vane had sent us the same dress.

Suddenly the leather felt as binding as a straitjacket.

Her eyes held my face and moved down, a curious smile playing along the edges of her lips. Her eyes flashed once, contemptuously, then she pushed past me in a cloud of musk and embers and disappeared into the crowd.

The lights dimmed and I heard Jamie saying Lexi's name, and then everything went dark. There was a blaze of light and she exploded onstage, her presence as demonic as the music pounding behind her. She began to sing, that broken, guttural voice I knew so well filling the room, and I forced myself to move, to walk backstage, my limbs languid, as if I were suddenly underwater. I knew if I continued to stand there and watch, self-doubt would swallow me whole, and I turned away before I sank to the bottom.

But before pushing through the door that led backstage, I took one last glance out of the corner of my eye and saw that Lexi had peeled off the black dress, the leather slipping to the floor like the soft, fetid skin of an overripe peach. She stood in front of the microphone clad in only a pair of black tights and a black satin bra, rivulets of sweat running down between her breasts. She shone like a star, all meteor and cosmic dust, and I pushed the door open and stepped inside, leaving her behind.

Ten minutes later, I stood in dimness before the spotlight came up, breathing in through my nose and out my mouth the way Jamie had taught me to calm my nervous system. Then there was the shock of light, like being burned alive, and I smiled and stepped toward the microphone, mouth opening, my voice rising out into the audience. Time folded in on itself, and then there was the sound of applause, overwhelming, the crowd on their feet, whistling and clapping their hands together, my name on their lips.

I knew Lexi was out there in the dark somewhere, glowering. I could feel her displeasure just as I could feel the perspiration sliding down my back, the leather trapping my sweat in its folds, oiling it. But it didn't matter now. I had never wanted us to be pitted against each other. But suddenly I didn't want to lose either. The longer I worked with Jamie, the more I'd begun to crave it. The applause. The validation. For the feeling that I was there in the world, present, important, indisputable—to never end. The stage was the only place now where I felt truly seen, where it was safe to expose the secret melodies that lived inside me.

I held my head high as I walked into the crowd, triumph like an unfamiliar drug coursing through the rivers and channels of my arteries, knowing as I moved that if it was truly a competition between Lexi and me, that against all odds, against even my own tendency to self-sabotage and despite all who might've been betting against me, that this time?

I had somehow come out on top.

KAYLA

"Someone *followed* you?"

Jamie stood in the quiet of his living room, staring at me uncomprehendingly, and I wondered then if maybe my workaholic tendencies had finally culminated in a psychotic break, one that had caused me to hallucinate the entire episode. But deep down, I knew it had happened. He'd been waiting for me. I knew in my gut that he was planning on following me home. And there was no telling what he would've done if he'd caught me.

When Jamie opened the door, it was all I could do not to collapse in his arms. But I also knew that we needed to talk, and no matter how much I wanted to, I couldn't touch him before that happened. As soon as I made it inside, I asked him to close the blinds, hovering nervously as he switched on only one lamp in the living room. Even so, I found myself drawn to the window, compulsively moving the blinds apart a crack and peering out into the darkness.

I pulled off my coat and threw it on the couch, sitting down and waiting for him to speak. Even in a pair of ripped jeans and a ratty gray sweatshirt, at least a week's worth of stubble on his jaw, he was beautiful, and there was the same undeniable pull between us. I wanted to go to him, wrap my arms around him, if only to feel the illusion of safety once again.

The kind that apparently didn't exist anymore.

"What *happened?*" he asked, pushing up the sleeves of his sweatshirt.

"I was leaving work," I said, walking over to the window once again. I moved the blinds back an inch to look outside, but the street was predictably empty. "And I noticed a guy behind me, maybe half a block away, watching me. He was wearing sunglasses and a black baseball hat, so I couldn't really see his face, but this terrible feeling came over me. It was getting dark, and I can't explain it, but I felt *really* unsafe, like I was being stalked. So I jumped into a cab before anything could happen."

"But . . . he could've been anyone, right?" Jamie said slowly. "I mean, it could've just been a guy in a Yankees cap. The city is full of them."

"But it wasn't," I said, coming over to sit beside him. "He was following me. I know it."

Jamie nodded. "OK, well, if that's true, why you?"

"I'm not sure," I admitted. "I think it might have something to do with the story."

"The story on Lexi?" We were mere inches apart, and I could feel the waves of heat coming off his skin. I forced myself to focus.

"I think I'm getting too close to something. Something people don't want me to know about. Powerful people. Like Christian Vane."

"Christian?" Jamie laughed. "What does that old letch have to do with any of this? I think he has enough distractions right now besides worrying about some puff piece on Lexi Mayhem."

"Gee, thanks," I said dryly, and for the first time that day, I smiled.

"Oh, c'mon." He chuckled. "You know what I mean. But seriously, how could he possibly be connected to any of this? Besides the fact that he once worked with Lexi?"

"That's just it. He worked with Lexi. *And Ava.* He's got a history of taking advantage of vulnerable young women—like Ava. Like his own assistants. Maybe that night on the roof, he took it too far."

Jamie just stared at me, and I wondered yet again if I really had lost it. "First of all," he said skeptically, "I think it's a *very* big stretch. Christian on a private jet to the Maldives or in a suite at the Plaza? Sure. Christian on a grimy rooftop on the Lower East Side after midnight? Not a chance."

"That doesn't mean it didn't *happen*," I insisted, pulling my legs beneath my body so that I was sitting on my knees.

"I've found over the years that the most logical—and the most boring—explanation is usually the closest to the truth," Jamie said firmly. "She jumped, Kayla."

"But there was no *reason*," I protested. "She was about to become a huge star. Why would she just end it all?"

"Because sometimes that's what happens!" Jamie said, his voice strained now. "There's no making sense of it. Sometimes there isn't one reason but a whole *lifetime* of them piled up on top of one another. I don't know what happened up there the night Ava died—I try not to think about it—but all I *am* sure of is that sometimes things are just what they seem. Ava took everything hard. She was intense, could be a little withdrawn. Performing was a struggle for her and she could get down about it. I don't know what happened that night, but I knew Ava. And because I knew her, I also know that her jumping off that roof wasn't a complete impossibility."

"But maybe there was—"

"Jesus, Kayla. Why is this so *important* to you? Ava? This whole story? I don't get it."

"Because it matters!" My face flushed with heat. "She had all that promise, and then she was just . . . gone!"

"You didn't know her," he said, his words clipped. He stood up and walked to the center of the room, running a hand through his hair distractedly. "You didn't love her. *I did*. And after she died, I lost it. Started drinking. Staying out all night in clubs. I was trying to drown the pain, or at least numb it out of existence. I was losing clients and people were starting to talk. One morning I woke up in some girl's apartment in a puddle of my own piss, and I said to myself, that's enough. I went to rehab that afternoon, threw some stuff in a backpack, and just showed up there. Sixty days. When I got out, I was drowning in debt, and I'd lost damn near every client I had. But it was worth it to get some clarity back. I started Rukus from the ground up, which *really* put me in the red. But I knew that if I kept on drinking, I would've died. I think maybe some part of me wanted that. Just to be with her again. She's haunted me for years. She just won't *rest*. And now here you are, digging her back up again."

"I know what that feels like," I said in a low voice. So low I wasn't even sure he heard me. I looked down at my lap, not wanting to meet his eyes. "Something happened to me . . . in high school. Well, not to me exactly. To my friend Astrid." I stopped. "But I guess to me too. Because if I'm being honest, I've never been the same."

"You mentioned her before," he said slowly, drifting back over to the couch, hovering there. "That a guy came between you."

Suddenly, it was hard to think, and the words hitched in my throat, stranded there like castaways. Was my heart still beating? I reached up, feeling for the pulse in my neck, and my fingers met a series of reassuring thuds. I could hear Jamie talking, his voice low and steady, but I couldn't make out the words. But I knew I had to keep going, even if it felt like I might die. Somewhere in the periphery, I was aware of Jamie sitting back down beside me, but I ignored the nearness of him, knowing that if I stopped speaking, even for a second, I might never start again.

"It was the end of our junior year. We were at a house party. That whole year she'd had a crush on Scott Alexander. Basketball star, senior.

Untouchable. The kind of guy who is so revered that he gets away with just about anything. You know the type."

Out of the corner of my eye, I saw Jamie nod, and I took a deep breath before continuing. "We were drinking tequila shots, and by midnight we'd already missed curfew. She was in the kitchen in her black T-shirt dress and red Converse high-tops, dancing with guys who'd never talked to her before—including Scott, who was suddenly hanging on her every word. The house was packed body to body, and I could barely hear her yelling over the music."

I stared at a section of hardwood floor in front of me. If I just concentrated on that, I knew I'd be OK. *Don't leave me, OK?* she'd said, leaning over and throwing her arms around me. I closed my eyes for a moment, Jamie and the room itself disappearing, and I could still feel her, sweaty and warm, could smell the sting of alcohol on her breath, mixed with the strawberry body spray she doused herself in every morning.

There was a boulder in my throat the size of a small planet.

"I'm here," I heard Jamie say, as if through a mist, his features shimmering in and out of focus. "I'm listening."

"But the thing is?" I swallowed hard, wanting more than anything to bury the words I knew came next. "I liked him too. Scott. And a few days before the party, he'd walked up to me at my locker after school and asked me to take a walk. We ended up on the football field, behind the bleachers, and once we got there, he pulled me to him and kissed me. But that night at the party, he'd barely even said two words to me. Instead . . . he was focused on Astrid, his eyes tracking her every move. And every time he looked at her and not me, something in my stomach would tighten a little more until I could barely breathe."

Jamie reached over and put one hand on my leg, his touch giving me the strength I needed to go on, to say the words I'd been avoiding for years.

"It got late. I got drunker, and I lost track of her. And then Danny Meyers cornered me in the living room behind a huge potted plant. Danny Meyers, this indie-rock dude who wore skinny jeans, a mop of blond hair always in his face. But I didn't care. Anyone could've had me that night, if only to keep the jealousy from burning me alive. When I finally pulled away, there was this terrible feeling in my gut. I pushed past him and out into the crowd, kicking aside red Solo cups and empty beer bottles, calling Astrid's name. I climbed the stairs and started opening bedroom doors, one after another."

I paused again, for the first time aware that tears were running down my cheeks. I could feel the heat of them turning cold as they met my skin and slid down, dripping onto my neck. It was a constant deluge with no end in sight. But there was nothing cathartic about it. It felt as if the crying were going on somewhere outside myself, in the general vicinity, while inside I was untouched by emotion. If Jamie was still in the room, I didn't register his presence. There was only Astrid and me, and the story that had haunted me for more than a decade.

"I got to the last door," I said, wiping my nose on the back of my hand, "and she was sitting there on the bed in the dark. She looked small, breakable in her white cotton bra. Her black dress was torn at the neck and hanging around her waist."

I stopped, needing to take a breath as my thoughts raced dizzily. I could still see her in the dark of my mind, her skin glowing in the moonlight, making her more ghost than girl. Tears ran down her face, but she made no sound at all. She looked right at me, her eyes wide in the darkness.

He hurt me, Kayla. He hurt me . . . inside.

Who? Who did this to you? I asked. But I already knew.

"Kayla?" Jamie said softly, his voice pulling me back into the present.

"She . . . she said that it was Scott. That he hurt her." I took a deep breath and forced myself to keep going, knowing I had to finish.

"I remember that I reached out and put one hand on her back, and she pulled away and bent over, rocking back and forth. She sank to the floor, and I crouched down, wrapped my arms around her as she cried. And in fragments, she told me what had happened. After I'd disappeared, the room had begun to spin, so she made her way upstairs to lie down. She must've passed out for a while, but when she came to, the bed was rocking, moving back and forth in a strange rhythm, and there was a heavy weight on top of her. She tried to push it off, but it wouldn't budge."

I could feel Jamie's eyes on me, the intensity of his gaze, but I couldn't look at him. My voice sounded hollow, robotic, and I felt as if I were floating outside myself, watching the scene from above.

"Do you want to stop?" Jamie asked, and I shook my head vigorously. I had waited this long to say these words aloud. I owed it to Astrid to finish.

And maybe I owed it to myself too.

"When she opened her eyes," I began again, my voice barely above a whisper, "he was on top of her, a hand over her mouth. She bit down on his fingers, and he slapped her face once. Hard. After that, she just lay there, too scared to move or cry out. He yanked her underwear down, pushing inside her so roughly that she shrieked, but he still had his hand over her mouth, and after a few moments, she went limp, waiting for him to finish. And when he finally did, he climbed off her, zipping his pants, and stood there on the side of the bed looking down at her. *Thanks,* he said, as if he'd just borrowed a pencil. And then he walked out of the room, leaving her alone in the dark."

Jamie was quiet beside me. The tears still hadn't stopped. They were falling of their own accord, unrelenting, like a hose I couldn't turn off. I fell silent, lost in the labyrinth of my thoughts. I could see it all in my mind, as if it were unfolding for the second time right in front of me. I could hear the party still raging downstairs, the bass thumping through the floor. And somewhere down there was Scott, drinking a beer with his buddies.

We have to go to the cops.

Promise me you won't say anything—to anyone, Kayla. Promise me.

But this was rape, Astrid. We have to—

No one will believe me. No one. He practically runs the school. You know I'm right.

But he hurt you. He's a scumbag. At least let's tell your mom, someone, any—

No one. Is going to know about this. And I don't want to ever talk about it ever again.

OK, I saw myself say quietly, and in that moment, she turned away from me, pulling the remains of her dress around her like a shroud.

OK.

"Kayla." I could hear the gentle sound of Jamie's voice, but I could not meet his eyes. I just wanted to finish, to get it all out. Like a bout of sickness I couldn't shake, I needed to finally be empty.

"She wanted to keep quiet. Begged me to." My voice was emotionless and flat as I spoke, as if it belonged to someone else entirely. "I kept my promise and said nothing. I tried to pretend it had never happened, but it hung there between us like a corpse. That summer we barely spoke. I would call and her mother would say she wasn't home. But I knew it was a lie. And all senior year," I said, my voice breaking sharply, "she ignored me. Walked right past me in the halls like I wasn't even there. She wore baggy clothes, ate alone in the cafeteria. Avoided me at graduation. She never spoke to me again." I swallowed hard, looking over at the window, wondering if the man in the black hoodie was outside, waiting for me to leave. "And every time I saw Scott? He smiled at me. Smiled in a way that let me know that he knew that I knew." I began to cry silently as I bent forward, the sobs tearing their way out of my chest, from the very heart of me.

What I couldn't tell Jamie—not yet—was that a few weeks after the party, I'd seen Scott in the hall near my locker, talking to a freshman girl. Avery was her name, young and blonde with legs like matchsticks. She reminded me of a bird just out of its nest, learning to hop tentatively on one foot before she could fly. He leaned in to whisper in her ear and I saw her freeze, her eyes meeting mine, her face going dead and still. And I knew he'd gotten to her too. The shame and regret, almost overwhelming now, were all over me, thick and noxious as vomit, so much that it could never be scrubbed away.

"Kayla," Jamie said, his voice jerking me out of the dark void of my memory. He moved his hand to my shoulder, and I forced myself to finally look at him. "It wasn't your fault. You know that, right?"

His voice was insistent, sure of itself. But he was also a man. He didn't, couldn't, understand the bond between women. Unspoken, intricate as lace and just as fragile.

"You were a *kid*," he said, folding me into his arms, and just the contact of his body on mine, his arms around me, made the tears come faster. I closed my eyes and breathed in the scent of him. Clean laundry, wood chips, and spring air.

"I stayed quiet," I said woodenly. "I did what she asked. And in that silence, I betrayed her, Jamie. I betrayed our friendship."

There was a long pause. Jamie rocked me in his arms, his face buried in my hair.

"Have you reached out to her?" he finally asked. "It's been a long time."

I shook my head, unable to speak, and somehow the shame of that admission burned worst of all. The cowardice of it. I'd told myself there was no way I could even begin to make up for all that had happened, all I had done and failed to do. Going off with Scott. Wanting him for myself. My horrible silence as I watched her walk past me in the halls, her eyes glazed and distant. My voice stolen like something out of a fairy tale. My overwhelming, pathetic weakness.

The adrenaline leached out of me, a river of curling smoke, leaving exhaustion in its wake. All I wanted was to sink into swift darkness, the quiet punctuated only by the intermittent thump of a car radio outside. Jamie held me, rubbing my back in tentative circles, as if I were fragile and unformed, on the verge of becoming. I let him hold me, and as I closed my eyes, I felt my own arms tighten around him until I was returning his embrace with everything I had, holding on tight, hoping he'd never let me go.

AVA

2006

After the showcase, the men surround me, a flower placed near the droning hum of a beehive, Christian Vane pushing through them all and taking me by the elbow, propelling me out of the crowd. There was a nimbus of strong cologne, citrus and sea salt. Lavender buds crushed beneath a bootheel. Fields of California sage. He leaned toward me, speaking platitudes over the crash of the music that surrounded us.

"You were incredible up there tonight." Behind the round lenses of his gold sunglasses, he leered at me, a smile on his full lips. "You'll join me at Balthazar," he declared, as if the matter had already been settled.

"I don't know if I can . . . ," I demurred, unsure of what to say, of what excuse I could possibly make. I knew that turning down Christian Vane was nothing less than career suicide. It had all been so improbable already, and I'd come so far, further than I'd ever dared to dream.

"You can and you will," he said firmly, brushing aside any chance of protest.

"Will what?" Lexi appeared in front of us, her hands on her hips, and I realized that Christian had been hanging on to my arm this whole time, tightly. Suddenly he released me, and I felt my body immediately relax.

"Perfect timing," he said, bending down to whisper in her ear. I watched as she threw her head back in soundless laughter. I missed her laugh, missed being the one to generate it, to coax it out of her, and I knew in that moment that she was lost to me forever. "I was just telling Ava how phenomenal she was tonight. She had the whole room in the palm of her hand."

Lexi gave him a tight smile. "Were you now."

Christian just stared at me as if I might slip from his grip if his attention waned even slightly.

"Where are we off to?" Lexi asked, lifting her chin, regarding me as if I were an irritating child clinging to the hem of her dress.

"Balthazar," Christian replied with a shrug, as if the choice were obvious. "I could use a good steak," he said as his eyes traveled the sparse lines of my body.

Before I could say a word, Jamie appeared, a hard energy emanating from his very presence. "Can I have a word?" he said in my ear, ignoring Christian entirely, and I shivered at the vibration of his breath against my skin.

"See you there," Christian said before taking Lexi's arm as they turned and walked toward the exit. As soon as they were out of earshot, Jamie grabbed me by the arm, pulling me over to the side of the stage. The speakers placed on each end were huge black specters, like gargoyles looking down on us.

"What was *that* all about?" Jamie shouted over the music, gesturing toward the patch of ground where I'd stood with Christian and Lexi only moments before.

"We're going to Balthazar."

"Oh, are we? Let me guess—I'm not invited? *Just me and the ladies tonight*," he added, parroting Christian's words from the last time he'd swept us away, closing the limousine door in Jamie's face.

I recoiled slightly, the chartreuse haze of jealousy tainting everything between us. Was this what awaited me every time some industry exec put his hands on me? I wondered as I looked at Jamie's face, tight with anger. I thought Ian had vanished forever when Lexi had banished him back to the island. But now I wasn't so sure.

"Let's not do this right now," I said, leaning forward and whispering directly into his ear. There was the scent of his sweat, sharp and sour, and I could smell the whiskey on him, too, how it turned his blood rancid.

He pulled back to look at me. "Do what? I'm not supposed to care about what my girlfriend gets up to?"

"That's the problem," I said, shaking my head. "I need you to be thinking like a manager right now, not a boyfriend."

"But I *am* your boyfriend," he said, pointing out the obvious. "Aren't I?"

"Of course," I said quickly. "But you're my manager too. And maybe it's crazy to think you can be both."

"You're going to leave me now too?" he asked, raking a hand through his hair until it stood on end, as if the restless energy he exuded had finally made it to the top of his head before exploding.

"What do you mean?" The words felt thick as paste in my mouth, and the final notes of the song faded away into silence.

"She just told me she's moving on. Apparently, she got herself some new manager."

"You're kidding," I said woodenly, even though some part of me had been expecting it. First me. Now Jamie. Who else would she leave behind before it was all over?

But it is *over,* a voice inside me said quietly. *Here's your proof.*

"Listen," he said, "if Lexi wants to play the game, that's her business. But you don't have to."

"But what if I *want* to?"

"That's up to you," he said coolly, his face expressionless. "But I can't guarantee Christian won't try something. It's never just business with these guys."

But it wasn't with Jamie either. Whatever was happening between us was so enmeshed in the rapid trajectory of my career that I could no longer untangle one from the other. The desire for fame mixed with my desire for him, for his hands on me, his mouth on mine. The stage, the microphone, the music that pulsed through me, saving me in a way nothing else ever could.

"Do whatever you want," he said, his voice tight. "You want to sell it all out for a record deal? Be my guest."

"Isn't that what we've been working toward all this time? A deal?"

"Not like this, Ava." The look he gave me as I stood there, my eyes pleading with him, stopped my heart. I reached out to him, wanting to take it all back, to make things right again and bring back the man I thought I knew.

But it was too late.

He dropped his arms to his sides, and before I could reach out, pull him to me, he turned his back on me, pushing his way through the crowd until I was left with nothing but a sick, empty feeling, my eyes smarting with unshed tears.

You better want this, that voice inside me whispered once again. *Really want it.*

It may be all you have left.

KAYLA

2019

I slept the night in his arms, both of us fully clothed, and in the morning, the early light streaking the room, tingeing it in shades of sepia and ochre, I made coffee in his pristine kitchen, carrying him in a mug. We sat there in companionable stillness, the scent of coffee beans perfuming the air, the sound of garbage trucks rumbling down the street. As far as I was concerned, the smell of coffee was right up there with baking bread, the scent of a lover's skin, and the hope-tinged perfume of lilacs in the spring, the branches heavy with blossoms. We didn't talk about the night before. There was nothing else to say. But something had shifted, and Ava's ghost was no longer between us.

The phantoms of my past had receded as well. Not for good, but far enough into the distance that for the first time in years, I didn't see Astrid's face each time I closed my eyes, her waiting for just the right moment to spring into the light. Now, a weight had been lifted, small and compact, but significant nonetheless.

"I don't want any more secrets between us," Jamie said, leaning against the headboard. I sat cross-legged beside him.

"Me either," I said, bringing the coffee to my face, inhaling the steam.

He took a sip from his own cup, bringing a hand quickly up to his mouth. "That's superhot," he said in protest. "Scalding, in fact."

"I like my coffee the way I like my men. Incendiary."

We grinned at each other like fools for a moment before he reached out, taking my free hand in his, stroking my palm with his fingers. The feel of his hands made me want to close my eyes, a cat luxuriating in sunlight, its eyes opening and closing in contented rapture.

"Seriously, though," he said, his pale eyes softening. "I want you to know me, Kayla. And I want to know you too."

"I think last night was a pretty good start," I said as he leaned over and pulled me to him. My mouth found his, my hands snaking around his neck as I fell back onto the bed, his solid weight on top of me, his hands tangled in my hair. He smoothed the sheaf of my bangs back from my forehead, my face exposed in its entirety now, his eyes searching mine. I pulled him to me, blotting out the world around us, my mouth on his collarbone, the silk of his throat, and I felt his hands on my waist, pulling down the panties I wore, tugging the meager scrap of fabric from my body and tossing it to the floor.

———

After Jamie headed off to work, I pulled on a pair of his ridiculously baggy sweats and a T-shirt and wandered into the kitchen to make another cup of coffee before I hopped the train back to Brooklyn. It was quiet and still, and the trees outside his windows were in full bloom, a profusion of pink and white blossoms that made me nostalgic. Spring was always a painful reminder of youth, what I'd lost and would never have again—that first flush of hopeful innocence. The box of coffee filters on the counter was now empty, and I began rummaging around in his cupboards, not finding any hidden within but rife with the knowledge that the man I was currently sleeping with had some sort of unnatural attachment to instant ramen.

I bent down, pulling open the kitchen drawers one after another, then moved on to a sleek midcentury sideboard leaning against one wall. When I opened the first drawer, it stuck a bit, and I pulled harder until it finally opened and I peered inside. It was jammed with paper. Envelopes, hundreds of them stacked on top of one another in a disorganized, chaotic pile. I picked one up, peering at the address label in the left-hand corner.

Phoenix Records LLC.

I stared at the envelope uncomprehendingly before opening it and pulling out what appeared to be a royalty statement. A statement addressed to Jamie. And below that, a list of songs. Songs I'd heard on the radio more times than I could count. Songs that made up the entirety of Lexi Mayhem's first two albums.

I pulled out more envelopes, my hands filled with them, opening them quickly. More statements, more royalties that Jamie couldn't have possibly earned. He hadn't even been her manager when those songs were released, and coupled with the fact that Lexi had never spoken publicly about her early association with him, the whole thing was utterly incomprehensible.

I shoved the pile of papers back into the drawer and shut it. My brain buzzed with static as I gathered up my belongings, throwing them into my bag in a jumbled pile, and headed out the door. I needed to get back to my apartment, where I could think clearly. There had to be an explanation. Something I wasn't seeing. But I couldn't escape the fact that this was the second time Jamie had kept something from me.

Once is a mistake, my mother had always said. *Twice is a pattern.*

When I arrived back in Brooklyn, I settled in at my desk, pulling up the liner notes again for Lexi's first album. I remembered that one of the songs on the royalty statements was "Poisoned Kiss," one of Lexi's biggest hits, a track that had gone platinum, topping the charts for more than thirty weeks and shattering Billboard records. I googled the lyrics, not even sure what I was looking for, fighting back the feeling I was running after phantoms. When the page loaded, I read the lyrics aloud, mumbling under my breath.

I fly through the air before I hit bottom. Your hands on my throat till I scream and turn rotten . . .

I sat back in my chair, a feeling of déjà vu creeping over me. Why were these words—lyrics I'd heard thousands of times before—tugging at me now? There was something new here, gnawing at me, even if I couldn't figure out why.

On instinct, I pushed back my chair and drifted over to the hall closet, extricating the large box of Ava's things from the top shelf—the box Irina had pressed into my arms as I was preparing to leave that day. There was so much more back in Ava's childhood bedroom, but this was all I'd been able to carry. I pulled it into the living room, then sat down on the floor, picking out one item after another, laying them on the floor as if trying to reassemble the pieces of a puzzle.

There were ATM receipts, pay stubs from the Cornelia Street Café, one lone earring, decorated with brightly colored beads that cascaded to the shoulder. Take-out bags and spare shoelaces, still in the packaging. Photos, their colors beginning to dull to a soft sepia, and pages and pages of lyrics, Ava's messy, loopy scrawl filling the pages, the paper soft with age, discolored along the edges. They covered everything, the pay stubs, the bodega receipts, each one filled with black or blue ink, Ava's words circling the perimeter of each slip of paper. It was almost as if the need to write had overtaken her when she was engaged in even the most mundane activities: checking her account balance, cashing a check—even buying groceries.

As I was putting the receipts and photos into neat piles, trying to create some kind of order, a line jumped out at me, written in green pen, the careful script circling the receipt from a Chinese restaurant. A string of words that, at first, I flipped right past. But something made me turn back, my eyes moving obsessively over what I could see now were the lyrics that I, like so many other people, knew by heart. But here the song was entitled "Twin Flame," and with that title, the lyrics, dark to begin with, took on a new and ominous twist.

I wait for you, alone in the dark. Your poisoned kiss shatters my heart . . .

I stared uncomprehendingly at the words until they ran together. Why would these lyrics be here, in Ava's things . . . unless she was the one who wrote the song?

I turned back to the pile of papers before me, bringing the receipts and journal pages into the light. My mouth hung open as I read. It wasn't just the lyrics to one song. Practically all of Lexi Mayhem's early career was here in this box. Songs that were inarguably written by none other than Ava Petrova. Who was now dead and buried. Who couldn't talk or explain.

Or even protest.

Holy shit, I breathed, my nerves tingling uncontrollably, the way they always did when I uncovered something big. Sitting there surrounded by Ava's possessions, the ephemera of her short life crammed into a few cardboard boxes, I couldn't stop my brain from repeating the same sneaking thought. Did Lexi Mayhem steal not only Ava's style and her music . . . but her entire career? Her art? The life she was supposed to have? Chills ran up and down my spine like the patter of tiny, icy feet against my skin. I remembered the first photo I'd found of Ava and Lexi together, the "Rock Star" belt firmly cinched around Ava's waist. The belt Lexi would go on to wear on the cover of *Spin* magazine only a year later.

The answer had been right in front of me all along.

Now Jamie's inclusion on Lexi's payroll made sense. He'd no doubt heard these songs before when Ava first sang them. Even if they were works in progress, he would've had to be at least somewhat familiar with them. I sat back, drawing my knees up to my chest, my eyes suddenly damp. He'd betrayed me right along with Ava—and he had loved her. And even though he hadn't said it, maybe he even loved me too.

Not that it had stopped him this time either.

But it was all bigger than just the slightly dubious act of paying a former manager for his silence. What I'd discovered in the ragged cardboard box on the floor in front of me, in the royalty statements I'd stumbled across in Jamie's apartment, all added up to one undeniable conclusion: that Christian, Lexi, and Jamie had *all* been incentivized by Ava's death, each of them profiting in one way or another by stealing her songs. Ava had lain in the ground beneath shovelfuls of dirt, her jade eyes closed forever, her voice stopped in her throat—while they raked in millions.

And it had made Lexi Mayhem a household name.

AVA

The anger welled up in me, unfamiliar and jarring, my nerve endings suddenly aflame. I was tired of men telling me what to do, and even more tired of listening to them. My jaw worked incessantly as I walked, grinding my teeth. Soon there would be nothing but shards of enamel, a gritty white powder coating my tongue. I stepped into the street, reaching one hand up and hailing a cab, the air pressing in like an unwanted lover.

Taking a cab was as out of character as my fury. Lexi and I had walked everywhere, claiming these city streets with the soles of our boots, each step we took marking them forever. *Someday they will say, Lexi Mayhem walked here, and here, and here,* she'd proclaim, her aim an arrow cutting the air, straight and true. I settled into the shadowed back seat, one thought repeating itself endlessly in my brain: No one was going to take my shot away now. Not Lexi. Not Jamie. I wasn't going to be left behind.

This time, I was playing to win.

When we pulled up in front of Balthazar, I handed the cabbie a ten-dollar bill and got out, smoothing down my dress. *You've got this,*

I told myself reassuringly as I took a deep breath in, letting it out and trying to release the fear that still flew inside me, unchecked. Even if I didn't believe those words the way Lexi did, I'd had enough practice to know I could fake it now.

The vast dining room was bright, a stage itself, a proliferation of crimson, so much red that it made me dizzy, like stumbling upon a crime scene. I walked past the long line at the hostess stand, head high, trying to act like I knew where I was going. And then I saw them, huddled in a group at a round table at the far end of the room. I strode purposefully, shoulders back, chin lifted in the way I'd seen Lexi command a room on so many nights that I could execute it perfectly, the look in her eyes, a cockiness tinged with coldness.

Like me or not, it seemed to say. *It hardly matters.*

As I approached, one of the men seated next to Christian nudged him with an elbow, and all eyes turned toward me. Lexi glanced up from her plate. Cyanide eyes. A poisonous green. There was a cocktail glass in front of her, cut crystal, filled with a dark liquid bordering on red. Or maybe it was just the reflection of all the scarlet surrounding us. She picked up the glass, swallowing hard, her eyes never leaving my face.

My phone began to ring, a reprimand, and I drew it from my bag. Jamie. My heart fell for a moment, a scab torn off, fresh blood streaming from the cut. But even so, I pressed "Decline," ending the call and switching the ringer to vibrate. I knew what he'd say, knew there was no way he'd forgive me for even showing up there in the first place. That I was just like Lexi, soulless, bloated with ambition. But wasn't that what all that rehearsing had prepared me for? It had led me to this moment, this room. To Christian, who had the power to change the course of my life forever.

"Ava!" Christian said, motioning for the waiter to bring another chair, his fingers snapping the air. "Finally." This was a man one did not keep waiting, and from the slight downturned cast to his mouth, it was clear I had displeased him. But I knew the fastest way back into the good graces of men like Christian Vane was flattery.

"I'm so sorry I kept you waiting," I said as I sat down, the tablecloth brushing against my bare knees. "I know how valuable your time is." I smiled, hoping I seemed apologetically seductive.

He nodded approvingly, the dour look replaced with a self-satisfied smile.

I was seated directly across from Lexi and Christian and right beside the man who had alerted Christian to my presence: Jamie's assistant. He wore an olive T-shirt under a black blazer, a pair of jeans torn strategically at the knees. He smiled warmly, perhaps to put me at ease, and I noticed that his teeth were slightly crooked on the bottom, the jaggedness almost charming in the room full of Botoxed foreheads and torsos sculpted in weekly Pilates classes. But what he was doing there in Jamie's absence was anyone's guess.

"You were great tonight," he said enthusiastically. "Just magic."

"What am I?" Lexi shot across the table belligerently. "Chopped liver?"

"Of course not," he replied, as if placating her were already second nature. "I'd think you'd be tired of me telling you how incredible you were tonight, Lexi—I've been repeating it since we left the club."

Lexi rolled her eyes, guzzling her drink as if gold coins awaited her at the bottom. My phone vibrated again in my bag, muffled by the din of the restaurant, and this time I ignored it, hanging my purse on the back of the chair so I wouldn't be distracted. I wondered if Jamie was pacing the length of his apartment, the phone pressed to his ear, waiting for me to answer. Or maybe he was outside the restaurant, peering in the windows, searching for the light of my face.

"Now, now," Christian said in a chiding tone, as if this were a kindergarten instead of a bistro. "Let's not argue. This is supposed to be a celebration."

Lexi laughed once, a short, dry snort as she stared blankly into her glass. There was something about the limpness of her posture that set off my internal alarms, the way her head was drooping slightly. It was uncharacteristic for Lexi to get sloppy when it mattered most. But how well did I really know her anymore?

Had I ever?

"How many drinks has she had?" I asked, turning to Jamie's assistant, careful to keep my voice low.

"Two, I think?" he replied with a shrug. "The label bigwigs were super impressed tonight. She's going to be a huge star," he said reverentially, changing the subject and looking over at Lexi. "She just needs the right material."

"I *am* the right material," Lexi pointed out, her eyes brightening for a moment before she fell silent once again. Her red lipstick was slightly smeared at one corner, and her dark hair fell in her face. I watched as she pushed it away with one hand, her onyx nails tangling in the strands.

"Ava, what can I get you?" Christian asked, gesturing at his own glass of champagne in front of him, bubbles frothing deliriously.

"I'm good," I said quickly, noticing that Lexi was now staring into space, her eyes strange and unfocused.

"You're not drinking?" Jamie's assistant asked me worriedly, and his hushed tone told me that the choice to abstain was probably a mistake. But if Lexi was going to get obliterated, I knew it was to my advantage to remain sober and clearheaded.

"I'm OK right now," I reiterated.

"But you *must*," Christian argued. "I can easily order another bottle," he said, reaching up to adjust the gold aviators hiding his eyes from view. I couldn't shake the feeling that behind those dark lenses was a void. Dead space. The sockets blackened and empty. And across from me, Lexi slid farther down in her chair with every passing moment. "They have *great* cocktails here," he said as he pushed the menu toward me.

I stood up and reached across the table, picking up Lexi's drink in one hand. I raised the glass to my lips and swallowed, the taste cool and sweet but with something metallic lurking just below the surface. "Happy?" I said with what I hoped was a winning smile, the kind Lexi wielded like a strobe light.

Christian laughed, shaking his head as if I were a delightful new toy, an amusement, and I supposed that as far as he was concerned, I was. He immediately turned his attention to Jamie's assistant and began whispering in his ear, the two of them laughing uproariously.

I took advantage of their distraction and looked over at Lexi. There was something wrong, I could feel it. I got up and made my way over to her chair, bending down beside her. "Hey, Lex," I whispered, my lips inches from her ear. "Are you OK?"

"I'm just . . . ," she mumbled, her eyes fluttering closed.

"Let's take a walk," I said, pulling her to her feet, her body dead-weight against my own.

"Where are you going?" Christian called out.

"Ladies' room." I smiled, wrapping my arms around Lexi as she leaned her head on my shoulder.

"Hurry back," Christian said, his voice a level threat. "We have a lot to discuss."

Lexi's head lolled against my neck as we moved, and her skin was hot, feverish. We made our way to the back of the restaurant, one slow step at a time, past the waitstaff, who stared, then averted their eyes. Lexi a dead doll, her lips parted and bloodied, a lion sleeping after the kill, her jaw slack.

"What did you take?" I hissed. "Dammit, Lexi, what the hell did you *take*?"

"Nothing," she slurred. "Didn't." I felt a cold stab of fear shoot through me, her voice fainter now, a light being gradually extinguished, the sound of it causing my stomach to turn sharply. *She'll be OK*, I told myself firmly, trying to quiet the panic that rushed through me with the speed of a train derailing.

She has to be.

I pushed the bathroom door open, finding it blissfully empty, and maneuvered Lexi over to the sink. I leaned her against the cold porcelain and ran the tap, wetting a paper towel and pressing it to her forehead, her feverish cheeks. I could see the rapid pulse of her heartbeat in her neck, and her eyes fluttered open for a few seconds, as if she were being rudely awakened, before shutting once again.

"We need to get you out of here," I said firmly, looping one of her arms around my neck and pulling her to her feet again. She had never been so heavy. "Hold on to me." Her grip tightened ever so slightly, fingers clenching. Her skin was pale and waxen, and I had never seen her so completely lifeless.

"I don't feel well," she whispered, her voice barely audible as I pushed open the bathroom door and the noise of the restaurant surrounded us.

"I know," I said distractedly as I pushed through the tightly packed tables, the line of patrons at the front door waiting to be seated, their bored expressions only shifting as they took in the spectacle we made, Lexi's feet barely moving as I dragged her high-heeled boots along the floor. I said a silent prayer that we'd make it to the front door without Christian or his minions noticing, and each step seemed to last an eternity. Finally, we made it to the entrance, and as a man dressed in a black suit, a crumpled fedora atop his head, held the door open for us, I breathed a sigh of relief. The deal didn't matter now.

Nothing did. Except for Lexi and me.

"You need a doctor," I muttered as she clung to me.

"No way," she mumbled. "I want . . . ," she said faintly, her words vibrating against my skin as the wind blew her dark hair into her face, "to see the stars. Take me to the stars." I pushed the silky strands from her eyes, and she smiled up at me, her lipstick hopelessly smeared now. "The moon. It's a full moon tonight. Take me home."

"Are you sure?" I asked worriedly, pulling her closer, using all my strength to keep her upright. She only nodded in response, and I felt my eyes dampen with unshed tears.

"I'm sorry, Ava," Lexi mumbled into my neck. "I'm so sorry, birdie." Her voice caught in her throat, and she let out a short cry, a desperate note stopping just short of a wail.

That's what she'd always called me. Her little bird. But now she needed me to take charge, and I knew then with a sense of overwhelming clarity that this was my one chance to right what had gone wrong between us. I wasn't going to let her down. Not now and not ever again. There was so much sadness in that cry, and I knew that if I really let her words sink in, if I let them matter in that moment, I'd crumple to the sidewalk, crushed by the weight of her body on mine.

As it was, I felt curiously detached, as if my head were floating somewhere in the dense banks of clouds suffocating the stars. There was the sticky-sweet stench of rotting fruit in the warm night, the noise pollution of buses and cars. The lights shone down, too bright, too fierce. Was it the stage or just New York? *This whole town is a performance,* Lexi had always proclaimed. I didn't know anymore whether it was true. A furry brown rat ran by my feet, scurrying into a pile of trash on the corner, and all I knew was damp and warm in my arms. She'd come back to me, if only for one night.

And we were going home.

KAYLA

2019

I brewed a pot of strong coffee, carrying the mug to my desk and sitting down in front of my computer, knowing what I needed to do before my fingers even touched the keys—detail all the possible suspects, expose the probable theft of Ava's songs, and delve into her alleged suicide. But something was still bothering me, tapping me rudely on the shoulder with one pointed talon, demanding my attention.

If all my years in the journalistic trenches had taught me anything, it was that without comment from Lexi, the narrative would be incomplete. And "incomplete" meant "refutable." But any effort I'd made over the last week to contact her had been thwarted smoothly at every turn. Every time I reached out to Ben, I'd been handed yet another roadblock, which I was beginning to become more than just a little suspicious of. "If she's unavailable, we can push by a month or so," Keats had said last time I'd talked to him. "Not to worry."

But the story he wanted wasn't the story I was working on.

I needed to talk to Lexi.

There was a loud bang from outside the window, and I jumped up, peering into the blackness, the pane of glass cool beneath the pads of my fingers, half expecting to see the shadowy figure of a man staring up at me. But there was only a large German shepherd on the pavement below, his nose buried in the depths of an overturned metal trash can.

I sat back down, the warm weight of the cup resting in my hands. Then an idea dawned on me, and I grabbed my phone, scrolling through my contacts. It rang once, going straight to voice mail and Simone's calm voice patiently explaining that she was unavailable. I pressed "End" and had just sat back in my chair when my phone immediately pinged with an incoming text.

Have you lost your mind? Why can't you text like a normal person?

I grinned, my fingers tapping the screen quickly before she disappeared in a huff.

My bad. Could use your take on something.

Shoot.

I think maybe I've cracked this thing wide open, but . . .

Guess you didn't take my advice.

Sadly, I did not. It was good counsel though. But I was in too deep already.

Forgiven. So what's the issue?

I need a quote from Lexi to make it fly.

And???

I'm not supposed to call her. Unless it's an emergency.

Still not seeing the problem.

I mean . . . it's not an emergency. Not technically. Plus, I'm kind of ambushing her.

Hate to break it to you, McCray, but you're a journalist. Comes with the territory.

I know but . . .

You think interviewing Joseph Kony in Uganda was easy? The guy runs a child army. Mayhem may be a celebrity, but you've got to approach her like you would anyone else. She doesn't get special treatment. Ask the uncomfortable questions.

It's not the story she thinks it is. Things have really come to light. Things she doesn't want uncovered.

Can you spill?

Not yet. Soon.

OK. Listen, it's Saturday morning and I'm hungover af from my sister's baby shower last night. Who knew these Brooklyn moms swill wine like Gatorade? I was not at all prepared. Just call her. What's the worst that could happen?

She could have me killed? ☺

Possible. But unlikely. Call her. I'm going back to sleep.

Three dots blinked, then went still. Before I could change my mind, I scrolled through my contacts again until I came to Lexi's name. I pushed the "Call" button, holding my breath as the number began to ring. It was eleven a.m. in New York and three hours earlier in California, so it was entirely possible that she'd still be asleep. I could feel myself sweating, my back slick with it. The phone rang three times, then four, and just as I was about to hang up, that throaty, low voice I recognized immediately filled my ear.

"Who's this?"

I cleared my throat nervously. "It's Kayla McCray, Ms. Mayhem. From *Rolling Stone*."

"I told you to call me Lexi." She laughed, and I could hear her unwrapping something on the other end, the sound of crinkling plastic like brush fire. "This is *cute*," I heard her say to someone in the room, her voice fading away for a split second before hovering closer again.

"That's true," I agreed. "Apologies, Lexi."

"That's better," she said with satisfaction. "But didn't Ben tell you? I'm in rehearsals for the new tour. Like twelve-hour days. I'm not even *sleeping*. I won't have time to finish the interview till next week."

"That's OK," I said quickly. "I just had one quick question I was hoping you might comment on."

"I'm listening." There was silence on her end of the line now, and I had the feeling that somehow, I'd captured her full attention.

I took a deep breath and went for it. "After her death, did you record songs written by Ava Petrova for your first two albums without properly crediting her?"

There was an intake of breath.

Not a gasp, but almost.

Then nothing.

I looked at my cell uncomprehendingly. She'd hung up on me. And that abrupt disconnection told me everything I needed to know—even if I still needed to get her to actually say *something*. If all my years as a reporter had taught me anything, it was this: refusing to answer a question, whether it be over email, phone, or even text message, was an answer in and of itself. It just wasn't one we often wanted to accept.

I sat back down at my desk, opened my laptop, and started writing, my hands moving across the keys until dawn covered the sky gold and rose, the light breaking through the low-hanging clouds like redemption itself.

The weekend was swallowed by work. I barely left my apartment. I barely even left my desk—I needed to get it all down, my hands sore and stiff, as if rigor mortis had set in. Yet I'd never felt more alive. Jamie texted and called, the phone lighting up the room late at night, but I ignored his messages, even as they grew more desperate, even as he began to ask why I wasn't responding. I couldn't imagine what I would possibly say to address the suspicions that now tainted our every interaction.

On Monday morning, I ventured into the office, working at my desk until almost noon, putting the finishing touches on the piece before emailing it to Keats. Which I was dreading. I knew he wasn't going to be thrilled, but I also knew, now more than ever, that this feature *needed* to run. Not just for Ava's sake but for my own. This was the biggest story I'd ever written, and even if I hadn't quite cracked every aspect of the conspiracy or explained the hows and whys as much as I'd hoped, there was enough damning evidence here to make figuring out the things I didn't know yet an inevitability.

At least eventually.

About an hour after I finally hit "Send," my extension rang, jerking me upright. Had he read it already? Was it as good as I thought it was? "My office, Kayla," Keats said the moment I answered. "Now." He hung up the phone abruptly, and I stood up as if in a dream and walked the short distance to his door, knocking sharply twice before opening it.

When I swung the door open, Keats was seated behind his desk, and across the room stood Ben, dressed in his usual attire, a suit, this time in a neutral beige that bordered on drab, his cell phone gripped in one hand. He looked at me, the fury plain on his face.

"How dare you," he said contemptuously. I looked from Ben to Keats, my expression betraying my helplessness. "This was supposed to be a straightforward piece about the new record and Lexi's move from pop icon to record exec. Not some exposé on some mediocre singer who flung herself off a roof."

"That's where you're wrong," I said, my voice tight with anger. "She was extremely talented. But that's not the point. I *just* sent Keats the story. There's no way he could've even read it yet." And even if he had, I knew Keats would never leak a story to a potential source before it was published. His ethics were impeccable. "So what are we talking about here?"

And then it dawned on me. Lexi had called him.

Of course she had.

"I'm killing the story, Kayla," Keats said levelly. "I'm sorry, but my hands are tied."

"But you have to at least read it!" I protested, moving closer to his desk, holding my hands out in front of me in the air. "I *know* she stole those songs—and that's the *least* of it." I turned to Ben, who was seething to such a degree that he resembled a volcano about to erupt. "If Lexi won't comment, then I'll ask you the same question: Did Lexi record Ava Petrova's songs and release them as her own?"

"Kayla," Keats said quietly, his tone a warning. But I had already gone too far.

"You know what? I *will* answer," Ben spat, striding over to me until we were only inches apart. For the first time I saw that he was disheveled, his normally smooth face covered in dark stubble that grew unevenly across his jaw in patches. "No. Of *course* she didn't. The entire accusation is preposterous, and if you so much as insinuate that Lexi

Mayhem stole *anything* in this article or in the press, if you so much as breathe a word of it to another living human being, you're looking at a lawsuit the magnitude of which your feeble little brain can barely *comprehend*."

We stood there sizing each other up. I knew that if I broke eye contact, I'd lose any upper hand I possessed, so I forced myself to hold on, my nails digging into the meat of my palms as if at any moment I might draw blood.

"Ben," I heard Keats say from somewhere far away. "That's enough."

Ben finally looked over at Keats, taking a few steps away from me, and my body relaxed an inch in that small distance now between us. "Is it? Then *handle* this, Keats. Because I don't think I need to point out that you're liable too." And before I could say a word, the door banged shut and Ben was gone.

"It's over, Kayla," Keats said the moment Ben was gone, as if I needed the reminder. "I will repeat this one last time: I'm killing the story. It's a dead end."

"But, Keats, are you really going to—"

"This conversation is finished," Keats snapped, standing up, "and you will be too if you don't start listening to me. What did I tell you, Kayla? To tread carefully, to share what you discovered with me before you accused anyone of things we can't take back." He heaved an angry sigh. "I have some serious thinking to do regarding your place at this magazine."

I swallowed hard. I was inches away from losing my job and I knew it. Maybe not even inches. Everything I'd worked so hard for was about to be swept away, as if a hand had reached down from above to grab it all, leaving nothing but an empty wasteland.

"Now if you'll excuse me," Keats said, pushing his glasses up on the bridge of his nose, "I need to clean up the mess you've made. I suggest you go home for the day while I figure out exactly what to do with you."

I nodded, opening the door and walking out. I knew there was nothing I could say that would help the situation any further. This was one of the times I hated my devotion to stories, to words themselves, where my reliance on them felt like a weakness rather than a strength. Because no matter how much they mattered to me, there was always the point in a communication breakdown when they lost their impact, their meaning.

When suddenly, they didn't matter at all.

I closed the door to Keats's office behind me, the finality of it piercing the muscle and sinew of my heart. My feet traversed the length of the newsroom, leading me to the front door of the office. I stopped there, my future stretching out before me uncertainly, the entire life I'd managed to cobble together for myself over the years hanging in the balance. I turned to face the vast, open work space for maybe the last time, unsure when or if I'd ever return.

———

I walked and walked, aimlessly at first, then making my way downtown. Even though the afternoon was sunny and mild, as I moved through the crowds, the potential demise of my career still haunted me, along with the memory of being followed, and I couldn't help stopping to look behind me every few blocks to make sure I was still alone. These were powerful people, as Keats had said, and not necessarily innocent ones. They had more to protect than the average civilian and would do just about anything to avoid a public record of their transgressions. They had the money, the clout, and the power to turn my lights out—and topple the entire magazine in the process.

My stomach plummeted as I realized that even after all my work, there would be no justice. No comeuppance for whoever or whatever had contributed to Ava's untimely death. In all likelihood, some intern was being paid to scrub away any mention of Ava online, denying her any kind of legacy. Before it had been only a hunch. But now I was sure of it. The stolen songs, the royalties. None of it could ever see the light of day—not without dismantling Lexi's entire career.

I lingered in front of the Strand bookstore, perusing the carts of cheap paperbacks parked outside. I could almost see Ava breaking into peals of laughter as Lexi held up some outdated sex manual from the seventies, the two of them flirting with the cute hot dog vendors on the corner, Lexi throwing back her dark mane and Ava smiling shyly, clutching Lexi's hand in her own. I was walking in their footprints, their friendship deepening with every step. And now it was all gone, subsumed by the vacuum of history, along with my friendship with Astrid and my trust in Jamie.

I let my fingers trail over the stacks of books before walking to the corner and buying a pretzel covered in huge chunks of salt, consuming it piece by piece as I kept moving. Did Lexi ever wake at night, I wondered, Ava's face glowing in the dark, conjuring her the way I did Astrid? In the past, I'd always thought of it as the other way around, her seeking me out from the labyrinth of the past. But now I knew that it was my guilt that brought her back, my guilt that wouldn't let her—or myself—ever rest.

I grimaced as I turned onto Cornelia Street and wished I'd remembered to toss a pair of sneakers in my bag. After walking twenty blocks, the black flats I wore dug into my heels with every step. I broke off another hunk of pretzel, stuffing it in my mouth and chewing hard, passing the carriage house Taylor Swift had famously rented a few years back, and before I knew it, I was standing in front of the Cornelia Street Café and its dirty, opaque windows and tattered red awning that was a shade closer to pink now. I could still make out the lettering on the sign, as the café had closed for good only a few months ago, but it looked completely abandoned, as if it had been unoccupied for centuries.

I moved closer, peering into the windows, putting my hands on the glass in front of my eyes to cut the glare. I could make out a few tables and chairs strewn around the room like skeletons, but not much else. Were the ghosts of Ava and Lexi still trapped inside, some version of their former selves doomed to polish glasses and pick up trays of food on an endless loop for all eternity? Did Lexi ever pass by in her black stretch limousine, I wondered, the tinted windows hiding her from prying eyes? Did she glance over at the faded awning and remember all she had lost? Or did she stare straight ahead, her jade eyes focused on the future?

I thought I knew the answer now.

She had lived not far from here—Broome Street, I remembered from the police report—and I began walking quickly, as if there were an imaginary force urging me on, picking up speed despite the pain in my feet. I knew that when I kicked my shoes off that night, they would be spotted with blood dried to the color of fallen leaves.

Lexi's building had been gentrified into ten stories of luxury condominiums now. Only in New York City could a two bedroom the size of a closet, *without* a doorman, be considered luxurious in any way. I held my breath as I hit one buzzer after another in rapid succession, knowing the odds were in my favor that a tenant was either expecting a visitor or had ordered food. After a few seconds, the door buzzed sharply, and I pushed it open and stepped inside.

I walked to the fire door, ignoring the elevator, and began the climb to the top. The hallways were clean, freshly painted a light, unobtrusive greige, the building quiet, as if it were wholly unoccupied. I walked up one flight after another until I reached the top and a door marked ROOF ACCESS, which I shoved open, bracing myself for the shriek of an alarm that never came. A sudden breeze whipped the dark strands of my hair across my face, and I pushed it away impatiently with one hand as I stepped out onto the roof. The sun was beginning to dip lower in the sky, and the light was a rare gold, full of promise.

The roof stretched empty before me, and I moved closer to the edge, wondering where exactly Ava had been standing when everything in her world changed forever. It was cooler up there, and I shivered, rubbing my bare arms to warm myself. The rooftops of Manhattan stretched out before me in an endless vista, and I wondered how a place so heartbreakingly beautiful could have produced such tragedy. I could almost see Ava perched on the edge of the roof, the wind blowing her platinum hair back from her face, her profile staunchly determined as she stared off at some unknowable future, far in the distance. There were secrets here, but the roof wasn't talking.

"What happened to you?" I whispered. "What happened up here?"

There was no answer. Only the rush of the wind among the buildings, producing a low moaning that unsettled me. Then there was the clicking sound of the door behind me shutting metallically, and I jumped, whirling around, one hand to my heart. And there before me was a man, his hands shoved deep in the pockets of his trousers, his gold Ray-Bans reflecting the light of the dying sun.

"What are you doing here?" I said, the confusion likely plain on my face.

He just smiled and took another step toward me.

AVA

2006

"Don't sleep. You hear me? Lexi, don't *sleep*," I said as we careened down the street, weaving in and out of the crowd. "Don't close your eyes."

But there was no response. As we stumbled along, every minute of our friendship raced through my mind. Standing side by side in her bathroom, her satin robe shining wetly in the early-morning light. Carrying trays of drinks through the café, looking up to meet her quick wink, a flash of warmth that I held close, that stayed with me the entire night. Her laughter filling my ears, the streets of New York, all the rooftops of the world. I hurried, knowing there was no time to waste.

That maybe there had never been any to begin with.

The climb up to the roof was hellish, the stairwell airless as a tomb, and I had to stop on the fourth floor, gasping and trying to catch my breath, my forehead beaded with sweat. Lexi lolled in my arms, somewhere between sleep and waking. "The stars," she'd mumble intermittently before falling silent once again, and that dead space worried me more than anything. At the top, I pushed open the metal door, my eyes searching the darkness, finding nothing but the twinkling skyline awaiting us.

I moved her over to one of the lounge chairs, our usual spot, and sat her down as gently as I could, her bare legs akimbo, sprawled out in front of her like a broken doll, her short black dress riding up, her skin glowing in the moonlight like abalone. The flash of her underwear, a series of thin cords wrapped around her hips. Her head thrown back, arms limp at her sides.

"I'm sorry," she muttered, opening her eyes to look at me, her expression solemn. I knelt beside her, pushing her hair back from her face, her skin damp beneath my palm, and I wondered again, despite her refusal, if I should do something more proactive than merely letting her sleep it off. What if she never woke up? *Don't even think that,* I admonished myself. *She will be fine. She has to be fine. She's Lexi fucking Mayhem.* "It's just you and me," she said, reaching out for my hand, and as her fingers closed around my own, it was as if the broken pieces of my life were suddenly made whole again.

"No," I said quietly, shame rising up to find me, "I'm the one who needs to apologize. I should've told you."

"It's OK," she slurred, her eyes shutting once again. "I love you," she said, the words almost soundless, but I could see her lips moving.

"I love you too," I whispered, watching her chest rise and fall.

There was a squeak, the same noise the rusted metal hinges on the door made each time it opened, and I turned to see Jamie's assistant coming toward us, a sheepish smile on his face, his hands shoved into the front pockets of his jeans, a messenger bag the color of coffee grounds thrown over one shoulder. He walked jauntily, as if coming to deliver good news.

"What are you doing here?" I asked as he arrived in front of us.

"I could ask you the same thing," he said, and I stood up.

"She was in no shape to stay," I replied. "But that still doesn't explain why you're here."

"She didn't tell you? Thought you two were thick as thieves." His tone was mocking, as if he knew some crucial shred of information that eluded me. I just stared at him, waiting him out. It was another technique I'd learned from Lexi. An effective one at that.

"I'm her new manager," he said, an edge of triumph in his voice. "You did me a real favor hooking up with Jamie."

I saw him for what he was: an opportunist. A bottom-feeder. A parasite.

"You told her," I said, my voice barely above a whisper. I reached up and rubbed my head, which felt curiously light, my body heavy and sweat-dampened. "You saw us that day. In the studio."

"You thought no one would notice?" He laughed, and in that moment, I hated him more than I'd ever hated anyone. The feeling was new to me, rushing through my system like amphetamine. "But listen," he said conspiratorially, taking a step closer, "you've got a lot of talent. You could go far with management that actually has a clue, someone who really knows how to play the game."

"And that, I guess, would be you?"

"Let's cut right to the chase," he said bluntly. "I want you to write for Lexi."

"Write?" I repeated, staring at him uncomprehendingly, my feet on the tar, sticky as honey. "Write songs?"

"What did you think I meant? Novels? Parking tickets?" He sneered, and in that moment, he looked so entirely smug that I would've denied him anything, if only out of spite. "Listen," he said, taking another step toward me, "you're an incredible talent as a songwriter. You have what Lexi doesn't. But with your songs, she would be unstoppable—and that's my job, to make her unstoppable."

"I get that," I said slowly. "But you seem to be ignoring the fact that I'm a singer too."

He ran a hand over his closely cropped hair, and I could sense his frustration beginning to climb. "Let's get real, Ava. You hate performing, and frankly I can see why—you don't really have the feel for it. Your voice is great, but you look like a comatose kitten up there."

It was a curious tactic, undercutting me to get what both he and presumably Lexi wanted, highlighting my insecurities until I folded like one of those cheap paper fans Lexi and I often bought on the streets of Chinatown. But before I could say even one word, he prattled on.

"This way, you won't have to deal with any of that anymore. You'll do what you do best—and make millions for it. We'll make a great team."

A team. One where I'd do all the grunt work while Lexi garnered the applause. The acclaim. Me in the shadows, hiding my face and shrinking from view. The place I'd always thought I belonged. The out-of-the-way place, where no one would notice me. Where I'd never have to step into the light. Sitting there, the knowledge crept over me slowly, unmistakable in its power. I didn't want to be that girl anymore.

I didn't have to be.

"Thanks," I said, with as saccharine of a smile as I could muster, "but I'm not interested in playing on your team. The funny thing about the word 'team'? There's no *I* in it."

His expression changed abruptly, a flicker of annoyance in his eyes. "You'll come around. And so will Lexi."

"I wouldn't bet on it," I managed to spit out through gritted teeth. Before he could answer, I bent to check on Lexi, who was still out cold. I shook her limp shoulders, but she didn't move. She smelled of something hard and chemical mixed with the oaken silk of whiskey. "Look at her," I urged him. He glanced over at Lexi, her head lolling to one side now, a line of spittle trailing from her lips. "How did she get like this, anyway?"

"She had a few drinks," he said dismissively. "I've seen worse."

And with those words, a flash of anger ignited in my chest, one that quickly burst into flames. I moved forward so that he was forced to take a step back, then another, and as I watched his expression shift from smugness to fear, a bolt of satisfaction ran through me. *Good. Let him be scared,* I thought as my feet moved of their own accord, forcing him away from her.

Let them all be scared now.

I focused on the fear in his eyes and kept moving.

"How would you know what she wants?" he snapped, the sarcasm in his voice urging me on.

"Because I'm her best friend," I answered as we approached the edge of the roof.

"Lexi doesn't have friends," he said, his eyes glittering with fury. "Just people she uses."

"You would know, right?" I raised one eyebrow, as I'd seen Lexi do so many times before. But at that moment I was wholly myself. He glared at me, and somehow, we had shifted and spun, pivoting so my back was to the edge of the roof now, my calves pushed up against the cold stone. The warm wind whipped through my hair, hurling strands of it against my face, into my mouth, and I pushed it away angrily, his face blurring for a moment before snapping into focus once again.

"She doesn't know *what* she wants," he said definitively.

"So you get to choose for her?"

"Eventually, she'll see how much I care, that *everything* I do is for her. She'll realize that we make sense—in more ways than one."

He was close to me now, too close, and the dizziness I'd felt since leaving the restaurant descended once again, threatening to engulf me entirely. I'd barely drunk anything tonight—except the remainder of whatever had been in Lexi's glass. I glanced over at her then, sprawled on the lounge chair, and my blood ran cold.

Lexi's drink.

Poison.

I forced myself to focus, to stand tall even as he pushed me closer to the edge, trying his best to dwarf me. But I knew now that no one could ever do that to me again. I may have been a little bird once, wings batting uselessly at the air. But now?

Now I was ready to fly.

"She will never love you," I said as his body erased the last shred of space between us. "No matter what you do. No matter what you promise. No matter how many songwriters you pay off." His face darkened in anger, but I stood my ground. Because what I'd said was the truth.

And somewhere deep inside, he knew it.

"You don't know what you're talking about," he growled, so close that droplets of his saliva flew at my face, a hard rain. "Lexi and I—" His hand flew out suddenly, his fingers hitting me on the chest, the rough tap of them, and I recoiled out of instinct, jerking my body violently backward, away from his grasp . . . but there was nowhere to go.

For a split second I saw his eyes widen, and then I was falling, plummeting over the edge of the roof, moving through space as though time itself were weightless and inconsequential. I was weightless, too, the rush of wind in my ears drowning out the sound of his words, the lit windows flickering past, gilded safety, my hands clawing the empty air. I closed my eyes, knowing that surely the end would come, as inevitable as gathering clouds and summer rain. The lilt of my mother's voice in my head, inexplicable and strange.

Lights out, Ava. It is time for bed.

Forgive me, I thought. Then: *Lexi.*

And everything went black.

KAYLA

2019

"What are you doing here?" I repeated.

"I followed you from the office, of course," Ben said as he sauntered toward me, taking in the view, the dying light gilding his silhouette.

"You're following me now?" I asked, adrenaline rushing through me.

"I don't have time for games, Kayla." He smirked, peering at me over his sunglasses as though I were being deliberately dense.

"So what are you doing here, then?" I said, taking a step backward.

"I'm so glad you asked," he said, his voice measured and even, as if we were having lunch at Tavern on the Green, not standing on a rooftop where a young woman once plummeted to her death. "You know, everyone has skeletons. Secrets. But that doesn't always mean they need to be dragged out into the light. I thought I could trust you to stick to the story you were assigned. Not become fixated on some two-bit singer who never had her day. Things are in the past for a reason, Kayla. Because it's *over*."

As I stood there looking at him, his expressionless visage, I felt a surge of anger ignite in me—at Ava's death, at the roadblocks that were routinely thrown in my way each time I got close to what happened that night, to the truth of her story.

"No, it's *not*," I said. The sun was dipping lower in the sky now, casting long shadows on the buildings across the way. "I know something happened up here that no one is willing to talk about. And I'm going to prove it."

I turned my back on him, trying to slow my breathing, and I realized with a sudden intake of breath that Ben's appearance on that rooftop was a calculated move, just like everything he did, and as I glanced up at the sky, a cold stab of fear ran through me. The sunset was a curious shade of violet, the clouds darkening, as though a storm were imminent. There was a small sound behind me, a scraping of shoes on pavement, and when I turned, Ben was inches from my face.

Too close.

Closer than he needed to be.

On instinct, I reached down into the outside pocket of my bag and flipped on my digital recorder, hoping he didn't notice the movement of my hand. But he was distracted, somewhere else, his eyes a flat glare. "No one will talk about it," he began, "because you're asking the *wrong questions* to the *wrong people*. Lexi doesn't know what happened that night because she was out cold. And nothing in Christian's superficial existence even *registers* beyond his hordes of groupies and assistants, his beloved gold records. His house in fucking Malibu. There's only one person who knows what really happened that night." He was sweating, his face sheened with it, his muscles tense, coiled, and there was an air of excitement about him, as if he'd waited a long time to say these words.

Thirteen years.

"You," I said quietly, fear blooming in my gut. "It was you."

His lips twitched, but he said nothing. I could hear Ava's voice in my ear, a curious lilt to her words. *Don't let him too close. It's a long way down, Kayla. Longer than you could ever imagine.* I had followed in Ava's footsteps, and they had led me here, to the same rocky precipice.

"She didn't jump," I continued, aware that I had started to tremble, my hands shaking as if I'd been plugged into an electrical outlet.

"Lexi needed those songs more than Ava ever did," he said, as if it had all been so easy. As if he'd done Ava a favor by stealing them. "They *needed* Lexi—her stage presence, her charisma—to make them really shine. I mean, I was going to get what we needed one way or the other"—he laughed—"but Ava thought it would be more fun to fight me. She didn't understand who she was dealing with. Not until it was too late."

"But *why*? There are a million songwriters out there hungry for a job. Why did it have to be *those* songs?"

"Because Lexi wanted them, OK?" he shouted. "It was obvious to anyone with a pair of eyes how envious she was of Ava's talent, those songs. They should've been Lexi's," he muttered, moving even closer. "And I got them for her—not that she ever appreciated what it cost me. Do you know what it's like, loving someone who treats you like *furniture*? Who looks right past you for years like you're not even there? Someone you've done everything for, sacrificed everything for, who never even *acknowledges* it?"

"Lexi asked you to get the songs? To get Ava to give them up?" I needed to keep him talking, to keep his words coming fast and loose.

"I've always known exactly what Lexi needs. I know her better than she knows herself. She didn't have to *ask*. All these years, I loved her," he said bitterly. "First her talent, her beauty, and determination. And later I even loved that airbrushed *thing* I created. But no matter what

I did, it was never good enough. No matter how much I love her, she looks right through me."

I went rigid, my body tensing.

"Ben," I said slowly, "what did you do?"

"Same thing I have to do now," he said, and I was all too aware of the millimeters of space between us, the edge unnervingly close.

It's a long way down, Kayla, Ava said again. *It will break you.*

They break all the little girls.

Before I knew what was happening, Ben's arms snaked out, grabbing me by the shoulders, his palms clammy against my skin. His eyes were unfocused, as though he'd gone somewhere else completely, a place I could never find him. My mother's voice flashed through my mind, her face, the way she'd peer at me over the tops of her glasses when she was lecturing me—or giving advice, as she called it.

If a man ever gives you trouble, Kayla? Kick him where it hurts the most.

And then run.

With all the strength I had, I brought one knee up firmly between his legs, and he let go of my shoulders instantly, crumpling to the ground, his hands clutching his groin as if to stanch a wound, his mouth open in a soundless scream. I didn't wait for him to recover. I ran, dashing across the expanse of the roof and yanking the door open so roughly that I wrenched my shoulder, wincing, but not stopping as I raced down the stairs. When I reached the glare of the lobby, I sprinted the last few feet to the front door, shoving it open with all my might. I bolted into the teeming streets, grabbing my cell phone and dialing the three numbers that would bring me to safety.

911, what is your emergency?

MAYHEM MANAGER ARRESTED OVER SINGER'S 2005 DEATH

New York—Ben Reynolds, CEO of Avant Entertainment Group, was arrested on Monday in connection to the 2006 death of Ava Petrova. Petrova, 22, who performed under the moniker Ava Arcana, was at the time an up-and-coming singer and close friend of pop star Lexi Mayhem. The case had been closed for 13 years after it was initially ruled that Petrova, who fell from the roof of a Broome Street apartment building, had died by suicide. Police initially sought out Reynolds for questioning after receiving an anonymous tip suggesting that he had further information about the circumstances of Petrova's death. He was subsequently arrested, but charges have not yet been filed.

Petrova, who was born in Kyiv, Ukraine, and immi-grated to Staten Island at age 5, was a fixture of the Lower East Side music scene in the mid-2000s and regularly featured on the same bill as Mayhem. Shortly before her death, Petrova was being hotly pursued by a number of record labels, including Christian Vane's Phoenix Records, but had yet to sign a deal. At the time of her death, she was writing and recording songs for what would have been her debut album. She is remembered as being a par-ticularly gifted lyricist by those who knew her, but today her music is all but completely unavailable.

A spokesperson for Avant Entertainment who has worked closely with Reynolds over the years said that Reynolds, who has handled the career of Lexi Mayhem since 2006, has taken an indefinite leave of absence from the agency he helped found.

Reynolds is currently being held in city jail with bail set at $2 million. He will make his first appearance in front of a judge tomorrow for his arraignment.

KAYLA

2019

When I walked into the office the following morning, shell-shocked and bruised after only a few hours of sleep, Keats immediately ushered me into his office, closing the door behind us. I'd phoned him from the precinct the night before, my voice strained with panic. I had no recollection of his words, but just the sound of his voice in my ear had quelled the last of the shock waves traveling through my body. But now, in the quiet of his office, I stared at the floor, waiting for what I was sure would come next—the instructions to clean out my desk, turn in my employee badge, and leave the premises immediately.

But instead, he reached out, laying a hand on my shoulder until I looked up. Keats had never so much as come within a foot of me, and now here we were, face-to-face, his slate-colored eyes peering at me worriedly. "Are you OK?" he asked, and with those words something in me broke wide open, and I buried my face in my hands. Keats folded me into his arms. I leaned against his linen jacket, breathing in the scent of his Old Spice cologne—"It's *classic*," he'd always claimed. "The furthest thing from outdated"—and the vanilla latte he'd probably been drinking before I'd arrived. My tears ran hot and fast, and after a few moments he released me, and we stood there eyeing each other awkwardly.

"I'm sorry," I said, trying my best to smile. "I just couldn't let it go."

"I know." He sighed, walking back around to his desk and sitting down, motioning for me to take my usual seat across from him. "I should've had your back. But I think there's a way to make it up to you."

"What's that?" I asked, reaching into my bag for a tissue and noisily blowing my nose. I watched in satisfaction as Keats visibly recoiled. He hated being reminded of the corporeality of the body, the vulnerability of it. It made him queasy, he'd told me once.

"We're running the story," he said firmly. "*Your* story."

"You mean Ava's story?"

"One and the same."

"But . . . we don't have a comment from Lexi."

"Sure we do," Keats said with a sly smile, crossing one leg over the other. "You called her, remember? 'No comment' *is* her comment. And if there's any blowback, I'll take the heat. We're going to run it on the website so it can publish immediately, but we'll do a print version in the next issue. A cover. Just like I promised. The draft's pretty good, but I think it's missing a crucial scene. I wouldn't usually want you in the lede of your story . . . but considering your source almost pushed you off a roof, I think this is an exception."

I nodded as Ben's face flashed before my eyes, and I shivered violently.

"One last question," I said, trying to shake the memory. "Are you doing this just because I was right and you were wrong?" I raised an eyebrow.

"'Wrong' is a *very* strong word, Kayla. One that has no place in this office." I watched his lips twitch as he fought back a smile. "I'm doing this because it's a great story. One that will make your name as a journalist. And because you've earned it."

I nodded, my eyes filling with tears once again.

"But you need to stop with the waterworks now, OK?" Keats chided gently. "I want to publish by end of day. The edits are in your email, so let's get to work."

———

As I left Keats's office, I reached up, rubbing my eyes, which felt gritty from salt and the lack of sleep. But I was determined to push through, if for no other reason than the fact that I could finally collapse and put the story behind me when I was done. When I got back to my desk, Simone raised her eyes from the screen of her laptop, looking at me expectantly.

"So?" she asked as I slid into my seat, swiveling around to face me. "How did it go?"

"I've only got a few hours," I said, exhaling heavily. "I need to get moving."

She nodded, her braids swinging gently around her face as she moved. Her brown eyes softened behind her glasses, and when she spoke again, her voice was lower, gentler than I'd ever heard it before. "Are you all right?" she asked, peering at me closely. "You wanna talk about it?"

Without warning, the tears threatened to well up again, but I knew I had no time for them now. The clock was ticking, and I had only a few hours to address Keats's changes and file the story before deadline. "Yeah," I said, blinking a few times in rapid succession and pulling my hair back into a knot, then letting it fall again. "But I can't right now."

She shrugged, then nodded again. "Hit me up when you're ready. We'll grab a drink."

If I'd been less exhausted, I might have laughed out loud. All this time sitting next to one another, and here it finally was: an invitation.

"You're asking me out?" I said archly, biting my lip to stifle a grin.

"Don't get crazy now," she retorted, turning back around to face her computer before I could say another word. And with that, I opened my laptop, popping in my headphones to muffle the noise in the news-room—laughter, a murmur of low voices, and ringing phones—and got to work.

———

Three days later, I sat at the dining table in Jamie's apartment, fidgeting awkwardly. We'd never sat so formally with one another in his space before, and there was a thickness in the air, a tension hanging between us. We stared at each other tentatively, as if afraid to speak. The room, his face . . . It was all the same. But now in only the space of a week, everything was different. That ease we'd shared seemed to have evapo-rated, and now I didn't know what to say.

So much had happened in the days after the story broke. The calls had started coming in right away: NPR producers, news-show bookers, everyone vying for a few seconds of my voice or my talking head on the screen to break down exactly how I'd found out Ben was a killer—and how he had maybe, almost certainly, tried to kill me too. My phone rang steadily, but my inbox and notifications experienced nothing short of a deluge. Plenty of it was praise, but the hard-core Mayhem fans were furious that their idol had allegedly stolen material from some "unknown peasant," as they were fond of calling Ava in the comments section, not to mention their vitriolic TikTok videos and Instagram posts, many of which called for my head, referring to me as a talentless hack.

"After things blew up," Jamie said, "I wanted to give you some space. But then I found myself texting anyway." He smiled tightly. "I'm glad Keats did the right thing. But damn, is there gonna be blowback." Jamie chuckled, shaking his head.

"There already is." I grimaced. "We heard from Lexi's lawyers pretty much the second that Keats hit 'Publish.' And Christian's been brought in by the DA for questioning. I heard they're opening an investigation."

"Couldn't have happened to a nicer guy," Jamie laughed. "But seriously, Kayla, that opening paragraph you wrote?" He pulled out his phone, the glow of the screen illuminating his face as he read. *"I never thought I'd be the type of reporter to break a fourteen-year-old murder case by accident, but as I stood on a rooftop in the Lower East Side, looking into the eyes of a killer, I knew with blinding certainty that it was precisely what I had done."*

"And he was moving closer."

"It's a great story," Jamie said, looking back over at me and placing his phone down on the table. "I think Ava would approve. It's weird, but for the first time I don't feel her around me now, that restlessness. It's quiet. Maybe she's finally at peace."

I nodded, then looked away. I'd woken the previous evening in darkness, Ava's celestial body shimmering beside the bed as she looked down at me, her face serene. She smiled, her eyes still full of secrets, and she reached out a hand, hovering it over my motionless form. But just as she was about to make contact, she was suddenly gone, and the room was still.

I did the best I could, Ava, I'd said under my breath. *But it's out of my hands now.*

"I owe her this," I said, remembering the look in her eyes, still haunted. "And I think you owe her, too, right?" I said, looking over at him, my voice sharper than I'd intended. "For letting them steal her songs—and profiting off it."

His body tensed as if he'd been slapped, and then he looked away, letting out a long sigh. "It's complicated," he finally mumbled.

"I'm sure that's what you tell yourself," I said, unable to keep the bitterness from my voice. "I saw the royalty statements, Jamie." His face fell ever so slightly, and he exhaled loudly. "I wasn't snooping . . . but I found them."

He nodded, looking away, the pain emanating from him palpable, as if he were disappearing into the mist of heartache surrounding him.

"It was a bad time for me, Kayla," he said as he leaned forward, resting his head in his hands. "Ava had only been gone six months, and I'd been drinking myself sick every night. Her absence, the way we'd left things between us—it tore right through me. And after I got out of rehab, there was nothing but bills and clients who'd deserted me. I was flat broke, and Ben had made it clear that he was taking the songs one way or the other. Then my mom got sick. Lung cancer. She was in and out of the hospital, and every day was a struggle not to drink, a struggle just to get out of bed. I was on my knees, Kayla. So . . . I took the money. I'm not proud of it, but I was a different person back then. I haven't cashed those residuals in years. I can't bring myself to. But if I'd had any idea what had really happened to Ava on that rooftop, that she'd died *defending* those songs, I never would've agreed to any of it. No matter what."

He got up and strode over to the sideboard in the kitchen, pulling out the top drawer and then a handful of envelopes, stacks of them filling his hands. "Look," he said, holding them out toward me, "I just shove them in drawers. It's blood money, and I don't *want* it anymore. Every one of those checks erases her a little more, and I can't live with it. I don't even open the envelopes anymore. I can't." He threw the pile on the kitchen counter, where part of the stack slid, in what resembled a kind of protest, to the floor. He sank to his knees, a sea of paper surrounding him. He cried quietly, the movement of his body and the tears streaking his face the only indication it was happening at all.

There was no choice. I went to him, kneeling on the floor amid that detritus, years of it. "It's OK," I said, pulling his hands from his face and wrapping my arms around him. I could feel the tension in his body lessening, and the back of his shirt was damp with sweat. I rocked him as though we both needed soothing. I closed my eyes, feeling the heat of his flesh sinking into mine.

"This is real," he said, gripping me tighter on the last word. "What's happening with us."

I nodded, certain he could feel it.

"I *want* this with you," he said as he drew back, wiping his face impatiently with one hand.

"Me too," I whispered, realizing that it was true. We were both held together with bits of tape and fraying twine, our hearts unraveling along the edges, but maybe sometimes people really *did* save each other. Or perhaps it was more complicated than that—maybe some people came into your life so that you could finally find the courage to save yourself.

Ava hadn't been able to do it; she had fallen a minute too late.

But me? I'd caught myself just in time.

KAYLA

2019

By the time I returned to Brooklyn the following afternoon, I was blank with exhaustion. I triple locked the front door, grateful that it was a Saturday, and walked around my apartment, searching behind doors and peering into closets, searching for Ben's face in the tangle of dresses and coats. Even though I knew that I was safe, or at least as safe as I could possibly be, each time I closed my eyes I was right back there on that roof—Ben, the dying sun, the vacant look in his eyes. And Ava's voice still calling out to me, high and sweet and knowing.

I climbed into bed, falling into a restless sleep, waking somewhere in the middle of the night and sitting up in terror, my heart pounding. I lay back down and dropped off once again, slumber overtaking me like falling off the edge of a cliff. When I opened my eyes again, it was two p.m. on Sunday, the afternoon light tingeing the floorboards with ochre and gold. I picked up my phone and saw the explosion of notifications—*Entertainment Tonight, Good Morning America*—before I put it back down, overwhelmed. There were a few missed calls from Jamie, too, and I sent him a quick text to put his mind at ease.

Slept like Rip Van Winkle. Guess I needed it. More soon xx.

I wandered hungrily into the kitchen, wondering if I should just order Chinese instead of attempting to cook. Like most New Yorkers, my fridge contained only bottled water and some leftover Thai noodles from a week ago that I probably should've tossed already.

I had my head stuck in a cabinet, my hand on a package of spaghetti, when there was a knock on my door, a series of sharp taps. "Who is it?" I barked, trying to sound tough or, at the very least, less afraid. Whoever it was, they hadn't rung the buzzer. There was a stay-at-home mom on my floor who sometimes asked me to keep an ear out for her newborn while she ran downstairs to grab a package. When no one answered, I gathered my courage and yanked open the door as if I were expecting a fight. And there, in the hall, stood a diminutive woman with platinum hair, enormous dark sunglasses swallowing the sculpted bones of her face.

Lexi Mayhem.

"What are you doing here?" I blurted out.

"I need to talk to you," she said simply, as though famous pop stars showed up on my doorstep every day.

I opened the door a crack wider but was still too stunned to step aside.

"Can I come in?" she asked, pushing her sunglasses on top of her head. "Or do you want to do this right here?"

The combination of Lexi Mayhem and the mundanity of my Brooklyn apartment was dizzying. Watching her walk around the living room, looking at the photos on the walls, picking up a small wooden sculpture from the Amazon that my mother had given me for my twenty-fifth birthday. Lexi's sheer magnetism overpowered the room, making it appear smaller, less substantial. She dwarfed everything she touched.

"Nice place," she said as she ran her fingertips over the back of an armchair tucked in the corner, the faded hue of a blushing peach. She wore a pair of black vinyl leggings and a black short-sleeved top that left her long arms bare, the material cinched at the waist with a wide patent leather belt. Balancing effortlessly on pointy-toed heels, she resembled a dancer, all lean muscle and endless legs. I looked down at the faded gray sweatpants and ratty T-shirt I wore, a shirt that had been tinged pink when a red pair of underwear had sneaked their way into a load of whites. I groaned internally, wishing I'd at least showered.

"Thanks," I said. "I like it."

"It reminds me of my first apartment in the city," she said, looking around the room. "Of course, this is much nicer." Her eyes, outlined in dramatic sweeps of kohl, lines so dark they appeared almost wet, took in the earth-toned rugs underfoot, my velvet thrift-store couch, the greenery overflowing from the corners of the room.

"The apartment on Broome Street?" I asked, wondering if I should offer her something to drink, then panicking internally.

She was over by the window, looking out into the leafy treetops, her expression pensive. "Yeah. It was kind of a dump, but I always felt at home there." She shrugged. "You've seen it?" She asked, looking over at me in surprise.

"Not really," I said slowly. "Just the roof."

She let out a sigh, walking over to the armchair her coat rested on and sitting down heavily, crossing one leg over the other, her face somber now.

"I take it you . . . read the story?" I asked tentatively.

"That's why I'm here," she said. "Things are different now and I'm ready to talk—do you want to get your little recorder thingy?" She gestured in the air, her fingers weighted with silver rings.

"Different how?" I asked, quickly grabbing the digital recorder from my bag and switching it on.

"I'm here, aren't I?" she said impatiently. "I came to you this time. Remember what you asked me on the phone? Let's take it from there."

"The phone call where you hung up on me?"

"Listen, I'm ready to tell you things that you'll never be able to get out of me again," she said, staring me down, daring me to argue with her. "This is your shot."

"That's not exactly true," I pointed out as I stood up and walked over to the desk, sitting down in my chair and swiveling it around to face her. "With all due respect, you can't control the narrative now. The story already broke. And whether it's to me or to someone else, eventually you're going to have to talk."

"Exactly," she said. "Everyone is going to come looking for Ava now—but you've already found her. I want *you* to tell her story. *Our* story. Mine and Ava's."

"I thought I already had," I said slowly.

"No," she said sharply. "That was *Ben's* story. Not mine. And certainly not Ava's. For the first time in thirteen years, he doesn't have a say in what I do anymore," she said, spitting out the words like a mouthful of tacks, her face flushed with anger. There was a beat while she composed herself, the tension that had sprung up so suddenly now dying down to a low hum. "He never should've had one in the first place."

"This follow-up feature you want me to write . . . Will it corroborate the fact that you agreed to steal Ava's songs after her death?"

A small sound escaped her throat. Not one of indignation or even protest but of pain, the hurt swift and sure. She turned her head so that her face was in profile, her jawline clean and smooth, her pale hair falling around her face like a promise. "It was never my idea," she said, her voice barely above a whisper.

"But you went along with it."

"Ben . . . can be very persuasive. And I was young. But that doesn't excuse anything." She was agitated now, on the edge of anger again. "He said she was gone anyway, that no one would ever find out—but even back then, I knew he was wrong. Knew that even if it stayed buried forever, *I* would know. Still, I didn't realize how it would stay with me, the feeling that I had betrayed her. I failed her *twice*, Kayla," she said, looking over at me, her face bleached bone white by the sun streaming in through the window. "Once on that rooftop. And then again after she died." Her voice cracked, rendering her instantly human, and she looked away again, unable to meet my gaze. No longer an immortal, just a woman sitting in my living room, her face racked with pain.

"It wasn't your fault," I said gently. "You were out cold. There was nothing you could have done to help her."

I heard her draw in a breath, and when she raised her hands to her face, pushing a strand of hair away from her eyes, I saw that they were shaking. "I . . . I woke up for a second that night," she murmured, and I leaned forward to hear her more clearly. "It was just a flicker. But I saw them standing at the edge of the roof. Arguing. I wanted to call out, to get up, but it was like I was trapped under a bus. I couldn't move. Couldn't *talk*. I tried to reach out my hand . . . and then there was nothing. Until the moment I woke up in my own bed the next day, and Ben was standing over me, screaming that I'd almost blown it." She shook her head at the memory. "I never drank again after that night. Ben made me think that maybe I . . ." Her voice trailed off, as if she couldn't bear to finish.

"That maybe you'd pushed her?"

"Yes," she whispered, and I watched as tears escaped the corners of her eyes. I'd read a story once about the science of tears, how when they were truly heartfelt and authentic, tears originated from the inside corners of the eye. But tears that were manufactured, designed to manipulate, sprang from the outside corners of the eye instead. Watching Lexi as she cried, I knew without a doubt that the grief I was witnessing was real.

"You believed him."

"I didn't know *what* to believe," she said, her voice thick with frustration and regret. "I could barely remember anything about that night. And in the weeks before her death, we'd been fighting, Ava and I.

Looking back on it now, it was all so stupid. How we let them all come between us." She shook her head in disgust.

"What happened after that?" I asked, wanting to keep her talking. "Walk me through it."

She took a deep breath, fidgeting with the ring on her index finger, spinning it around. "Christian signed me a few weeks later. He wanted the album as soon as possible. I didn't have enough songs. Not even close. And there was no time—he didn't want to wait. So Ben started saying how much sense it made to use Ava's songs. To . . . take them. He wouldn't stop talking about it. He said it was logical, really, that she would've wanted me to have them, that she'd practically agreed before she'd jumped anyway. But I *knew* Ava, and there was no way she'd do that—not even for me. Those songs were everything to her. But I was grieving and barely going through the motions. I could hardly get out of bed. He knew that, of course. The deal, the music, being a star—it was all I had left. She was my best friend, and then she was gone. Oh, I don't expect you to understand," she said in exasperation as a tear dripped off the point of her chin. "How could you?"

Astrid's face appeared suddenly, and I could feel her there with us, filling the room with the scent of summer berries, her hopeful grin breaking what was left of my heart.

But this time I let her stay.

"I understand better than you think," I said quietly. "I had a best friend once too. And I let her down. I live with that guilt every day."

A look of understanding passed between us. It was in her eyes—they saw me down to the bone. The secret heart of who I was and what I'd done. But now, I didn't mind being exposed. It felt like a relief. With each person I told, the tiniest fraction of weight lifted from my shoulders, freeing me a little more.

"Ben pushed and wheedled and threatened, and finally I just gave in," she said, her eyes awash in tears. "I was so *weak*." Her voice was full of disgust, and I watched as the most famous pop star in the world wiped her nose on her own sleeve the way four-year-old Lexi Gennaro might've once upon a time. "I just wanted it so badly—the fame. The money. The power. We bought Irina that house, but it didn't erase the feeling that no matter what I did, Ava's death would hang over me for as long as I lived. I hated myself for years. I still do." She looked up, her face set and determined. "But now I'm going to make it right."

"What do you mean?"

She walked over and sat on the couch, directly across from me now, leaning forward so that her elbows rested on her knees, her face in her hands. "I'm going to devote myself to mentoring young female artists—I'll sign them to Underworld and give them the push Ava never had. And the first record I plan to release is *American Girls*, the debut album by Ava Arcana. Jamie has all the masters. My fans will recognize some of the tracks, songs they've already heard on my first two albums, but there's a ton of material that's never even seen the light of day. Ava was so talented. Such a good songwriter." Her jaw tightened. "I was so *jealous* of that talent, wanted it for myself, wanted to know what it was like for it to all come that easily. But at the end of the day, that talent belonged to her alone. And now I'm going to make sure everyone knows her name," she said, her eyes alive with purpose. "And they'll know what I did too. There's no hiding it anymore."

"Are you worried about that?" I asked gingerly, not wanting to dissuade her but wanting to be realistic about what this revelation would do to her career—detonate thirteen years of work in a few hundred words.

"I've spent most of my life worrying. Scared that no matter how well Ben hid our tracks, someone would find out. I've lived all these years with that guilt, and that worry kept me up at night, made sleep impossible. I've dreaded this day, praying to god that no one found out.

But now that it's here? I'm relieved." She sat back against the cushions. "It's time to let the curtain fall."

———

Two hours passed before I walked her to the door, my stomach empty and rumbling, my brain on overload. My voice recorder was maxed out, my notebook full of scrawled pages of notes. I'd written so quickly that my writing was practically illegible in places. But despite all I'd heard and the work that lay ahead of me, I wasn't tired. I was more awake than I'd ever been.

"I'll be in touch," I said as I opened the door, "if anything else comes up." She tied the belt of her coat around her waist, cinching it tightly, then reached up, pulling the sunglasses from the crown of her head.

"One last thing," she said. "I was wondering about your friend . . . Do you still talk?"

"No," I said quietly. "I've thought about it. But I haven't reached out. I don't know why. Maybe because I know she doesn't want to hear from me."

"You might be surprised," Lexi said with a shrug. "I never got to make things right between Ava and me. I was angry about her and Jamie, and I was jealous of her talent. Worst of all, I was afraid she'd make it and I wouldn't. I let that fear run my life, and it cost me the person who knew me best, the person I was closest to. So many years have passed since she died, and I've never had a friendship like that again. Partly because I'm scared. And partly because I don't think I deserve it."

The admission hung there in the air, her words triggering a flood of recognition. There was a long moment where we simply looked at each other, two women standing in a doorway. Not a pop star and a journalist but two human beings. Flawed and imperfect but somehow achingly present.

"So, make it right," she said, sliding her sunglasses over her face, a blank canvas once again. "What's the worst that could happen?"

Before I could answer, she'd turned on one heel, waving over her shoulder, her long nails flashing in the light like opaque parings of the moon. I closed the door behind her, leaning against it heavily. I felt as if I'd just run a marathon, my muscles warm and spent. The work of confronting the past was exhausting, dizzying. Maybe that was why I'd avoided it for so long.

I moved slowly to my desk, sitting down and opening my laptop, clicking away from the story in progress. I opened Facebook, typing Astrid's name into the search engine, holding my breath, and the page loaded. And there she was. Older but with the same apologetic half smile I remembered from our youth. *Make it right,* Lexi had said. But it wasn't that simple, was it? Just because I apologized didn't mean Astrid would forgive me or even want to hear me out. And who was the apology really for anyway, I wondered. Me or her?

I clicked through the photos on her Facebook page, the same ones I'd ruminated over a thousand times before: Astrid in jeans and a white sweatshirt, a purple kite in one hand. An expanse of blue sky and grass so green it looked almost artificial. Astrid in a chair, looking back over one shoulder, holding a glass of red wine, an amused glint in her eye, as though the photographer had caught her unaware. Astrid at two or three years old. Braids and a white pinafore, her grin so open and pure that she might have been smiling with every cell of her being. So different from the way she'd walked the halls senior year, her eyes cast on the ground, shoulders hunched, a curtain of hair hiding her face from view.

The hurt in her eyes every time she saw me—and then quickly looked away.

I grabbed my cell and punched in the number I knew by heart. I'd looked it up so many times that my fingers moved effortlessly across the screen. It rang once, twice, and I held my breath, squeezing my eyes shut. I could see us there in the void of my vision, two small girls in a blue plastic pool, frog decals at the bottom, our chubby arms looped around one another, the chemical-coconut smell of sunscreen in the air. I could still feel the weight of her tiny hand in mine.

Holding tight.

There was a click and then her voice, questioning, halting, a little lower, but otherwise just as I remembered. So familiar that I was crying before I'd even uttered a single word.

Oh Astrid, I thought, clutching the phone as if it were her fingers. *Finally.*

"It's Kayla," I said, taking a deep breath and opening my eyes. "I know it's been a while . . . but I was hoping we could talk."

ACKNOWLEDGMENTS

Every book is challenging in its own way. But a novel written during a global pandemic is a different beast entirely. To that end, this book could not have been written without the support of the following individuals: Les Morgenstein; Josh Bank; Gina Girolamo; and the entire team at Alloy Entertainment, particularly Joelle Hobeika and Viana Siniscalchi, who believed in Ava's story—and my ability to tell it—from the very beginning. Your brilliance, humor, and inexhaustible patience made this a far better book than it would've been otherwise, and I am forever grateful. Everyone at Lake Union Publishing but especially my rock star editor, Alicia Clancy, for giving Ava the perfect home. Gina Frangello, for her endless text threads, late-night phone calls, and for cheering me on when I needed it most. I owe an enormous, unpayable debt to Willy Blackmore, who has read everything I've written for the past sixteen years. Without his insightful critique, this book would still be languishing in my hard drive. And finally, nothing I will ever write could even come close to overshadowing my greatest accomplishment: my magical unicorn-girl, Story Blackmore. Your determined spirit and enormous capacity for joy are a daily reminder of why we are all here— and what a marvel it is to simply exist. Everything I do is for you.

ABOUT THE AUTHOR

Jennifer Banash is a former professor of English and creative writing, and author of the novels *Silent Alarm*, a finalist for the American Library Association's Best Fiction for Young Adults; *White Lines*; *Simply Irresistible*; *In Too Deep*; and *The Elite*. Jennifer is also the former cofounder and editor of Impetus Press, a small, independent publishing house that championed works of literary fiction with a pop edge. A native New Yorker, her first apartment was an illegal sublet located next door to the Hells Angels' former headquarters on the Lower East Side of Manhattan. For more information, visit www.jennifer-banash.com.